# DEFENSELESS

THE BOOK FOLKS

# Chapter 1

**Wednesday, May 9**

I woke with a start, my heart racing. The sound came from inside the house. My body flashed hot. Should I wake Lee, a blurry form in the darkness?

The door flew open, and a huge flashlight beam skipped around the bedroom.

The light settled on me. Lee screamed. The beam moved to her, and she clutched my shoulder.

My throat constricted, but I yelled, "Hey. Who are you?"

"Shut up," a man said. "Boss, come here. We got some folks home tonight."

He flipped on the bedroom light to reveal two men in black ski masks, tee shirts, and dark pants.

"Aw, crap," the other one said.

The one at the light switch pulled a gun from his belt and pointed it at me.

Lee moaned.

"Just be cool," the gunman said. "Keep real quiet, and things will be okay."

His partner turned toward him. "Let's just back out of here."

The gunman didn't move.

Lee trembled. "Stay behind me," I whispered.

"You don't have anything to say about it." The man with the gun stepped forward. "Let's have the lady stand up." He jerked the barrel up and down at

Lee.

My pulse pounded. "Look, just take what you want and leave. Please. We don't want any trouble."

The man with the gun crossed to the foot of the bed. His partner pulled a pistol from his waistband.

As the gunman came around the end of the bed, I inched my body against Lee. The gun focused on me.

The gun barrel stopped two feet from my face. I looked up. The gunman licked his lips. From the doorway I heard a low and commanding growl, "Let's go, partner."

"I'm not going anywhere until I see some more of this pretty woman." There was a slight hesitation. "And maybe a little more." He reached down, grabbed the sheet, and ripped it away. We both jerked back against the headboard. I felt powerless, sick to my stomach, ashamed. I was defenseless to protect my wife. She sobbed, and it flipped a switch somewhere in me.

"Touch her, and I'll kill you."

"I got the gun. I get what I want."

From the doorway the other gunman said, "I said let's go. I don't want this to get out of hand."

The man in front of me turned to look at his partner. I jumped toward him, but got little traction from the bed and went down. He turned back with a sick smile. I finally got to my feet, legs against the side of the bed. My breathing came hard from anger more than exertion. I stared at the ski mask. His right arm extended straight out from his body directly at me. His fist gripped the pistol, and his index finger wrapped around the trigger.

He turned his eyes toward Lee and smiled bigger. I glanced to see Lee naked, holding her arms around her chest, legs curled under her. She looked back, her face twisted with fear. I caught a quick blur of motion, and the pistol slammed into the side of my head. My knees buckled, and I grabbed my head. My eyes watered, but I straightened up, gritted my teeth. The pain seemed to drive away the fear.

"Since you pulled that little stunt, I'm definitely going to have a piece of that." He jutted his chin at Lee. The gun moved closer to my face. The black hole made little circles in the air. "You interfere, you're dead."

I leaned back away from the gun. Instead of scaring me, it made me think of something I had heard. Someone told me that most people who flaunt a weapon seldom have the guts actually to use it. I looked at the man in the ski mask and decided that, without the gun, he was nothing but a wimp. He sickened me.

Instantly, the anger surged, and blood pounded in my temples. Then I lost all capacity to think. I lunged past the gun and slammed the heel of my left hand into his jaw. He jerked back. The gun thundered. I twisted to gain my balance and tried to grab him around the neck. I heard another gun roar, and my right shoulder exploded in pain. It threw me against the wall, and I slid to the floor, grabbing my collarbone, gasping.

I looked up and saw the gun barrel descended toward me. I pulled back expecting to hear the gunshot, but a second set of legs tangled with the gunman's. The man and the gun twisted away.

"Let's go."

"Get your hands off me, Liam."

"No. We get out of here. Now. Neighbors will be calling the cops." The second gunman shoved my attacker toward the bedroom door. I rolled over, crying out at the pain in my shoulder. I crawled to the foot of the bed and pulled myself up. I lunged to the doorframe, leaning on it. Across the room, the front door hung open. Blood seeped through my fingers pressed against my chest. I grabbed the back of the sofa, a chair, pushed against the fireplace, and stopped in the open doorway.

A car door slammed, and I jerked my head toward it. I saw the second door slam on a nineties-era Dodge pickup truck parked in the shadows down and across the street. The engine started, and the tires spit smoke as the truck fishtailed from the shoulder. As it passed under a street lamp, I saw the backside of a faded white cab and bed with a Florida plate on the bumper. It skidded around a corner, leaving a swirl of dust.

"Lee!" The agony in my collarbone was excruciating. "Lee!"

She didn't answer.

I pressed my open hand against my right collarbone. It was thick with blood. The pain, like a fire, spread through my chest and arm. I took one deep breath, and the pain exploded. My knees buckled once more, and I gripped the doorframe with my bloody hand to keep from collapsing.

I staggered toward the couch and grabbed it. If I went down, I wouldn't be able to get back up. I shuffled along the couch toward the bedroom door. I had never felt pain like this. I focused on where to put my hand as I moved. The pain wanted all my attention, but I needed help.

I made it to the bedroom door. My bloody hand slipped, and my chest slammed into the frame. I clutched the wall inside the door and dug my nails into the gypsum board.

"Lee, help me."

She lay slumped over. I saw blood, a crimson river that covered her chest and oozed onto her legs. Was it my blood? She didn't move. "Lee!" Panic overcame my pain, and suddenly my legs strengthened. I pushed from the doorway to the foot of the bed and clawed my way up the sheets using my good arm. I tried to grab her with both arms, but the right one wouldn't work, and I twisted in pain.

"Lee, Lee, no."

I turned her face toward me. Her hair was matted. I could see little slices of her half-closed eyes. I pressed my ear to her chest, laying my ear in warm blood, but didn't hear a heartbeat. My fire-filled shoulder pushed against her body, and I wondered if we would die like this. Fear filled me. It clutched me and squeezed. I was afraid Lee would die. I was afraid I wouldn't be able to do anything about it.

I pushed up but slipped and fell against her. I got to my knees, wiped my slick hand on the bed, and reached for the phone. I hit 911.

"Nine-one-one. What's your emergency?"

"Help, help me. We've been shot." I went slack and dropped off the edge of the bed.

\*\*\*

I lay in the dark. My body swayed to the left. I rocked toward my right and slammed against my injured right shoulder, causing me to cry out in pain. A hand cushioned my right side as the bed moved under me. I heard clanking, like opening the silverware drawer, and a muffled siren. That's when I felt belts holding me to the bed. It startled me, and I thought of Lee.

"Lee!" I whispered.

"It's okay. You're going to be okay. You've lost a lot of blood. Just lie still."

I saw the shadow of someone on either side of me but couldn't focus. The pain engulfed my chest and continued down into my right leg. My shoulder hurt deep inside but didn't sear like a flame anymore. I couldn't feel my right arm, but I felt cold sweat on my face. The shadows faded to black.

Light flashed against my eyelids. I heard a rattling sound, voices. I pulled my eyes open. A person in scrubs pushed my bed, and another walked next to a drip bag hanging next to my head.

"Lee, Lee," I croaked.

"Easy, Mr. Stone. You're going to be okay."

"My wife, I..."

"You're headed into surgery, Mr. Stone. You've been hurt very badly."

I closed my eyes. I felt a hand in mine and tried to grip it, but I didn't have the strength.

I heard a faint voice. "He doesn't know."

I made out the sound of a heart monitor beeping and inhaled the scent of hospital. I thought there were voices, but they seemed too far away for me to grasp.

"Mr. Stone. Mark Stone. Can you hear me, Mr. Stone?"

*No, I can't. I don't want to hear you. I just want to sleep.*

"Mr. Stone." The tone startled me. "Mr. Stone. Mr. Mark Stone. You can go back to sleep in a few minutes."

What?

With effort, I fluttered my eyes and saw rectangles of diffused light. Forcing them open, I focused on a man in aqua scrubs and woman in similar scrubs. She held my hand.

"I'm Dr. Carpenter, Mr. Stone," said the man, "your anesthesiologist. I need to be sure that you have no problems with the anesthesia. You're doing fine." He smiled again. He leaned forward and put a stethoscope against the upper left side of my chest.

I jerked as he moved his hand across my chest. It triggered my memory of Lee's bloody chest. I clenched my eyes.

"Lee." I whispered.

I felt the nurse squeeze my hand. "Doctor, his wife," she said.

"Can you?"

I couldn't open my eyes. I just held her hand. I felt her face move closer to mine.

"Mr. Stone, I'm so sorry. Your wife was fatally injured."

# Chapter 2

**Thursday, May 10**

The hospital room was dark. My eyes were grainy. The bed was hot, and I hurt all over. The room seemed to spin. When I closed my eyes, I saw Lee, with her bloody chest, slumped lifeless in the bed. My wife, lover, friend, gone.

I could have done something to save her. It should have been me, not her. I should have protected her.

When the killer's eyes had raked her body, I should have slammed him to the floor and beaten him senseless.

I pounded my left fist against the bed rail. The IV in my arm twisted under my skin, and I fell back on the bed. My breathing came hard. I clenched my teeth. After a time, I calmed, lost focus, and drifted to sleep.

**Friday, May 11**

I opened my eyes at the swish of the door to a room flooded with daylight. A man walked in, and my eyes were drawn to his red vest bulging from a navy sports jacket. He pulled a leather wallet, held it a couple feet from my face, and said, "Lieutenant Beauchamp." I saw a gold badge and picture ID, but nothing was clear. My mind wasn't working. I looked at him and heard the wallet flop shut.

His round face hid behind a neat ginger beard. "Mr. Stone, I'd like a few words. Are you well enough to talk?"

"Sure." It came out raspy, and the effort sent slivers of pain across my chest.

"Before we do…" Beauchamp looked back at the door. "We need to take care of some formalities. You consent to providing some physical data, don't you?"

I wondered what he meant.

Beauchamp turned toward the door. "Gentlemen?"

The door swung open, and two technicians with tackle boxes came in and stopped next to Beauchamp.

"Mr. Stone?"

"What?" I didn't understand.

"We need DNA, check for GSR, scrape your nails, that sort of thing." I heard something in his voice. He bounced gently on the balls of his feet. "Mr. Stone, what you tell us and what we learn with forensics will help us catch your wife's killers."

My throat constricted at his last words. I closed my eyes and nodded.

The technicians set to work. Beauchamp stood out of the way, holding his jacket lapels, and grunted a response when a technician asked him a question. I complied with their requests. After a few minutes, one tech said they were done, and they left the room.

"Mr. Stone, I would like for you to take me through the events of three nights ago."

Panic shot through me. "Three nights?"

"Yes." He seemed to catch the tone of my voice. "If you're not up to this now, I can come back tomorrow."

"No. I want you get started on it." My eyes burned, but I fought it off. "You need to find who did this."

"Okay, I'm starting a digital recorder." He placed it on the nightstand and opened a pad. "Just start at the beginning. Tell me everything that happened."

I told him everything. He asked a few questions to

clarify a couple points, some of which didn't make sense, but it didn't matter to me. I wanted his help. I wanted the killers caught. He circled back to a few points I thought I had made clear and asked questions about them. When he asked if I was sure, I didn't like it, but I answered anyway. I was exhausted by the time he stopped. "I saw the truck they used. I want to make sure you have its description."

"Yeah, yeah, I got it." He flipped his pad shut and picked up the recorder.

My eyes closed. I didn't see him leave the room.

## Monday, May 14

I sat in the backseat of the limousine as it crept along the crushed shell pathway among the graves. My mother sat next to me, my dad next to her. I felt her concern for me. The ride from the hospital had been quiet. Earlier, I had asked them to pick up a suit from the house because I wasn't ready to go home, not without Lee.

They had made arrangements for the funeral once my discharge from the hospital had been finalized. I knew I would have to go home soon. At least for a few days they would be staying at our house, and I would sleep in the guestroom.

The limo stopped. A cluster of folding chairs filled a funeral tent on a gentle rise a few hundred feet away. Eight men in black suits carried a maroon casket under the cover and placed it on a lowering device. Heat waves shimmered from the top of the tent. A dark blue sheet of plastic topped a mound of dirt to the side of the tent. A stream of people made their way to the gravesite. I didn't want to get out of the cool, idling car, but the driver came to my door and pulled it open.

My mom took my left arm, and we waited for my

dad to join us. We walked side by side slowly up the rise. Within thirty seconds, sweat rolled down my temples. I stared at the thick St. Augustine grass as it crunched under my shoes. My mom's heels sunk in the heavy turf. She seemed to walk on tiptoes.

The sling strapped my right arm to my chest. It kept my shoulder and collarbone immobile and trapped the heat. My shoulder hurt, but I wondered if my irritation from the heat was going to surpass the pain in my shoulder. The last row of chairs came into view, and I stopped.

At funerals, I'd always stood in back of the chairs or sat in the last row, but most of the chairs were full, and the crowd was still growing. My mom tugged on my left arm. "This way, Mark." We moved around the end of the chairs and slid in between the casket and the first row, stopping at the middle. My mom and dad sat, but I stood, staring at the casket. I didn't want to sit. I touched the top of the casket. It swam into focus as I saw a tear splash next to my hand. My knees buckled, but I remained upright. I heard my mother sob.

The minister began his remarks. He appeared fragmented as I saw him through my tears. I hoped he was able to help the others who listened. I realized that whatever he said, it wasn't for Lee.

She wasn't here. I finally sat but continued to stare. It was just a box, a pretty box. I focused on the streams of sweat rolling down my face, into my blazer, and into the fabric of my shirt. The inside of my sling became a sponge for half of my body. I had thought it would be good to be here to say goodbye to my sweetheart.

My heartbeat ramped up. I couldn't say goodbye. She wasn't here.

When we were together, it was wonderful. We were

comfortable, happy. I think we both took life for granted. Now that it was ripped away, I could see that. I needed Lee, even when I hadn't realized that I needed her. All our plans and goals were gone, never to be. I loved our life, our house, being together, not because I wanted them, but because we both wanted them. Now, I didn't want any of it. Losing Lee meant losing my own life. I didn't care anymore. I thought I was going to say goodbye to my love. But, I couldn't. Somehow, I'd missed it.

The panic ebbed, and a smoldering anger grew in its place.

I stood, ran my hand across the top of the casket, turned, and moved to the end of the front row of chairs. The minister stopped, and everything became quiet. I walked past the little crowd and down the slope away from the gravesite.

# Chapter 3

**Monday, May 28**

I pushed open the back door to Johnson and Kinley, the largest and only architecture and engineering firm in the city. My shirt stuck to me from the two-minute walk from the parking garage. I was glad no one stood around the back door smoking. The firm spread over all four floors of the building, and my workspace was on the third floor, which was dedicated to the engineering department. I took the elevator.

Murmurs echoed throughout the third floor from behind head-high dividers. I was glad to get to my office without running into anyone. I powered up my computer while I hit the phone message button. It told me I had thirty-seven messages. I slammed down the phone, and pushed away from my desk. I ran my fingers through my hair as I walked a small circle. Calculations, specifications, drawings, schedules - they didn't seem to interest me anymore. Nothing interested me anymore.

I decided to risk it and headed for the coffee machine at the end of the building. If I ran into anyone, I would just blow the person off. I simmered with anger. I felt more irritated than angry; it was like sandpaper against my skin that occasionally rubbed a raw spot. When I turned from the hallway into the mini-kitchen, Chief Mackey was pouring a cup of coffee.

I smiled. He was one guy I was always glad to see. "Chief, how is it I never see you without a cup of coffee?"

He set down the pot and reached for my left hand. "Mark, let me say how sorry I am for your loss." He maintained his grip and squeezed my forearm in his other hand.

"Thanks, Chief." A few seconds passed in silence, and he dropped my hand. "Let me get you a cup." He pulled a mug from the cupboard and filled it. "You know why I'm never without a cup of coffee? Twenty-four years in the Navy. If I didn't have the right mixture of coffee in my blood, I'd go into a coma."

I'd heard it many times, but I still smiled.

"Chief, if I'd run into anyone else but you, I would've turned and walked away. I can't deal with it. People are so…"

"I know. But, hey, we can talk about other things. Come on." Chief Mackey turned and opened the door to the balcony.

Before the door shut behind us, the heat got to me.

"It's too hot. Let's go down to the second-floor conference room." The small conference room was perfect for informal meetings between departments but not used very often.

We pulled chairs and dropped into them. The lights were low, and the room was cool. I plucked at the front of my shirt, sucking in the refreshing air.

"How's the arm?" He nodded at my sling.

"It's my shoulder and collarbone area. A bullet went right through just below my collarbone."

"What caliber of gun?"

It had never occurred to me to find out. "I don't know."

Mackey looked at me like he couldn't believe I didn't know. "How's the pain?"

"It's bearable most of the time. What bothers me more is that I don't want to be here, at work. I feel compelled to be here, but I really can't do anything with my right arm in a sling."

"You want to do something else?"

"No, that's not it. I just...I just don't feel like working. I don't want to talk to people. I don't want to deal with the petty work or the politics around here."

Mackey laughed. "Sounds normal for this place."

"Yeah, I've probably said the same thing before. But then, it was just standard-procedure complaining."

"I think the big boss would understand if you asked for a leave of absence. After all, getting shot is a new thing for J and K. You've set a new precedent."

"I guess a leave of absence is a good idea."

As Chief Mackey took a slug of coffee, I said, "I just don't know what to do."

"What do you mean? Take a trip, rest, go to the movies. Get well."

"That's not it. I'm restless. Most of the time, I'm just angry. I feel aimless. And helpless."

Mackey leaned forward. "Mark, I can't imagine how you feel. I don't know what I would do if I lost my wife. But, I know you. You're not a quitter."

I gazed into my cup and took a sip, trying to keep from choking up. I looked up. I knew he felt bad for me.

"Look, Mark, you need to go to the cops and find out what's going on with your case. That'll help. You'll see there's progress and hope for finding her killer."

"It's only been a few weeks. You really think they've made some progress?"

"Man, don't you watch CSI? They have ways of solving crimes these days that would have been considered black magic ten years ago."

I smiled. "Yeah, I guess so."

"You know who's on the case?"

"I think so. A detective came and interviewed me at the hospital."

"Good. Go see him. He'll be straight with you."

"Okay, you're probably right."

"You have anything for protection?" Chief Mackey squinted at me.

"What do you mean?"

He bent forward and pulled a small black pistol from below the table. He laid it on the table. "Buddy, you've suffered a break-in, robbery, assault, and worst of all, you lost your wife in the whole mess. I have a concealed weapon license. No one would do that to me. And no one would do that to you, either, if you had a gun."

"But, you're former Navy. I'd expect you to be good with a gun."

"Mark, you have the right to protect yourself. Especially in your own home."

"I've never thought about it."

"What if someone breaks in again?"

"I'm not sleeping well. The slightest noise and I'm awake. I'm sleeping in the guest bedroom. I just can't imagine lying in our old bed."

"Well, maybe you'll wake up when someone tries to break in, but then what?"

I looked back into the dregs in my cup and saw the whole scene of waking naked and defenseless to the sight of intruders. I shuddered. Glancing at Chief Mackey, I shrugged.

"Look, come on down to the gun club, and I'll show you a bit about shooting, some tips on how you can protect yourself. If you're interested, we'll sign you up for a weapons class. You can get your own concealed weapons license. Even if you don't want a license, you have the right to own a gun and protect yourself, especially from a break-in."

"Okay, I guess I can do that."

"Have you put in a security system?"

I shook my head.

"A well-known company, like ADT, allows you access to data on your house on the Web anywhere. That is a good start. Now, we've just had a product presentation here at J and K about a new system that monitors the perimeter of your property as an advanced warning. Pretty cutting-edge stuff. The manufacturer wants us to consider specifying it on high-end homes. It's pretty amazing. You can piggyback the monitoring system onto the ADT security system data feed, but only you have access to it. Hey, I'll e-mail you a link to the product specs, and you can check it out."

Chief Mackey looked at his watch and slapped the table. "Just remember, you have friends. You need anything, let me know. Hey, I got to go." He swiped at his pistol, and it disappeared.

I returned to my office. I picked up the phone and hit the "delete all" button. I felt good for resolving all thirty-seven messages in a matter of seconds. I pecked at my computer for a few minutes with one hand, composing my request for a leave of absence. It frustrated me, and I leaned down and pulled the plug on the computer.

I looked around my office, and nothing jumped out at me. I decided to go see my boss, who was tucked away in his corner office.

"I have to request a leave of absence. I really can't work."

"I understand. You'll need to come back in a day or two so you can hand off your projects to one of the other engineers. I'll see who's available."

I nodded. "Just let me know when you have it set up." I headed for the door.

"How's the arm?"

I held up my left hand and nodded as I walked out of his office.

## Tuesday, June 5

The installation tech the security system company had sent was good. It was a sign to me that the product and the company were reliable. I watched as he installed and tested a sensor on every window and door in the house. He even put one on the yard shed. He explained how it all worked and showed me how to operate the control panel. When he asked about my sling, I told him I'd gotten shot in a break-in a few weeks ago. At that, he offered to come over anytime if I had any trouble with the system. He showed me how to access my security system on my cell phone and laptop. Impressed at its sophistication, I asked him if he knew about a new perimeter-monitoring system that could sense people or vehicles as they entered the property. He said as far as he knew, there was nothing like that on the market.

As the tech left, I ran into the mailman at the front door. I signed for a registered letter. When I opened it, I was shocked to find a check from our life insurance company for a death benefit in the amount of one hundred thousand dollars.

## Thursday, June 7

It took me a while to find the checkbook and deposit slips. Using one hand, I became frustrated digging through the papers on the desk and rifling through its drawers. Apparently, Lee didn't keep the checkbook and deposit slips there. I checked all the logical places in the house with no luck. I exhaled a laugh when I found them in a spare dresser we kept in the closet, in the bottom drawer, in a Tupperware container under some old skirts. I loved that woman.

*\*\*\**

When I went into the bank lobby, the line for the tellers looked daunting, and I turned toward the assistant manager's cubicle. She saw me and stood as I walked toward her. Her dark hair and round face seemed familiar.

She smiled. "Can I help you? Oh, how did you hurt your arm?"

I didn't want questions. I cleared my throat. "Gunshot. Can you deposit this for me?"

She took the deposit slip and check from me and sat down. She filled the slip and stopped. Looking up with a big smile, she said, "You must have won the lottery."

My eyes burned, and I swallowed. I shook my head, not trusting my voice.

She looked back down, quickly scanning the paperwork. "Oh, you have to sign here."

I took the pen with my left hand and squatted. She watched me struggle for a moment and then said, "Here, let me hold it steady for you. By the way, how's Lee? I haven't seen her for a while."

I set the pen down gently without looking at the woman. I pressed my lips together and held up a hand. The woman hesitated, picked up the slip and check, and left. I felt like screaming. *She's dead! It's my fault she's dead and here I am getting money for it. I don't deserve it. It should have been me to die and not her. I didn't act soon enough, or forceful enough.* I leaned on the desk and put my head in my hands.

The woman came back in her cubicle quietly. "Mr.

Stone, I'm sorry. I just saw the details on the check saying it was a death benefit for Lee Stone. I had no idea." She touched me on the shoulder. "Please, accept my sincere apology and condolences."

I nodded and wiped my nose.

She came around her desk and sat. "If you don't mind, how did she pass?"

I let out a long breath. "Shot to death."

## Wednesday, June 13

I had a hard time getting used to the female voice from the security system panel mounted on the kitchen wall. She told me that there was a fault on the front door, which meant that someone had opened the screen door. The doorbell rang. When I opened the front door, the FedEx guy had an envelope for me to sign. Inside the envelope, I found an official notice from our home mortgage company. Due to Lee's death, our mortgage insurance policy had paid off the balance on the loan on the house. The notice informed me that I had to sign an affidavit, and the company would finalize it.

I set the papers on the dining room table, recalling eight years ago when we'd closed on the house. Lee and I had argued about paying the extra for mortgage life insurance. She had won the argument.

In the end, it didn't matter. I had lost in the worst way. "I would much rather have a mortgage and a life with Lee," I said to the empty room.

## Friday, June15

I pulled on the glass door stenciled with "Police Department, Apopka Springs, Florida." Inside, the entry vestibule was cool and modern. A raised reception counter with an elderly woman sat across a ceramic tile floor. As I approached, I noticed she overfilled a police uniform. She heard me come in but didn't glance up when I stopped at her station. I stared at a crooked part in her gray hair for ten seconds, then fifteen seconds. She finally looked up, noted my sling, and said, "Well?

"I'm here to see Lieutenant Beauchamp." I laid his card in front of her.

"He expecting you?"

"I don't have an appointment, but I'm sure he'll be interested in meeting with me."

"If he's here. Name?"

"Mark Stone."

She picked up a handset and punched a few numbers. She spoke in monotone. Hanging up, she pointed to the right. "Go through those doors, down the hall, and up the stairs at the end. Detectives are in the old building second floor. Can't miss it." She turned back to her desktop without looking at me.

"Thanks, you've been a big help." I made my way through the doors and down the hall. At the stairway, the building's architecture changed from modern and professional to simple, rustic wood. I had a faint recollection of the police headquarters renovation ten years ago when it had tripled its floor space and quadrupled the garage. The city had hired a firm from Tallahassee instead of J and K, no doubt a back-scratching deal.

I climbed the worn wooden stairs. They had depressions on both sides like wheel tracks in a dirt road. They creaked, each one with a slightly different pitch than the others. A ten-foot-wide landing at the top fed three different directions to wooden doors with frosted glass in the top half. The door in front of me was painted with the word "Detectives." I opened it to find a waist-high, wooden rail across the front of the room and an empty reception desk to the left.

Inside the rail, a handful of desks, filing cabinets, and chairs sat in a pattern that clearly denoted individual territories. Detectives sat at two of the desks, and I recognized a red vest. Beauchamp looked up and waved me in. I pushed through a spring-loaded gate and worked through the maze. Beauchamp stood, hooking his thumbs on each side of his vest, and watched me approach. He motioned to a wooden chair on the left side of his desk.

"Mr. Stone." He offered no handshake. Beauchamp cleared his throat. "You were on my list to contact today."

"Really? I'm glad to hear that. It's been a few weeks, and I'm anxious to hear about any progress on my wife's murder."

"Yes, yes. As a matter of fact, the department has completed the crime scene investigation."

"So, you have some good evidence to go on?"

"Well, evidence, at least." He clasped his hands on his belly.

"What about the bullet that went through my shoulder? Did you recover it? What was it?"

He glanced at my sling for a few moments, seeming to weigh his answer. "We have it, and it came from a .38 special."

"And what about the gun that killed my wife?"

"Nine millimeter."

"Can you trace either bullet?"

"No, neither one is in the federal records. But, look here, Mr. Stone, I was only going to contact you today to let you know the crime scene investigation was complete, as I said, and that you have been cleared as a suspect."

"When did I become a suspect?" It came out hard. My cheeks grew hot.

"Standard procedure. Husband is always the prime

suspect." Beauchamp waggled his head as if he were lecturing a child.

"What about real suspects?"

"Not your concern."

The heat from my cheeks spread throughout my body. "It's my only concern!"

Beauchamp jerked his head and looked down his nose at me. He pursed his lips as if he had something to say but was holding back.

I spoke through clenched teeth. "Do you have any leads from the crime scene?"

"I can't comment on an ongoing investigation."

"But, she was my wife. I'm sure you can comment to me."

He gave me a blank look, looked at his desktop, then looked back at me. Ten seconds ticked by. Then I realized the truth.

"You don't have anything, do you?"

"We're working on it."

"What about the description I gave you of the getaway vehicle?"

"Mr. Stone, your description is pretty flimsy. What you describe could be any of a great number of trucks."

When I clenched my fists, pain shot through my right shoulder, and I closed my eyes. A piercing pain hit me when a vision of Lee's lifeless body flashed in my mind, and I thought again that it was my fault she was gone. I missed her, but more, I needed her forgiveness. When I opened my eyes, Beauchamp hadn't moved.

"When you did your investigation at my house, did you stand in my front door and look across the street like I did when I spotted the getaway vehicle?"

"Yeah, I did."

"But, did you do it at night?"

"Mr. Stone, I'd say it's impossible to see any detail in the dark like that. You were wounded, probably in shock. I can't rely on your description. It is too nebulous."

I was deflated by Beauchamp's dismissal of the only real evidence from that night. I had only small bits of information about the crime, and I depended on him to make something of those small bits. He was my only chance. My greatest hope was that the detective could track down the vehicle from my description. "You're the professional," I said, even though I didn't believe it. "You need to find those murderers, now."

He stood, pulling on the bottom of his vest. "You have a good day, now." He waved his left hand toward the door without looking at me.

On the stairs, a tread creaked especially loud, and I stopped. It was clear Beauchamp wasn't getting anywhere. I didn't want to think he was lazy, or that he didn't have the skills. Replaying the conversation, I realized he was hoping the crime scene investigation would drop something real into his lap, and when it didn't, he was stuck.

Until that instant, I'd thought he was my only chance, but he wasn't even that. I couldn't sit around and wait. I had to do something, but what could I do?

It was my fault Lee was gone. I couldn't save her, couldn't do a thing to stop it. But now, I had to do something about it. The stair creaked under my feet as I swayed back and forth with each conflicting thought.

I'm going to find those killers. I don't know how, but I am going to do it, and they're going to pay for it. I have to... for Lee.

# Chapter 4

**Friday, June 15**

It didn't matter that I had left the windows down and parked in the shade of a small tree. I folded myself into the oven that was our nine-year-old Stratus and struggled left-handed to get the key into the ignition. As soon as it kicked to life, I flipped the air to high. It never ran on less than maximum when I drove.

I looked over at the modernized building. "Beauchamp is an idiot."

I dialed Chief Mackey and touched the speaker button.

"Hello, this is Mackey."

"Chief, it's Mark. Got a minute?"

"Always."

"Hey, when are you going to the gun range again?"

"Anytime you want. I don't have any set plans."

"What about today?"

"Sure, if you want to make it later in the afternoon."

"Sounds good. You pick the time."

The roar of the cool air filled a short pause. "How about between four-thirty and five? You remember where it is?"

"Yeah, sounds good. See you then." Once I had all the windows up, I worked my way out of the police headquarters parking lot.

"Pick one to start."

There were three pistols and clips on the plywood table in front of us. We stood on a wide concrete floor under an open wooden frame holding up a shingled roofed. Chief Mackey had given me a tour of the club, and it impressed me. We were on the firing line of the fifty-yard range. It was separated from the hundred-yard range by a high earthen berm. The three-hundred-yard range was on the far side of the hundred-yard range. Each range had to be at least seventy-five yards wide. The shingled structure with the concrete floor ran the length of all three ranges. A tall berm closed off the end of each range. Mackey had placed two wooden target supports seven yards downrange from our position. On each one he had taped paper targets.

"What is the smaller black one?" I nodded at the tabletop. Sweat dripped from my chin, and I was grateful for the shade.

Mackey picked up the pistol and its clip. Holding it barrel-up, he said, "Double-oh seven."

"What?"

"The early James Bond carried this gun. It's a Walther PPK." He chambered a round. With both hands on the grip, he faced downrange and fired it rapidly eight times, each shot whip-cracking in the air between us. He popped the clip, slapped it on the table, and held the pistol up for me to see. "The only difference is that this is a .32 caliber, and Bond used a .380."

He amazed me. "You're good."

"I don't know. Did I hit the target?" We turned, and I counted eight holes in the paper.

"Only eight times. I'd say you're good."

Smiling, he put the gun down and picked up the one next to it along with its clip. "Now, this is a 9-mm, very similar to a .380." He loaded and shot at the other target. The gun boomed through the foam earplugs I had jammed in my ears earlier. Mackey's pace was measured. I smelled the gun smoke. After eleven shots, he released the clip and set down both pieces. He squinted at the target and nodded.

"Eleven for eleven. I think you may be an expert."

"It's easy to hit a target that's not moving. And I've practiced a lot, but I wouldn't say I'm an expert."

"Okay, what's the last one?"

"You don't recognize it?"

"No. I've never shot before, remember?"

"Yeah, but this is an icon." He picked it up and twisted it back and forth for me. "Don't you watch movies?"

"Sure. It seems familiar, but I couldn't say what it is."

"A piece of history. This is a 1911 .45. This is the pistol every combat soldier carried in World War Two and every other military conflict until Iraq. Let's see how it does." He showed me the clip and slid it into the pistol. He fired seven shots. I felt the concussion of each one. It was so loud I didn't think I was wearing earplugs. With each shot the muzzle flipped up, even though he held it tightly in both hands. He calmly lowered and aimed each time. He slipped the clip out, and placed both on the table.

My ears rang. Mackey smiled at me, tipped his head downrange, and said, "Shall we take a look?" He picked up two more paper targets and the roll of duct tape.

We left the shade and walked to the targets. The first one now held eight small holes and seven large holes.

"Chief, I know I am a total novice at this, but even I know excellence when I see it."

He taped up the two new targets over the old ones. "I'm just showing off. And having some fun at it."

As we walked back, he said, "You want to have some fun? You should try it."

The short walk had triggered another round of sweating. At the table I wiped my free hand on my shorts. "I'm not sure I can handle a gun. I'm not left-handed. And, the .45 scares me."

"I don't think you'll have a problem. Try the .32, and take it slow. I'll help you." He fed small cartridges into the clip for the Walther, then set it down and picked up the pistol. He showed me how to hold the pistol and aim it. He gave me a short lecture on using a two-handed grip and how it helps to stabilize the gun. There was a moment of hesitation when he realized how limited I was with my right arm in the sling and how I held the pistol in just my left hand. He shrugged and continued. He slipped the clip into the gun and urged me to take a shot.

The little gun kicked up as I took my first shot and missed the target entirely. Mackey gave me a nod and waved downrange. I pulled the trigger again and missed the target again. Mackey told me to squeeze the trigger slowly, and on my third try, I hit the target. I smiled and hit it again. When I had exhausted the clip, four of the eight shots had found the paper.

"See, you can be an expert, too." He took the gun from me and ejected the clip.

"That's fun, but I think I'll hold off on any more until I can use both hands."

"No problem. We can do this anytime you want. By the way, what did you hear from the cops about Lee's case?"

Beauchamp's smug face came to mind. I had been

having so much fun, my worry about the murder and the ineffective cop had been pushed aside. I clenched my good fist and looked for something to hit.

"I take it things are moving slowly." Mackey pulled the orange foam plugs from both ears.

"They're not just slow. They have nothing." I pulled my plugs, and it felt good.

"Come on, surely the crime scene techs came up with something."

"Not according to Beauchamp."

"Who?"

"The detective on the case. He's an idiot."

"What's their next step?"

"I don't think they have one."

"What about you?"

I rolled and pinched one of the foam earplugs. No matter how hard I squeezed, it expanded back to its original form. "I'm going to try to track the killers down myself."

Mackey surprised me. "Good for you," he said with a nod. "Anything I can do to help, just let me know."

"Thanks. I just don't know what to do."

Mackey turned to the table to pack the guns. Over his shoulder he said, "Mark, grab the broom and sweep up the empty brass."

As I swept up the shells, he collected the wooden target supports. He set them against the table and said, "I think I saw you flinch when I shot the .45."

I thought he was trying to be funny. "What of it?"

"I just want to say, you can't be afraid if you are going to try to go after the guys who killed your wife. You can't flinch, and I don't necessarily mean with a gun. It could get dangerous, and if you're afraid or not committed to what you are doing, you could get killed yourself."

It was like a lightning bolt had exploded a few feet away: an instant of pure terror and a concussion that knocked the wind out of me. When the instant passed, a massive steel lock snapped shut, and I was totally convinced, totally committed to finding the killers and making them pay.

# Chapter 5

**Saturday, June 16**

I stepped out our front door and into the wet heat. Its grip never seemed to fade, even at eight in the morning. On the drive home from the gun range I had decided Mackey's warning was credible. I felt fat and slow, and I didn't want that to keep me from doing whatever I had to do to track down Lee's killers. I couldn't remember the last time I'd tried to do any workout.

At the end of the driveway, I shifted from a walk to a jog. I knew the route through our neighborhood but didn't know if I could run the one mile I had planned. Within a few steps, I realized that I had to hold my right arm against my body with my left hand. The sling was too loose, and my arm jarred with each step. Even holding it tight didn't mute the pain in my right shoulder. Each time my right foot came down it sent a shock of pain into my shoulder. Maybe it was too soon to get started on this.

The thought triggered old memories of excuses I'd used to try to minimize my training workouts. College cross-country is a team sport, regardless of how you look at it. Once I didn't make the starting team, I'd realized I couldn't take short cuts. After that, I'd never quit. I'd never given in to any excuse to cut it short. That thought pushed me now. I had started, and I wouldn't quit.

My breathing came hard, and it rasped in my throat. Sweat rolled off my face. I tried again to recall the last time I had worked out. It must have been years ago. My lungs and chest hurt. I couldn't get enough air. My legs began to burn. I picked out a huge pine tree a few hundred yards ahead and focused on it. I knew I had to get my mind off of the pain.

Lee, this is for you. I am doing this for you. I am going to find your killers and they are going to pay. But how?

I realized that the cops always started with the crime scene. But, I was there. I already knew more than they did. The thought came back, and I questioned if I really knew the crime scene. I had not gone into the master bedroom since coming home from the hospital with my mom and dad. We had gotten most of my clothes and other things and moved them to the guest bedroom. I'd kept the door closed. I just did not want to relive Lee's murder.

But maybe, that is just what I have to do. I have to start somewhere.

I wiped sweat on my left shoulder and looked ahead. I glimpsed my house two blocks away. I had fallen into a rhythm of breathing and slapping the pavement with each stride. It was nothing like the old days, but I sensed that it could come back if I could stand the pain in getting there.

I leaned forward and stretched out my stride. My pace increased a little, and I held it until I hit our yard.

It took me the best part of a half-hour to get control of my breathing. I sprawled on a towel, nearly lifeless on the couch. Dusk settled, and I accidentally rambled down memories about my life with Lee. Each memory seemed to fast-forward to the scene of her lifeless on our bed. I imagined Mackey's pistol in my fist, the barrel against the killer's head while I ripped off his ski mask.

I didn't want to dwell there. But, the one thought that dogged me was that I had always hoped to get back into shape for Lee. She'd always looked good. She said I looked good, but I could see what she saw, and I was ashamed, at least thirty pounds ashamed. The mantle clock showed that it was close to an hour before I stopped sweating. My shirt was drenched, but I felt recovered from the exhaustion. I thought it would help me stick to the running program if I made a daily record, and I owed it to Lee to keep up the program. I needed strength to persevere.

It took three tries to get off the couch to head for the kitchen. Lee kept a notebook on a shelf with her cookbooks, and I found it easily. I dropped to the kitchen table and flipped through pages covered with her notes. I could see her scribbling some and smiled. When I found the first open page, I wrote the date with the number one behind it and how long I had run. I left the page open and dropped the notebook on the dining room table as I headed to the shower.

Later, cool and dry, I put my hand on the master bedroom door. I swung it open and stood in the doorway. The room was stuffy, even with the air running in the rest of the house. I opened the drapes to early-evening sunlight and decided to start my investigation by going through the sequence of events of that night. I sat on the bed where I had been when the killers had come through the door. The room didn't look anything like my memory. I imagined Lee next to me and moved to the position where I'd confronted the killer. As I stood, I looked back at the bed and saw Lee, naked and afraid.

My knees buckled, and I dropped to the floor. *My actions had gotten her killed.* Until that moment, I hadn't made the connection. I leaned against the bed and sobbed. Not only had I failed to protect her from getting killed, but I had started the chain reaction that had caused it.

The room was dark when I finally straightened up. I wiped my face on the bed one more time. I was determined to follow the sequence all the way through. I remembered the gunshot and put my hand over the upper part of my sling, turning to look at the bullet hole in the wall. I touched it, picked at it, but it didn't shed any clues. I walked through the steps that had followed. I went to the front door, opened it and stared down the street, seeing the truck speed away in my memory.

At the bedroom doorway again, I studied the room for a long time. There had to be something I could use. Disjointed scenes of that night flashed in front of me, but a fleeting thought haunted me. Something I couldn't grasp. The harder I tried to define it, the more it retreated. I gave up and decided to try to walk through the events from the killer's perspective.

Back at the front door, I tried to imagine what the killers would do. I knew from the police report and from filling out the insurance forms that they had taken things before breaking into our bedroom. I moved to the small alcove that we called our den and stood next to the desk. I could imagine them searching it and grabbing what they could. But, the desk gave up no insight into the killers. From there, I was sure they'd begun to look for more likely places to steal things. One had made his way to our bedroom. He had passed the shelving unit where we kept all kinds of things. I stood again at our bedroom door. I was the killer. I turned on the light and pulled my gun. In front of me were a defenseless, naked couple, and a single bullet hole in the wall on the far side of the bed.

I pounded the doorjamb with my fist. "What am I

thinking? There's nothing here."

I walked across the bedroom, stopping in the doorway to the master bathroom. Inside the glass-walled shower, a drip fell every few seconds from the showerhead. I opened the door, stepped in, and tugged on the handle. The dripping stopped. I didn't know how many times I had done that. Lee had never seemed to shut it off completely. My eyes were drawn to the soap dish holding the yellow bar of soap. Cracks spread across its dry face. My throat constricted, and my eyes welled with tears. Lee and I had always shared the bar of soap, and we had a tradition that went back years. Every bar of soap became part of the next new bar of soap and could be traced back what we called generations. I had forgotten what generation this bar was. I turned to the top of the glass wall on the right. I put my hand up near a number, written on the glass with the bar of soap when it had been hard and fresh: a hazy number 338, in Lee's handwriting.

When we'd first married, Lee had started a tradition that had endured many years, through the good times and the bad. We always showered together, and she showed me how to blend the sliver of the used bar of soap into a fresh bar of soap. Both pieces had to be in full lather, and then she would compress the small piece into the larger piece. When it dried overnight, it would be melted together as one solid bar the next time we used it. I had resisted at first, telling her it was silly. But, when she'd kept at it, and even started to keep track of the generations, I became as committed to it as she was.

One time, angry with her, I used the last of the soap and threw away the sliver. By the time I realized how foolish I had been and was ready to apologize, she had already started a new generation with the new number 1 written in soap on the glass wall. She never mentioned it. Today, I still regret throwing it out. When we accidentally ran out of soap on occasion, it also ended the chain of generations, but we always started over.

I pried the bar of soap out of the dish and held it to my nose. I had always been able to smell it on Lee, but I knew I would never breathe it in on her again. As I lowered the bar, I accepted that she was gone. It wasn't that I had any hope, but I had stayed above the concept of not sharing the rest of our life together. The soap smelled like the bar, not the fragrance of my lover. Only her body could combine with the soap to create her unique and desirable scent. And I would never have the chance again.

If she had been there, I would have promised her I would keep the generations going. It was a small thing that we could continue to share, even if she wasn't there. We had both worked to keep the generations going, but it was her signature, a part of her that I could keep.

What I couldn't accept was that she had been taken from me, ripped from our life together. I squeezed the bar with rising anger. Someone had broken into our house and destroyed our life. It was raw and brutal, and I wanted justice. I slammed the bar on its ceramic ledge and spun out of the shower.

Walking across the bedroom from the bathroom, I came to a sudden stop. The vision of the killers' truck speeding away replayed in my memory. In the vision, I saw something I hadn't remembered, a heavy-duty trailer hitch protruding from under the rear bumper. I knew it then. That kind of hitch wasn't standard on pickup trucks and was typically used on trucks that often pulled heavy loads. It was distinctive, a detail that would make it stick out. I had the key to finding the truck.

***

Five hours and fifty websites later, I knew every detail of Dodge pickup trucks from 1994 to 2002. There were quite a few variations, but now I knew the differences. The one I was after fell between 1998 and 2002. I had printed out a photo of the exact version of truck locked in my memory; just as I had guessed, the trailer hitch was not a standard Dodge option. It was an after-market item that had to be custom-fitted for heavy-duty towing. The truck in the photo I had printed didn't have the hitch. For that, I printed a separate photo.

## Monday, June 18

Once again, the elderly receptionist in her police uniform did not look up at me for a long pause. When she did, there was no recognition. "Yes?"

I laid Beauchamp's card in front of her and held up a manila folder. "Is Detective Beauchamp in? I have some new information on my case. I'm Mark Stone. My wife Lee was murdered."

She reached for the phone and punched in a few numbers. When she'd finished, she waved toward the right and started to give directions.

"I know where to find him."

When I pushed through the little gate into Beauchamp's area, he saw me and nodded, but didn't rise. The area was quiet, with one other detective hunched over his desk and on the phone.

"Detective, I have some new information on Lee's case."

It was as if I'd slapped him. He jerked back with wide eyes.

"What information?"

"I recalled more detail from the night of the murder."

"Are you saying you didn't tell the whole story in your previous statement?"

It was my turn to feel slapped. But, I didn't react, though I felt my heartbeat rise. I stared down at him for a few seconds. "I just said that I recalled more detail."

"What have you got?" He nodded at the old wooden chair at the side of his desk, then turned, closed a folder on his desk, and pushed it aside. I sat.

"You remember the getaway truck?"

"Mr. Stone, we've been over that."

"It's key to the murder, Detective." My heart began to pound, and I felt my cheeks and neck burn. I could feel myself a step away from rage. "It's the only link to the killers."

"It's not hard evidence."

"There is no hard evidence. You told me that. So, you have to start with something. That's what I brought you today. You want to see it or not?"

"Okay, but no guarantees."

I looked at him for a minute, letting my anger bleed off.

He grew impatient. "Mr. Stone, what have you got?"

I opened the folder and spread the two full-page color photos on his desk. I told him about recalling the special hitch and then about the research I had done. I explained to him my guess of '98 to '02 model years, based on its appearance and features.

"Detective, you recall the last time we spoke? You said that my description was too nebulous. This is now specific."

"And?"

"Look, it had a Florida plate. Get a listing from the state for all the trucks from ninety-eight to oh-four. Then, start eliminating the trucks that don't match the body style or other features. I'm sure you can narrow it down to a very manageable list."

"That sounds very simple, Mr. Stone. I assure you, it is not. Let's say we do it. How does that lead us to the killer?"

"When you have a suspect for any other crime, don't you do a line-up where the victim points out the criminal? Once you have it narrowed down, I can pick out the right truck."

"Really, Mr. Stone."

His tone told me all I needed to know. "You aren't going to even consider it."

"It is a long shot in my opinion. And, one that will get us nothing but trouble."

"Why?"

"First, I don't trust your memory. Second, you identify the wrong owner, and we have a lawsuit on our hands."

I stood quickly and left. It was the only thing that kept me from putting my fist through his teeth.

# Chapter 6

**Wednesday, June 20**

"We don't get a lot of gunshot rehabs here." The therapist smiled as she looked up from the file. She wore a brightly patterned set of scrubs with an oval nametag that said Rachael. "But, don't worry, we know what we're doing."

"I'm sure you do."

"The record says you had some major surgery on it. I hope you don't mind, but I'd like to take a look at it before we get started." She dropped the file on the desk and came around.

I stood and pulled my tee shirt over my head. She put her hand lightly on my shoulder and pushed her reading glasses higher on her nose. A light scent of her perfume caught up with her. She looked at my collarbone, my back, and then again at my upper chest. She made some notes in her file.

"Okay, you can put your shirt on. We're going to go through a series of simple exercises. You'll need to do these periodically for the next few weeks. I'll show you how they're done, and we'll do a set of them today. I'll give you a schedule and a cheat sheet to follow for doing them at home. Are you ready to get started?"

We started with what she called some simple stretching moves. She should have called them torture moves. White-hot pain stabbed down my arm and across my chest. She saw my grimace and seemed to take it a little slower. The stretching lasted about ten minutes. When we stopped, sweat rolled off my face and drenched my shirt. She made another note on the file. "Have you been moving your arm at all?"

"No, I've been wearing the sling since leaving the hospital. Should I have been?"

"Some people do. You seem to be in pretty good condition. I kind of expected you to have done some exploratory movements. But, it's okay." She smiled.

"I've started up a running routine."

She raised her eyebrows. "That's great. But, check with me before starting any other type of sporting activity, at least until we're done with our course of therapy, okay?"

"Sure. Perhaps it would have been more accurate to say I've jogged around my neighborhood three times in the past few days. No so life-threatening, although I thought it was."

She smiled. "Now we're going to start on some real exercises."

We began by using a small dumbbell and doing four different exercises, each one repeated ten times. When I realized we were going to repeat them, I grabbed the other small dumbbell and did the same exercises with my left hand. We repeated each set of the exercises four times. I couldn't remember when I'd worked so hard. The pain faded, but the sweat continued to roll off my face. My tee shirt was soaked from the neckline to my navel. When we took a break, I sat on a stool with my hands on my knees, breathing hard.

"You're a good patient, Mr. Stone. I haven't heard a peep out of you."

"Thanks." It came out sounding like a hiss between two quick breaths.

"Most of my patients would be into the whining stage by now. What's your secret?"

I held up my hand and took a few deep breaths. "You don't want to know. What's next?"

She looked at me and turned to the file. "We are going to do a few more stretches, and we'll be done."

She stepped behind me and told me she was going to assist. She put one hand on my back and gripped my right wrist. Then, she lifted my arm and pushed on my back, pulling my arm toward my back. Electric pain shot through my chest, and my breathing ramped up. In a silky voice, she told me to relax. I could no more relax than fly to the moon. It hurt so badly I began to twitch.

"Still no complaints, Mr. Stone?" She maintained the hold on my arm.

"I focus my anger on the pain." It came out between gritted teeth.

She slowly lowered my arm. "We have to go up now." She raised my arm above my head and held it. The pain wasn't as bad. "And why are you so angry?"

I blurted out the story of Beauchamp's ineptitude over the murder of my wife. I told her how I had narrowed down the vehicles and given him the information, how he'd dismissed it, and how I was back to square one, with no hope in sight.

She seemed to take the rest of the stretching easy on me, or maybe I was just getting used to it. She worked on me for a few more minutes before saying, "Okay, we're done. Why don't you sit down and catch your breath while I make some notes in your file?"

After a few moments, she put down her pen and pulled off her glasses. When she looked up at me, I noticed a thin sheen of perspiration on her face. She didn't seem to be aware of it. I liked her. She worked hard and cared about her patients; at least, that was what she'd shown me.

"I don't want you to think I'm meddling…." Her voice trailed off, but her gaze remained on me.

I didn't know what she meant. "Yes?"

"Why don't you just go down to the local motor vehicle office and ask about the truck? Maybe they can give you a list of all the years and models that cover the specific truck you want to find."

"I don't think they give that kind of thing to regular people."

"I assume you need to change the legal name on your car title and registration. Right?

"I never thought about it, but I guess so."

"Go down there to take care of that, and while you're at the counter, just ask them."

"I still don't think they will help me."

"I learned something from my dad. He always said that if you don't try, you'll never know."

"I'll think about it."

We scheduled my next visit and took care of some paperwork. As I was leaving she said, "By the way, you don't need to wear that sling anymore. But, when you visit the motor vehicle office, it probably couldn't hurt to have it on." She gave me a wink and said goodbye.

When I got to the house, my shirt clung to me. I slipped on running shorts and shoes and ran for twenty minutes. I grabbed a towel when I came back inside and wiped my face three times before I got my fourth run noted in my log. I also noted the first physical therapy session with Rachel under the same date and underlined her name.

### Thursday, June 21

I took a number and looked around. The place was packed. I wondered if the motor vehicle office was ever anything but busy. I found a seat and waited. A half-hour later, my number came up, and I went to the counter, carrying the number slip in my right hand, which was supported by my sling. The number-taker pointed me to an open window across the room. As I approached, I read a little placard in a brushed aluminum frame: Sue Brown, Records Specialist.

"How may I help you, sir?" A middle-aged woman with curly, dark brown hair gave me a sincere smile. Maybe it was the sling effect.

I explained that I needed to change my vehicle records and why. I pulled them out, along with a sealed death certificate. Miss Brown was quite efficient, and it was over quickly. When she asked me if there was anything else she could help me with, I hesitated, started and stopped, and finally got it out that I wanted to help the police solve my wife's murder. To do so, I needed a list of specific trucks that fell within a few years of age, that I would narrow the list down and turn it over to them for finalizing the search. Unbelievably, Miss Brown seemed to consider my request. After a few moments she said, "Let me get the division supervisor."

I watched her walk away. She stopped at the biggest desk and leaned in to speak quietly to an older woman. They came back to Miss Brown's window, but she didn't look at me.

"Mr. Stone, have you ever heard of the Drivers Privacy Protection Act?" The other woman's voice was blunt and carried across the room.

"No. I just wanted…"

"Now, see here. Only the police are entitled to the type of information you want. You should leave the police work to the police."

"Yes, Ma'am." I gritted my teeth and made my way out.

# Chapter 7

**Thursday, June 21.**

I couldn't slam the door, and there was nothing I could hit. I clenched my fists, my muscles twitching with rage. I had to do something. I pulled the car out of the parking lot, the tires screeching on the hot pavement. I knew the edge was near. A part of me wanted to go on a rampage. I felt I deserved it. Instead, I pulled into a McDonald's and changed in the bathroom. I locked my sport bag in the car and took off running in the blazing heat of the afternoon.

I ran on the sidewalk of a large avenue on the north side of Orlando. My arm and chest hurt from yesterday's workout with the therapist. I started out running too fast, and my throat burned, but the most painful was the blazing sun. Sweat poured off my face. I looked forward to the intermittent shade of street side buildings. Various small businesses lined the avenue, none of which held my interest. I didn't know where I was going; I just wanted to burn up my anger. At a major intersection, traffic was heavy, and I didn't want to wait for the light, so I turned and kept pounding ahead. As long as I concentrated on the pain and heat of running, I lost track of my rage. I settled on a challenging tempo and kept running. I cut through traffic and ran in the direction that seemed to offer the least resistance. The road hit a "T" where it ran into a lake. When it split left and right, it changed names. Due to all the lakes and ponds in central Florida, this was a common thing around the area. My legs felt strong, and my breathing was steady. I turned right and kept going. Most of the pain seemed to drop off as I kept running. I concentrated on maintaining my tempo.

Exhausted, I stopped and looked around. I spotted a bench near a small lake and slumped into it. I was happy with my breathing; it wasn't ragged or short. It felt like a great run, a distance I hadn't run yet in my new running program. The contentment of completing such a good run made me feel good. I had lost the angry edge and the feeling that I wasn't getting anywhere. I almost came to accept the situation.

The sun hit the top of the trees around the lake. Evening shadows began to creep across the bench. I realized that I didn't really know where I was. Or, to be more precise, I didn't know where my car was parked. I guessed it was more than a few miles away. I felt a light stiffness when I stood up. I knew I needed to head generally north, but until I found a street I knew, a general direction was the best I could do.

It was fully dark when I saw the McDonald's where I had parked. Thirty minutes later, I was home. I grabbed a large glass of water crammed with ice and drank most of it nonstop. I carried my sport bag and rest of the water to my recliner and dropped into it. My shirt was damp. The room was dim, partially lit from the kitchen. I set the glass on the floor next to the chair and closed my eyes. *How am I going to find Lee's murderers?*

I heard my cell phone ring, and it made no sense. I blinked awake while the phone continued to ring. It took a few seconds, but I realized it was in my sport bag. I pulled it from a pocket on the bag on the fifth ring.

"Hello." It came out as a croak.

"Mr. Stone?" The woman's voice seemed familiar.

"This is Mark Stone."

"Mr. Stone, I hope I am not calling too late. This is Mrs. Brown. I wanted to call earlier, but wasn't sure that I should."

"I'm sorry, but do I know you?"

"I took care of your records at the motor vehicle office today."

I remembered seeing her name on the placard at her counter. "Oh, yes, I remember you. Thank you for your help."

"I feel bad for what my supervisor did to you. I'm sure you were very embarrassed."

"No, I didn't care about that." The anger snapped back in place. "She is just in line with everyone else when it comes to bringing justice to my wife's murderer. No one can help."

"That's why I am calling. I might be able to help."

"You can help?"

"First, I want to know if you meant what you said. Are you going use the information to help the police? Or are you just some weirdo?"

A tingle of hope flitted in my chest. "No, Mrs. Brown, I am at a dead end right now, and so are the police. I'm desperate to make some progress, desperate to give the police a lead." The phone remained silent, and the tingle died away. "I actually asked the detective, Lieutenant Beauchamp, exactly what I asked you earlier today, to get a listing of all the Dodge trucks from the right years and to whittle it down by eliminating the ones that don't fit the description. From there, he could make a much smaller list to investigate. He told me it was a waste of time."

"He must be an expert detective."

"I think that's the only kind they hire at the Apopka Springs Police Department."

"Right."

"Mrs. Brown, how about we meet for lunch tomorrow to talk?"

"I think that's a good idea."

We set a time and a place and said goodnight.

## Friday, June 22

I waited in the cool and calm of the country club restaurant. The décor and furnishings focused on elegance and comfort. I had never been to this golf course. Mrs. Brown had suggested it, since she thought it was a spot that was guaranteed not to attract a lunch crowd from the motor vehicle office. It seemed strange that she would help me. There was no doubt that her help would entangle her in breaking, or at least bending, motor vehicle division policy. I would gladly accept her help and not think twice about division policy.

Mrs. Brown appeared at the hostess station. I stood. She saw me and made her way across the dining room. She wore a conservative sundress with wide straps. I guessed she was five to ten years older that I was. I felt a pang for Lee.

"Hello, Mr. Stone." She pulled the chair opposite mine and sat.

"Mrs. Brown."

She tilted her head. "Do you mind if we get rid of the Mister and Missus?"

"Fine with me, but I have a very important question. Why do you want to help me?"

She looked me in the eye. "Six years ago, my husband was gunned down in broad daylight near a major intersection. His murder remains unsolved today."

"I'm sorry."

"Mr. Stone – Mark – I don't expect his murder to be solved. It's too old a case. But, you seemed sincere in your approach, how you explained that you could actually help solve your wife's murder."

"It's going nowhere right now. It could end up just like your husband's case. I couldn't live with that." I realized that was what she lived with every day. "I'm sorry, I didn't mean to…"

"It's okay. I didn't take it that way."

The waitress stopped at our table, took our order, and left.

"Mark, whatever I may be able to do, it can't come back to me." She twisted her napkin, saw what she was doing, and put it down.

"That's the last thing I would do. If you can help in any way, I will be grateful. And I won't say or do anything to connect it to you."

"The computer system we use at the tag office is very powerful. I can take the parameters you have and enter them into the database and search for matches. I just need the right time and opportunity. I can save the data on a USB drive. It's quite quick, and I can wipe the system clean of all traces of my searches."

"That sounds great. Sounds like you've thought about it."

"It didn't occur to me until I saw what my supervisor did to you."

My lunch with Sue turned out to be the best thing, the most positive thing that had happened since before Lee's murder. I had hope. The killers were out there, and this was the first step in casting the net for them. Sue told me she would text me with any progress.

After Sue left, I got my sport bag from the car, changed in the washroom, and did a very difficult run.

As I was running, I thought about it and decided that it was reverse psychology. It was difficult because I had been feeling good instead of angry.

**Tuesday June 26**

Orange and gold light splashed on the wall from the setting sun as I sat at the dining room table. My left hand held a towel to my neck and cheeks, soaking up the rivers of sweat rolling off my face. My running log held eight entries and twice as many dried drops of sweat. I entered number nine and pushed the notebook away.

# Chapter 8

**Wednesday, June 27**

Sue was exactly where she'd said she would be, the floor covering area of a Lowe's on the north side of Orlando. I was a few minutes late coming from my third physical therapy session with Rachel. Sue seemed to be deciding on a large throw rug and had a few items in a shopping cart. She heard me approach and turned to smile.

"What do you think of this one for a living room?" She gripped the edge of a large rug hanging from a rack that held ten different styles.

It took me by surprise. I looked at the carpet and back at her. My apprehension vanished, and I laughed. The rug was covered with various-sized squares of brown, green, and rust. "It might be a trick to get that to work."

"I think I might be able to pull it off. My therapist says I need to push my boundaries, break old patterns."

"Does offering to help me fall into that category?"

She furrowed her brow. I couldn't tell if it was quizzical or a sign of irritation. "No, I don't think it does." She turned back to the rug.

"I actually like the rug," I said.

"I do, too. But, I'm going to have to look at the living room carefully before I commit to it." She put her hands on the cart and turned it my way. "I've got the thumb drive for you." She snapped open a large purse wedged into the child seat of the cart. She pulled the drive out by a lanyard and swung it toward me.

"I really appreciate you for doing this for me. I hope you didn't take any crazy chances to get it."

"No, it was simple. We often do our own work in searching the database, and I just mixed this little project in with a couple others I had yesterday."

"Thanks, anyway." I gripped it and imagined getting to work. We walked out of the rug aisle and turned down one with wood flooring.

"You had told me that you needed to research 1998 to 2002 Dodge pickups. When I first looked at that range, it turned out that there are over fifty-eight thousand pickup trucks for those years registered in Florida."

"Oh, no." Beauchamp's smug face came to mind. "Maybe the detective was right."

"I knew that would be overwhelming, so I narrowed it down to Orange County and the four surrounding counties."

"How many trucks did that turn out to be?"

"The list I have is a little more than 4,900 trucks."

I shook my head. This was going to be tougher than I thought. "Well, thanks."

"Mark, I have a friend in my support group whose mother's home was burglarized a few months ago. It was such a traumatic experience for her mother that she talked about it for weeks. I mention it because Dana – that's my friend – told me that her mother said the crooks drove off in a truck like the one you're trying to find. She was cleaned out, and the burglary hasn't been solved."

"I wonder if your friend will let me talk to her mother."

"I was thinking the same thing. Let me call Dana

and ask her."

Sue called Dana from the wood flooring aisle and set it up for us to meet her at her mother's house.

*** 

Forty minutes later, a petite, middle-aged woman answered the door and hugged Sue. She let us in, and Sue introduced me to Dana, who introduced me to Phyllis. There was no question that Dana was a younger Phyllis. Dana offered us coffee and I immediately liked her. There seemed to be no misgivings on the part of the mother and daughter about my strange request to meet with them, and I wondered if Sue had talked to Dana about me before her phone call at Lowe's. We pulled chairs at the kitchen table, and I let my concern fade.

"The coffee's great, thanks."

"Dana said you wanted to ask about the robbery." Phyllis held her cup in both hands but looked directly at me.

"From the little that I heard, it seems similar to the break-in at my house. I thought if we compared notes, there may be some detail that might help the cops solve both of them."

"I would be more concerned about helping the cops solve your wife's murder." Sue's voice was low. Dana and Phyllis both nodded. That confirmed it for me. Sue had told Dana, and she'd probably told Phyllis. I was glad it was out in the open, but I felt an uptick in concern that Sue might have told more than she should. I didn't want her to lose her job or go to jail for what she had done for me.

"Yes, of course. I don't mean to be unkind, but solving her murder is all that matters to me. And I hope you can help."

"I hope I can." Phyllis smiled.

"If you don't mind, can you tell me what happened when they broke in here?"

"Sure. I don't know if you noticed, but my house here is pretty isolated. It's just what we wanted when my husband and I bought the place years ago. The state park comes right up to the property line on two sides, no one lives across the road, and my only neighbor is to the south. And they're never home. We don't get much traffic here, so we notice it when we get it. That day, when I came back from the grocery store, I saw a Dodge pickup parked a few hundred feet down the road. I came in through the garage with a couple bags. Something didn't seem right, and I walked into the living room to find the front door open. I looked out it in time to see the pickup pull away. When I went into the master bedroom, it was a mess. The French doors leading to the pool deck were broken and leaning open. It seems as though the crooks put a foot on one door and just pulled the other door until the deadbolts splintered the wood frame."

"I'm sorry to hear that. Did they get anything?"

"Money, credit cards, important paperwork. My identity was stolen, and it's been a huge problem. If Dana hadn't done so much to help me, I'd still be in a fix."

I didn't know what to say, but I shook my head in sympathy. I pulled the truck picture I had printed from the Internet and showed it to her. "Is this what the truck looked like?"

"That's it."

"I hate to ask you this, but how did you know it was a Dodge pickup?"

Phyllis pushed back her chair and turned toward the door leading to the garage. "Take a look here."

She swung open the door and flipped a switch.

I leaned out the door. The exact truck from the photo sat in the garage.

"Don't ask me about Chevys or Fords. My husband bought this one new in 2002, but then he passed away two years ago. It's all I drive."

"Did you happen to see the plate when they drove off?"

"No. As soon as I saw it, I ran to phone the cops."

"You tell the cops what kind of truck you saw?"

"Of course, but there's been no progress, and I don't expect any. I've taken care of the identity theft and gotten new credit cards and so on, with Dana's help, and life's back to pretty much normal."

"That's good." I sat quietly for a few moments, thinking about what had happened to Phyllis. "I think that there's no doubt these are the same criminals who broke in my house." Another thought popped up. "Phyllis, could you tell how many people were in the truck?"

"I'm pretty sure there were just two. I seem to recall seeing two heads through the back window of the truck."

"When did your break-in happen?"

"It was April 4th."

"I think this means they're local. Two break-ins approximately a month apart, two guys using the same truck."

"I think you're right." Sue slapped the tabletop for emphasis. "And, it seems like they're still out there."

I thanked Phyllis and Dana for their hospitality and help. Sue said she was going to stay and visit with them for a while. I left and headed home to get in a late-night run before getting to work on the data Sue had provided.

# Chapter 9

While toweling my hair dry, I stopped in the kitchen to put on a pot of coffee. The coffee maker clock showed 10:57. While it gurgled, I fired up my laptop in the mess that was the dining room table. Once I had a large mug of coffee, I sat at the computer and stuck in the USB drive.

It was empty except for a single file just under 400 KB with a .csv extension. I was very grateful to Sue for that type of file. It imported directly into my spreadsheet program. I often used a spreadsheet at work as a tool to make complex calculations and extensive lists, and I was proficient with spreadsheets. The comma-separated variables of the .csv file dropped into individual columns. I immediately scrolled to the bottom of the sheet. There were 4,937 Dodge trucks in the list. My heart dropped. If I spent one minute on each truck, it would take me more than eighty-two hours.

I scrolled back to the top and started naming each of the columns of data. The first column was the year of truck. Then came the owner's last name, the owner's first name, and middle initial. I knew this data wasn't useful at the moment, but it would be prime information in the end. I kept naming the columns and stretching them to fit the information in each. It came to twenty-seven columns of data. For information that I didn't think was immediately useful, I shrunk the column size to provide only a glimpse of the data. One of the columns I shrunk contained the truck serial number. I didn't see how I could use it at the moment; I didn't even know which truck might be the one the killers had driven.

One column that seemed important was the color of the truck. I started at the top of the list and scrolled over to that column. The first entry had a black truck. I deleted that row. The next row held a blue truck. One row at a time, I either kept or deleted each entry. When I'd deleted row number one hundred, I hit the save button and got up. I rubbed my forehead and walked into the kitchen. I refilled my mug, and the clock said it was few minutes before midnight.

"Let's see, a hundred entries is about two percent. This isn't going to work."

I sat back down and looked at the first entry. I copied the owner's name and pasted it into Google. It came back with more than ten pages of entries for that name. Out of curiosity, I searched the entries until I found the owner by the same address as the one on the DMV record.

While I was looking, I saw an advert for an online company selling data about people. I clicked on the ad. It advertised its people search capabilities. It also promised to provide information on background checks, criminal records, property records, phone numbers, e-mail addresses, social network affiliations, and property and neighborhood reports. I checked on the fee. For $59.95, you could enroll for a year. I was amazed that this kind of information was readily available. I didn't like it. But, if I found the truck owner, this information might be useful. I paid with a credit card.

It also offered an identity protection feature that I immediately took. One of the ways it protected your identity was by limiting the information available on this and linked websites.

I realized that this wasn't helping me with the analysis of the data on trucks. I seemed to be hitting a stone wall. I couldn't think of any better way to research the list than what I had been doing. I knew it was going to take a lot of time, something I didn't feel I had. I clicked on my favorites list and saw a half-dozen of the sites I had used and saved when I had done my initial research on the types of Dodge trucks. I clicked on one. While it was loading, the little digital clock in the task bar told me I had been sitting at the computer for almost six hours. I shook my head. I had narrowed the list by fewer than a hundred items in six hours.

The site included a number of sub-pages for various topics related to the trucks. I clicked through a few of them and hit one called "service." I was about to click to the next page when I caught sight of a chart with the heading titled, "Decoding the Serial Number." I stopped in time and scrolled through the chart. "No way!" I slammed my fists on the table. I knew in an instant that this was the key to my search. The chart was like a tree. It broke down the serial number into a definition of each of individual features of the truck. For example, one digit indicated the engine size, another indicated the paint scheme, another indicated the body style, and so on. I printed the chart and jumped back to my spreadsheet of four thousand trucks.

First, I saved the original list as a new file name so that I would have an original and a work file. I created a data table based on the serial number and its breakdown. I then used some of the data-sorting tools built into the spreadsheet and created an automated way to sort the trucks to fit the information I knew about the truck the killers had used. The first run I did was to search for white trucks. If the truck in the list wasn't white, the spreadsheet dumped the listing. I knew the truck was a two-door, extended cab with a short bed. I ran that and dumped all the ones that didn't match. I eliminated dually trucks, diesel trucks, long beds, and two-tone paint schemes. I thought about the heavy-duty towing hitch. Trucks could be bought that were set up from the factory for frequent towing. I knew it was a risk, but I decided to run it anyway. I also eliminated any trucks that were V6 engines, reasoning that the smaller motor would not be suitable for heavy-duty towing. I did a few more runs, eliminating trucks with things like chrome wheels and heated mirrors.

I saved the final list with a new name. I was about to print it out, but I sat back and took a sip of cold coffee. I smiled and nodded, not at the coffee, but at my progress. I knew I had taken some risks, mostly because I was so interested in the bottom line. But, I also knew that the risks were calculated. If the truck was used for pulling a trailer, it was very likely that the buyer knew that in advance and bought it that way. It was likely that it was still white. I thought through my choices for eliminating trucks based on features like these and nodded again. I was pretty sure of my approach. I hit the print button, took my cup into the kitchen, and noticed a glowing horizon. The clock showed 6:39. I went back into the dining room and pulled the sheets from the printer. The last entry was 47. The list of thousands had become a list of 1% of the total.

I clicked off the light and wandered into the bedroom. I hoped I could sleep, knowing that the sun was ready to bake the day.

**Thursday, June 28**

The room was stuffy. I rolled toward the nightstand and pushed the pair of Lee's panties off the face of the digital clock. Before Lee died, she had kept the alarm clock on the nightstand on her side of the bed. She used to keep an old pair of my under shorts over the face of the digital clock to kill its brightness. I missed her dearly and felt some tiny connection by adopting her approach to the alarm clock. It read 1:38 PM. I turned away, and my first thought was that I needed a map. I imagined a large map with all the roads and highways in central Florida. I then realized that it would have to be large.

After a shower, I jumped back on the laptop and started a local search for the map. I called the store and asked if it had one in stock. An hour later, I left the store with a huge map, a package of fine-tip white board markers, and a moleskin hardback notebook.

I pulled down a couple unremarkable pictures from the dining room wall and tacked up the big map. It was over seven feet long and over five feet high, in color, and laminated. There was a separate little booklet indexing all the streets. Most of the streets included the address range as well as the street name. It was impressive.

I spent the next four hours marking the exact location of each one of the 47 trucks on the list. I used a deep blue marker to draw a circle around groups of addresses that appeared relatively close together. There were seven groups. I was going to research one group at a time. I capped the marker and looked at the map. I pointed at it. "I know you're in one of those groups. And I'm coming for you."

I changed clothes and went for a run.

# Chapter 10

**Friday, June 29**

It was a few minutes after 9:00 AM when I eased the Stratus to the curb two houses away from the first house on my list. I didn't see a Dodge truck in the driveway. The house was an older cinder-block house with a single-car garage. A car sat in front of the garage door. I eased the car down the street and looked carefully at the driveway and along the far side of the house. I pulled over on the next block and made notes. The driveway seemed to indicate that another vehicle normally sat behind the car parked in front of the garage. There was an oil stain about ten feet behind it. I also noted that there wasn't another vehicle in the side yard. I doubted the truck would be parked in the garage; it seemed too small for a truck. I made a note to check back on this location.

I punched the next address from my list into my phone map app. It wasn't far. I was glad I had taken the time to group the addresses, making it quick to get from one to the next.

There was no truck at the second address. It didn't have a garage. I made notes and drove to the third address.

I didn't see a truck until I got to the sixth address. I ruled it out, since it didn't have a hitch of any kind. But, I was irritated. I sat for a while and considered the problem, but the air-conditioning in the Stratus didn't work so well when it sat and idled, and I started to sweat. I slammed the steering wheel and pulled out. I couldn't think of a better way to investigate the list of trucks. It wasn't a big list, but I wanted to make quicker progress.

I got lucky on the next address; there was a truck, and I eliminated it immediately. I spent the next three hours visiting the rest of the addresses. At the last one, I summarized my findings: two addresses out of twelve had a truck in plain view. I'd eliminated a total of two and needed to find the other ten. I figured that the trucks were used for work, and that was where they were during the day. I would have to change my strategy and come out early on Monday morning and try to catch the trucks before the owners headed out for work.

I made my appointment with Rachel on time, and working with her distracted my thoughts of futility. She had such a great attitude that it rubbed off on me. This was our fourth session together, and she seemed more of a friend than a therapist. When we were done, the positive feelings encouraged me to get in a run, even though I had thought of blowing it off for today. I asked her to let me leave my car parked in her lot for an hour while I ran. The way she agreed to it made me feel that I was supposed to leave it there without even asking.

On the way home, I decided to swing past the first house I had checked early in the morning. It hadn't changed; there was no truck. I made my way out of the residential area and onto I-4. Within a quarter mile, traffic came to a standstill. I looked for a way out, but I was totally blocked in. Within a few minutes, the air conditioner started to blow warmer again. I wondered how I'd gotten to this point. I was hot, and not just from the furnace called Florida.

Normally, on Friday evening Lee and I would be headed home from our jobs to meet up and do something, or just to be together. I slammed the wheel. We didn't deserve this. I pictured the hooded killer and wanted to kill him.

## Saturday, June 30

It was before 7:00 AM when I went out into the garage. I turned toward the car that Lee had normally driven. It was a three-year-old BMW, and we'd called it the family car. I decided to change things up and use it today. If anyone had seen me sneaking around the neighborhoods yesterday, the BMW would be something totally different. I had reconsidered overnight about looking for the trucks on Monday morning. I'd realized that early Saturday morning might be the best time to go to look for them. Unless somebody was gung-ho about doing a home project and had headed for the hardware store early.

I swung the driver's door open and slid in. I breathed in Lee's scent. I had to grip the wheel to keep from collapsing. The pain was like a blow to the chest, knocking the air out of me. My eyes burned, and I sobbed. I took a deep breath, trying to inhale all of her, but the scent had faded. I looked at the passenger seat and saw her there the last time we'd driven the family car together.

The weekend before she was killed, we had driven to Cocoa Beach. On the way, we'd joked that it was our own Cinco de Mayo holiday, just because it was the 5th. We normally didn't think too much of that holiday, but it had just worked out that way. We'd played on the beach, and the water temperature had already been in the eighties. It had felt like bath water. Lee had looked so good in her bathing suit. I wasn't ashamed to tell her that she was hot and really turned me on. I was careful not to say, "Even after eleven years." She'd told me I looked good, too, and I knew she meant it. We'd had a great time, gotten too much sun, and stayed until well after sunset.

I leaned over and saw some beach sand on the floor mat. It convinced me that it wasn't a dream. We had actually gone to the beach together.

I kicked the air conditioner to maximum and backed out the car. I didn't need the map or phone GPS system. I drove right to the first house on the list. The truck was there, and I eliminated it from the list. Next house, same thing, and again on the next address. I got lost looking for the next address, oriented myself, found it, and scratched it off the list.

In three hours, I visited all ten addresses on the list and found and eliminated eight more of them. That was a pretty good average. I had accomplished a big step, thirty-seven to go.

I got on I-4 again, and it was smooth sailing. And the air worked great. When I got home, I prepared my notes and strategy for moving to the next group of addresses. As dusk approached, I changed into my running gear. I took the BMW, hoping for a scent of Lee again, but it was gone for good.

I pulled into a park that was nestled into an older neighborhood a few miles from our house. As a park, it was a throwback. Most parks these days are pieces of land bulldozed to death during the construction phase of a subdivision. This park had history. It was also unique for Florida. A spring-fed creek flowed through it, but the other side of the park was hilly and wooded, a kingdom of squirrels. The creek had created a vast swamp in the lowlands. In ages past, a garden and flower club had adopted the park, and various portions of it had been planted with all kinds of exotic plants and flowers. Also in ages past, the club had funded construction of a wooden boardwalk through the swamp. Lee and I had visited the park on occasion, and it was always too hot and humid, especially on the boardwalk in the swamp. There were picnic areas and trails that ran next to the creek and up into the trees. It was especially hot today.

As I ran the trails, I tried to convince myself that the extra heat made the workout that much more efficient. It didn't work. Rasping breaths tore at my throat. Fire spread through my legs. I was determined to stay at it for at least forty minutes, and I ran the same circuit three times. I guessed one circuit was just about three-quarters of a mile. The stifling heat and humidity on the boardwalk came toward the end of the circuit. The third time through it, I knew I couldn't make another time around. And then came the final hill.

I leaned against the trunk of the BMW, breathing hard, wishing I were dead. The sun was long gone. I knew it would take at least an hour for me to stop sweating. I grabbed my phone and a towel and walked to an ancient picnic table, where I sprawled on the bench seat. For twenty minutes I used the towel and slowly brought my breathing under control. The workout was good for me. Each time, the pain lasted only so long, and then I felt good, a justifiable weariness. I had accomplished something worthwhile. Each workout was a single step toward a meaningful goal. Where I had grown soft, I would be strong. Where I had taken shortcuts, I would become enduring. I moved toward a condition where I could depend on my body, and that was part of my goal. But, mostly, I was alone. I had no partner, no helper, no one looking out for me. I needed to find Lee's killers. I wanted to be prepared when I did.

The towel became saturated and pointless. I draped

it over the edge of the table and stuck my earphones in my cell phone to call Sue. She answered on the third ring and seemed genuinely glad to hear from me. I told her of my progress on her file. She was incredulous that I'd analyzed the data in one night. She became even more amazed when I told her of my progress in investigating actual vehicles. At one point, she became quiet and asked me if I shouldn't turn over the data to the cops and let them take it from there.

"It's simple to investigate and eliminate trucks from the list. Wouldn't it be better if I went to them with only two or three possibilities?"

"Sure. It would save them a lot of time and effort."

"More importantly, they wouldn't have any reason to delay checking into just a couple of them."

"Sounds like you would be serving them up on a silver platter."

"Do you realize that I would know in very short order who killed my wife?"

She didn't reply for a few moments, and I wondered if I had hit a soft spot considering her husband's unsolved murder.

"Mark, I've got an impression from you, and I am a little afraid to ask, but would you like to go to church with me tomorrow morning?"

I didn't answer at first. I didn't want to consider the question. Adrenaline dumped into my bloodstream, and my heartbeat began to increase. I felt my anger rise. "No. I don't see any point in talking to God right now."

# Chapter 11

**Sunday, July 1**

I went out early and was driving in the dark toward my first address by 5:30. There were five addresses in the group I had targeted for today. I found the first address just at first light and immediately eliminated a truck sitting in the driveway. Things went well for three more addresses. At 8:30, I found the last address in a very well-to-do neighborhood with expensive homes around two lakes. Central Florida was like that. A common practice was to build a housing development with a lake, pond, or even a swamp as the centerpiece. The houses near the lakes were the most expensive, whereas homes a bit farther away were not as impressive or costly. It all depended on how close to the lake the house was built. Some developments didn't even offer homes that were not directly on the lake.

Address number five was a mansion. A tall, wrought iron fence with arrowhead-tipped pickets surrounded the place. A motorized gate crossed the driveway, which wandered about a fifty yards through a stand of pines. The garage didn't face the road but was along the backside of the house. Beyond the house was a manicured lawn that extended to the lake, where a massive dock jutted out a long way. I could see a parking area in front of the garage, but not the garage itself, as a wing of the mansion stuck out and hid the garage doors. But, I could see the nose of a Dodge truck parked just past the protruding wing of the mansion.

I took all of this in as I rolled slowly past the mansion. I had become concerned about parking while investigating an address. Since starting the search for trucks, I had tried to stay inconspicuous, but I had still been subject to curious stares by people out for walks or a target for barking dogs. For this address, I had to take a closer look, but I didn't want to come back around immediately and park. I left the area to find a 7-11, where I bought a small coffee. I took my time getting back to the mansion and finished the coffee before I got there. As I drove past, I noticed that the fence on one side, about two hundred feet from the house, followed a drainage ditch through the pine trees. The neighbor's fence stood on the opposite side of the drainage ditch, leaving a ten-foot gap between the two fences. On the other side of the mansion, only one fence stood on the property line. Both fences on either side of the place marched all the way to the shore of the lake.

I drove past and parked in a place I judged to be inconspicuous. The neighborhood was so well-to-do that it didn't have sidewalks. The area was quiet, and I walked along the side of the road. When I came to the mansion with the truck, I crossed the street and worked my way down to the drainage ditch. It was marshy in the very bottom, so I climbed along the slope next to the fence by the mansion.

I stopped when I was deep into the lot and across from the truck. From there, it was inconclusive. I needed to see if it had a hitch. I kept moving toward the lake, trying to get a better angle on the back of the truck. When I could finally see it, I was thirty feet from the lakeshore. I gripped the fence posts and moved my head, trying to see through the stand of pines. It had the right kind of hitch. But, something was off.

"Hey! What're you doing there, boy?" The man's bark came from behind, and I turned to look. Thirty yards away, a white-haired man pointed at me and walked from the neighbor's dock toward me. It was just what I had feared.

I lifted my open palms toward him at about shoulder height. "It's okay, sir. Don't worry. It's not what you think."

"What're you doing here?" He approached his fence on the other side of the ditch.

I went down the slope, jumped the mushy part of the ditch, and came up to his fence. It was as tall as his neighbor's, and I ended up looking through the steel pickets face-to-face with the man. "Sir, I'm a private detective working with the police to try to identify a vehicle involved with a recent crime."

"You accusing my neighbor with a crime?" He grimaced.

"Oh, no, no. It's just that a truck like his was seen at the scene."

"Well, why don't you go knock on his door instead of sneaking around out here?"

I looked back at the house and the truck. From this angle, I saw a crease leading to a dent in the right rear fender, something my target truck didn't have. "How long has the fender been wrinkled?"

"Why don't you ask him? I've never seen his truck when it didn't have the damage."

"Thank you, sir. You have just cleared his truck from suspicion." I jumped the ditch and headed toward the street. I didn't look back. I hustled, trying to not appear any more suspicious.

Sweat poured off my face when I reached the

street. I finally turned, saw the old man still standing by the fence, and waved at him. He turned away. I made it to my car as fast as I could.

## Monday, July 2

There were seven addresses on the list for today. I was very apprehensive about this group. If yesterday's houses were expensive, today's probably belonged to millionaires. I didn't expect the potential suspects on the list today to be violent criminals.

I drove the BMW to an area known as Windermere Oaks. Sixty years ago, it was just a small town well outside of Orlando in the midst of a chain of lakes that created exclusive tracts of land between the lakes. Someone with money had built out there, and before it could get regulated and standardized, it had grown up as a very exclusive and costly place to live. Multi-million dollar homes sat on estates, and two country clubs had worked their way in around the estates.

I slowed as I came near the first address. It surprised me, because it was one of the ancient clapboard houses that had made up the original little township. In the gravel driveway was a dirty white truck without a hitch. A single asphalt road twisted through the original township, and I didn't even stop when I saw the truck. I felt grateful to have an easy one.

The second address was a tough one. A concrete block wall that stood ten feet high surrounded the estate. Thick, swirling stucco decorated the wall. Intermediate concrete posts, three feet square and two feet higher than the wall, stood spaced out at twenty feet along the length of the wall. It reminded me of the Great Wall of China, and probably cost more, too. Maybe that was intentional. A matching gatehouse sat next to the main entrance gate. Through the gate I glimpsed a mansion that evoked the glory of Athens. Other than the impression through the gate, I saw nothing of the grounds or the mansion because of the perimeter wall. It seemed a stretch to think the owner would take his truck into town and rob homes for a living. I decided to move on to the next address.

I talked my way past a guard at a gated community and found the next address. I saw the truck and eliminated it. On the way out, I asked the guard about one of the nearby country clubs. The next address I needed to visit was a golf-front home on the course. He said that it was restricted for use by residents of the development and their guests. I thanked him and pulled out. Down the road, I pulled off and used my phone to search the Internet for homes for sale in the country club community. I found a few for sale and made notes on the addresses and the listing realtors.

I pulled up to the country club gate for the development that held the next address. The security guard came out, and I rolled down the window.

"I'm here to meet with Blakely Realtors and look at the house for sale on Whitford Court."

"Good morning, sir. If you don't mind, pull up over there. You can wait for them there." The guard pointed to a wide spot inside the gate.

I gave an impatient huff and slapped the steering wheel. I jammed the shifter into gear and pulled up to the spot. I sat for three minutes, got out, and slammed the car door. I marched to the guard hut. He had the door open before I got close.

"Look, I know where the house is. Just send the realtor over when he gets here." It came out forcefully, leaving no room for argument.

He gave me a gentle wave. "No problem, sir."

I pulled away, heading in the direction of Whitford Court. Once out of sight, I made my way to the address I actually needed. I found it and the truck. It was a beautiful home with the garage around back. I could easily see the truck as I drove by. I turned around and looked again as I drove the other way. It didn't match my criteria, and I crossed it off the list before I made it back to the guard shack.

I pulled up to the exit gate. The guard showed surprise at seeing me. I jabbed a finger at the gate and jerked my thumb up. He got the message and opened the gate.

I eliminated two more trucks easily and headed for the last one on the list. It was a massive estate, similar to the one I had seen earlier where I couldn't even see inside the tall wall. This one had a wall just as big. I drove past the main entrance and saw nothing of the place. A road ran along the north side of the estate and turned onto it. I followed it and passed a service entrance, looking through the gate for any sign of a truck or a way in past the guard. I had no luck and kept going. I turned around when I found a cross street a half-mile farther down the road. As I came back toward the estate, a white Dodge truck pulled out of the service entrance loaded with palm fronds. I followed it and made sure it did not meet my criteria. When it came to the main road in front of the estate, it turned right, and I turned left. I pulled into a parking lot when I got back into the township and made notes about the day's progress.

I felt good. I'd come to find seven trucks and had ended up eliminating six of them. I left the seventh one on the list, hoping to eliminate it one way or another. I was down to twenty-six trucks to find. I was sure the killers were in that group. I felt close now, and I shivered. I knew I would find them. When I did, they would pay.

I put the car in gear and headed home to get in run

number thirteen.

# Chapter 12

**Tuesday, July 3**

By 8:30, I had found five of the eight addresses on my group for the day. Each one eliminated a truck from the list. I approached number six to find a vacant house and a "For Sale" sign in the front yard. I pulled in the driveway anyway. I got out and checked the house. I peered in the front door window to see bare floors and walls. I went back to the car and called the realtor's number from my cell phone. I gave my name and asked for the agent whose name was on the sign, a Mr. Garrett. When he came on, he asked me if it wasn't a bit early for a house tour.

"No, Mr. Garrett, I don't need a tour at this time, just a little information."

"Okay, how can I help you?"

"How long has the house been vacant?"

"It's been on the market for five months, but the owners vacated it three months ago."

"Do you know why?"

"The husband had a job-related move, and they couldn't wait for a sale to move."

"Where did he get transferred to?"

Mr. Garrett hesitated. "I didn't say he was transferred."

"Well, where did they go?"

Garrett's voice seemed to harden. "I don't see how that matters to a house sale."

"I would like to speak to…." I picked up my list and checked the name. "Mr. or Mrs. Hollenbeck."

"Mr. Stone, I don't know what's going on here, but neither I nor our office gives out the names of our clients until we have a contract. How did you know the owners?"

"I was told who they were. Now, are you going to tell me where they are, or not?"

"I'm afraid not, Mr. Stone."

I hung up.

I went to the next two addresses on the list and eliminated only one of them. There was no truck at one of the addresses. I drove home, made my notes, and fired up the laptop. I used the name and address of the Hollenbecks to look up their old home phone number. I called it and got a recording to call them at a number with a 305 area code. I wrote it down and called it. A woman answered.

"Is this Mrs. Hollenbeck?"

"Yes, who's calling?"

"Sorry, wrong number." I hung up.

I logged onto my subscription to the Internet service that provided information on people. The service included a feature to use a person's phone number to look up an address. I entered the Hollenbecks' new phone number, and it came back immediately with an apartment address in Homestead, Florida. I printed a map to the address.

I got in the BMW. Unfortunately, any trace of Lee's scent had dissipated. I worked my way to I-4, and headed south. I took the exit for the Florida Turnpike and hit the gas. The BMW cruised with smooth power and is easy to handle at high speed. I had driven the turnpike a dozen times or more and it was always boring. The best part is the speed limit. It's officially 70 MPH, but it is well known that anything under 80 is okay. I set the cruise control for 78. I'd spent more than twenty bucks on tolls by the time I made my way around Miami three and half hours later, where the Turnpike officially ends at Homestead. The sun had died somewhere in the Gulf of Mexico when I started looking for the apartment complex.

When I found it, I passed it by on purpose, trying to do a quick survey before entering the lot. It occupied a large plot of land on a corner of two boulevards. It had four entrances, two on each street. I didn't know its layout and didn't know where to start looking for the truck. I pulled into the parking lot and drove slowly down an aisle of parked cars. The parking areas had overhead lights, but they were dim and didn't cover the area well. I spotted a handful of Dodge trucks of various colors. It made me think that I should check every line of parked cars, just to make sure I found the Hollenbecks' truck. After twenty minutes of cruising up and down the parking area, I found three white trucks that fit my criteria. I didn't care which one was the Hollenbecks'; I would check on them all.

I drove near the first one and came to a stop. I had to jump out to check the rear of the truck for a hitch. A car was parked just behind it and blocked my view. It didn't have a hitch. The second one didn't have a hitch, either. The third one had a hitch. I parked the BMW in an open slot. The car came with a maintenance and minor repair kit strapped in the trunk, including a mini-flashlight. I got in the trunk and pulled out the flashlight. I walked over to the truck before flipping on the light. At the back I clicked on the light and then knelt down to inspect its hitch. I had my head down and was scrutinizing the hitch when I heard yelling. I snapped the flashlight off and stood. A plump woman in a uniform ran toward me. She yelled something at me, and I took off. I didn't run straight for my car but across the lot, hoping to lose her. At the end of a row, I dropped down below the level of the parked cars. I peeked through a car window and saw the security officer fifty yards away, swiveling her head in every direction, trying to spot me. I crept along the car, then ran across an aisle and worked my way to the BMW. I opened the door when I thought the woman was looking the other way and slid in, closing it as quietly as possible. The security officer was stalking the far side of the parking area when I started up the car and pulled out onto the boulevard.

I made my way to the Turnpike and headed north. I mentally prepared my notes for the notebook. The truck had a hitch, and it was a heavy-duty hitch. It was a cheap one, though, and not the same as the one I knew from seeing the real one and doing the research. I would eliminate the truck; it didn't matter if it or one of the other two trucks was the Hollenbecks' truck. None of them fit the bill.

About twenty minutes down the Turnpike, I saw flashing blue and red lights in my rearview mirror. I immediately thought that the security officer from the apartment complex had identified the BMW and called the cops. I slowed and pulled over. While the officer took his time getting out of his cruiser, I panicked, trying to think of what to tell him if he accused me of suspicious behavior at the apartment complex. I had no excuse except to deny I had been there. I rolled down the window when I saw the officer move up along side the car.

"Sir, may I see your license, registration, and insurance?"

I handed them out the window, and he told me to

stay in the car while he retreated to his cruiser. When he came back, he had me sign a speeding ticket, gave me my documents, and asked me to drive safely.

I drove the speed limit back to Orlando and got home well after midnight.

# Chapter 13

## Wednesday, July 4

It was a struggle, but I went out early again, before first light. This seemed to be the best way to do my truck investigations. Not many people get up and get going that early. With the holiday, I hoped no one was up and out. I had a list of five in this group. I drove to an area of central Florida near Orlando, with older homes and a lower standard of living. The neighborhood was plain, and some of the yards didn't have a lawn - more like patchy dirt than a lawn. Cars or trucks sat in some of the front yards. Some of them clearly didn't run. I found four out of the five trucks in no time. I decided to try back later in the day for the fifth one. With the holiday, I didn't know what to expect, but it had been a successful day, even if I didn't find the fifth one later.

I went to a barbecue restaurant that was part of a chain throughout the South. Lee and I used to eat there a couple times a month. They had some all-you-can-eat specials, but I had learned that they were really too much. I used to leave the place with pain from eating all I could eat. The restaurant was crowded, but I wasn't in a hurry.

It was early afternoon and like a furnace outside when I left. My cell phone rang just as I got to the car. It was Chief Mackey.

"Hi, Chief. Happy Fourth."

"Hey, Mark. What are you up to?"

"Just wondering what to do besides sweat."

"How would you like to come out to the shooting club and see an exposition of cowboy shooting?"

"What the heck is cowboy shooting?"

"It's pretty cool. These guys dress up like cowboys and use old-style pistols and rifles and compete in a timed course. I'm surprised you haven't heard of it. It's a nationwide competition. They even have their own magazine."

"Sounds interesting. Are you going to shoot?"

"No, I'm not a cowboy shooter. But, if you want to try it, I have a few friends who are in the competition, and I'm sure they would let you try it."

"No, I don't think so, but can you bring a couple of your pistols and we shoot a little on the range?"

"Sure, the competition will be over by four. You have any particular gun you want to shoot?"

"I like the 1911 and the Walther."

"Okay, but you are going to have to buy your own ammo in the future."

We made arrangements to meet at the club in an hour. I was looking forward to watching the competition, but the idea of shooting Mackey's pistols really sounded like fun.

The cowboy shooting competition was a blast. The participants dressed up like Old West cowboys and cowgirls and even had names like Cypress Sam and Swamp Molly. The marksmanship was incredible. They moved from station to station, shooting at moving and non-moving metal targets that made a wonderful plinking sound when hit. There was even a quick-draw competition, although they didn't shoot at each other. I was stunned to see that the art was alive and well.

Afterward, Mackey and I shot some paper targets

with his pistols. I felt much more at ease than when I'd worn my sling. Mackey showed me how to shoot the .45-caliber 1911 with both hands, and it still kicked and boomed like nothing I had ever encountered before. It wore me out shooting three full clips. In contrast, I could easily control the .32-caliber Walther. It seemed to fit my hand really well. When we were done and cleaning up, I asked him, "Would you like to sell your Walther?"

"I could tell you really liked it. I wouldn't sell it to just anyone, but since you're asking, I'd consider it."

"I have no idea what a gun costs. What would you take for it?"

"I paid $550 for it maybe six years ago. How about $750, and I'll throw in a hundred rounds of full metal jacket ammo?"

I thought it was a reasonable price, and we agreed. He gave me the gun and the ammo, then told me I could bring the money by the office tomorrow and he would give me a receipt.

"You haven't said a thing about your investigation. How's that going? The cops making any progress?"

"I've made some good progress. The cops haven't." I told him about the information from the DMV, my analysis of it, and the ongoing field research. I could tell he was impressed.

"I knew you were a resourceful guy, but it's incredible how far you've gotten."

"Thanks, but I've had some help, you know."

"Mark, I want to make sure you understand something about owning a gun. I trust you and know you'll do the right thing, and, of course, you have every right to defend yourself. But, you can't pull that gun anytime you need some courage. You can't use it to threaten or force someone to do what you want. You do that, and you're no better than the criminals who killed Lee."

"Thanks. I understand and agree with what you're saying. I'll keep it in mind."

"You should take a self-defense class as soon as possible. As a gun owner, you need to be careful and not put yourself at risk."

"I know, I'll look into it." I suddenly had reservations about the gun.

He said he was headed to a cookout, and we both left the club.

\*\*\*

I drove back to the neighborhood from that morning, heading for the address where I had struck out. I was going to do a drive-by just to see if anything was there.

It was the truck.

I caught my breath and gripped the wheel. I was by it, and I didn't know what to do. I kept going and decided to circle back, park down the street, and try to get a closer look on foot. I circled the block and stopped about six houses away on the opposite side of the street. When I put it in park, I slipped my hand in the door pocket and lifted out the Walther. The glossy black steel pistol felt smooth and slippery. A curved tip on the clip stuck out from the bottom of the grip. When I wrapped my hand around it, my pinky finger curled around the curved tip and snuggled the grip into my hand. I thought about the pistol as I held it. I put it back in the pocket. I didn't want the temptation.

I got out of the Stratus and locked the door. I stood still and looked up and down the street. It seemed quiet as I stepped to the sidewalk. The sun was low; I guessed it would be dark in an hour. I walked past the house on the far side of the street, staring at the truck the whole time. It had the exact trailer hitch, and all of the other features I remembered fit. It fit the neighborhood and the profile of the type of person who would be a criminal. I crossed the street three houses beyond it and walked back toward it. There was no sidewalk on this side of the street, and I walked along the edge of the road. When I got to the truck, I stopped and looked around again. I didn't see anyone, so I walked up along the passenger side and around the front. There were no distinguishing marks or features I could use to eliminate it. I stopped at the driver's door. The window was open, and I put my hands on the bottom of the opening and leaned inside to look around.

I heard a soft noise and felt a blow smash into me just below the point of my hip. It threw me forward; I hit my head on the mirror and spun around, landing on my hands and knees.

"Just what do you think you're doing?" It was a growl as vicious as any wild animal.

I looked up to see a beefy guy with a ball bat aiming another blow at my head.

"Wait!" I held up my hand. The pain burned from my hip to my toes.

"I told you I saw someone snooping around." This was another male voice, but I couldn't see him. I concentrated on my attacker.

"Wait. I'm not here to steal anything. Please, hold it a second." I breathed hard, trying to absorb the pain. Panic gripped me as I thought this might be Lee's killer. Would he recognize me? Would he kill me, too?

"Gary, let him be a minute. It don't look like he's going anywhere soon." A woman's voice came from the doorway of the house. "You didn't have to hit him with the bat."

"Woman, I got a right to protect my stuff. I don't like people sneaking around our house."

"Mister, you better have a good reason to be here." She may have saved me, but she didn't sound happy about it.

I rolled onto my butt and leaned against the truck door. My leg wouldn't work. I was caught and terrified. Sweat rolled off my forehead into my eyes, mixing with the tears. I looked up at Gary. He was big, and big around the middle. He had a full beard with streaks of gray. He didn't quite fit. I tried to get a look at his buddy, but he stayed behind Gary. I took a chance. "I'm a private detective working with the police on a recent violent crime. We got a tip that a truck like the one used was in this neighborhood."

"I ought to bust your head." Gary pulled the bat back like a major leaguer waiting for a fastball.

"Hold on, Gary." The woman came down the stairs. "Let's find out about this before you go off the deep end." She stopped next to him. She was thin. "Okay, Mister, when was this so-called violent crime committed?"

"May ninth."

"I thought you said it was recent. No way it was this truck." I noticed she hadn't said there was no way it wasn't Gary or his buddy. But, Gary eased down the ball bat, and I took that as a good sign.

"Okay, I believe you, Ma'am. But, now, don't take this the wrong way: how do you know it wasn't involved?" I wiped my face on one shoulder and then the other. I started to get my breathing under control.

She went around the front of the truck and opened the passenger door. I heard her in there a few seconds, and she came back. She carried a few sheets of yellow paper. She looked at them and then turned to me. "We just spent every penny we had to get it fixed. It was in the shop from April 27 until May 18. We would've had it sooner but didn't have the money to get it out." She waved the papers in front of me until I took them. I scanned the dates and the repairs. They'd rebuilt the transmission, and it had cost them over thirty-five hundred dollars.

I felt foolish.

"Ma'am, I'm sorry to have bothered you." I handed the papers back.

Gary dropped the tip of the bat to the ground. "Why don't you just get the hell out of here?" His voice didn't carry the animal ferocity from earlier, but there was no friendliness about it.

I rolled to my hands and knees, reached for the truck bed rail, and pulled myself to my feet. My right leg shot with needles of pain, and my foot was numb. I limped to the end of the truck, using it for support. I didn't know how I was going to make it to my car.

I stumbled across the street and didn't look back. I kept my right hand on my right hip as I hobbled down the sidewalk. I didn't know if it helped or not, but was afraid to pull it away. It was deep dusk when I got to the car. I wanted to sit in it and rest, but I needed to get out of there. I might have eliminated another truck, but wasn't completely sure.

# Chapter 14

**Thursday, July 5**

I couldn't get out of bed when the alarm radio snapped on. I couldn't even move. My entire right side ached. I turned off the radio and let the inky darkness persuade me back to sleep.

The clock showed 11:37 the next time I looked at it, and a headache had now joined the attack on my body. When I made it to the bathroom, four aspirin preceded a very hot shower. As I enjoyed its soothing massage, I wondered if Rachel had any therapy suggestions for a busted-up hip. I couldn't imagine any training runs for at least a few days.

There were seven addresses in today's group. I thought about picking it up again tomorrow, but I didn't want just to sit around all day. That would reenergize the headache for sure. I was drawn to the prospect of making progress. I felt that I had momentum and wanted to keep moving.

When I tried to fold myself into the driver's seat of the BMW, a bolt of pain streaked down my leg, and I sucked in a long breath through clenched teeth. I headed for Kissimmee, which on the south side of Orlando. The area had numerous housing developments of all ages, and I didn't look forward to searching the winding residential streets. But, it paid off quickly. It seemed that the day after a holiday was a good day to stay home. I found and eliminated five out of seven trucks by late afternoon. Most of the time, I just drove by the address, and the truck sat in the street or driveway.

The first one I couldn't find was the second one on the list, and I circled back by the address toward the end of the day. It was a single-family home with a small car in the driveway and a white picket fence around the front. A woman knelt on a concrete walkway leading from the driveway to the front door and pulled weeds from a decorative rock bed. She hadn't been there when I'd driven by earlier. I wanted to finalize the list for today and had an idea to try to make it happen.

I pulled alongside the curb at the front yard, certain the woman had seen me stop. When I finally made it out of the car, I hobbled to the front and leaned on the hood. By the time I got there, she had come to the fence. "Good afternoon, Ma'am." I knew she had seen my limp.

"Is there something I can do for you? Are you okay?"

"Old war injury, don't worry." I gave a dismissive wave. "I'm actually here to take a look at your Dodge pickup truck. You have a white one, don't you?"

"We have one, but what's this about?" She didn't seem defensive, just curious.

"Ma'am, I represent a consortium of lawyers who have brought a class-action suit against Chrysler regarding the defective plastic used in the dashboard of Dodge pickup trucks from 1994 to 2004. Maybe you have heard about the suit?" I had read on a website that there really was a lawsuit regarding the plastic in the dashboards. It seemed to be a design and material failure, and the suit had been going on for years.

"No, I hadn't heard, but our dash cracked and split

apart years ago."

"Yep, that's what the lawsuit's all about."

"My husband has the truck at work today. Can you come back later this evening or on Saturday?"

"Sure. And, thanks for your time. Sorry to drag you from your work."

"No, I'm glad you did. I needed a break." She wiped her forearm across her forehead and shook her hair back. I got the impression she didn't quite want to end the break.

"Well, thanks again." I used my hands to help me stumble along the driver's side fender. I smiled at the woman as she watched me. "Oh, by the way, does your truck have a trailer hitch?"

She tilted her head in surprise. "We have a ball on the bumper to pull our jetski trailer. Why?"

"Oh, they're looking into a possible faulty design of the heavy-duty kind of hitch. But, I don't think you need to worry. You have what they call a bumper hitch." I pulled open the driver's door, climbed in, and started the car. I gave her a gentle wave and put it in gear. I caught sight of her in the rearview mirror standing by the fence.

I drove by the second address that hadn't had a truck earlier in the day. It still had no truck, and I drove home at sunset.

## Friday, July 6

My leg felt better when I got up on Friday. I slept later, on the theory that a Friday after a day after a holiday was as good as the holiday itself for folks to stay home. There were eight trucks left to identify, including the ones I couldn't find last Monday, Tuesday, and yesterday. That left five new addresses to search. I was going to try to revisit the three I couldn't find once I'd finished all of the ones on the original list. Of the five left, three were on the northeastern fringes of central Florida, and the other two were on the opposite corner of the map.

I set off for the first three, driving northeast on I-4, and crossed the St. John's River Bridge at the tail end of rush hour. It seemed my assumption about a Friday after a holiday was right; there were virtually no cars on the bridge or the highway. I found my target addresses in Debary, Deltona, and Deland. I saw and eliminated two out of three trucks. The last stop in Deland was the no-show, and I didn't feel like giving it a few hours for a second pass.

I had plenty of time to make my appointment with Rachel and got to her studio early. She had no other patients and took me early. When I came through the front office to her work area, she saw me limping.

With overly arched eyebrows she said, "Don't tell me you've been shot in the leg. PT on legs costs more."

I laughed. "And I would gladly pay."

I told her about the ball bat, and she took pity on me and massaged my leg before starting on our normal routine for my shoulder.

The massage and workout cleared the pain in my leg, and I decided to try a run. When I asked Rachel if I could leave my car in her lot again, her response made me feel proud, like a determined Olympic athlete on the field of competition. I liked that woman, but I ended up not liking the run at all. It killed me. She was gone when I got back. I sat in the car with the air running at maximum for a half-hour.

I headed home but pulled off the highway when I saw a sign for a Cracker Barrel restaurant. It always had room for a single or a couple, and I got in right away. It was Lee's favorite place to eat, and it brought me a tiny connection to her.

# Chapter 15

**Saturday, July 7**

I took a big detour around the attractions as I headed toward the Haines City area. I didn't care that it was farther taking the roundabout way. I hated driving through the tourist areas. Once I confirmed the truck in Haines City, I drove up US 27 to Clermont and found that truck. It was a big circle to drive and late afternoon when I got home.

I ran off my frustrations on the West Orange Trail, an asphalt path that ran for miles through Orange County, although for my sixteenth run, I didn't do miles. I cooled down and dried off on my way home.

When I sat at the dining room table, I caught up my running log and added a note about yesterday's session with Rachel. Afterward, I updated my notes on my investigation and the truck spreadsheet. For any vehicle that I had eliminated, I filled the row on the spreadsheet with a light blue background color. For any vehicle that I had checked but was not able to verify, I filled the row with a light yellow background. When I'd started my investigations, all the rows had had a white background. Now, the spreadsheet was almost totally blue, with only four yellow rows showing trucks I needed to investigate.

I sat back, took in the overall spreadsheet, and felt a sense of accomplishment. When I made the spreadsheet fit the screen though, I jerked upright with a feeling of dread. As an engineer, I often used spreadsheets and did various analyses of data on projects. They help to plan projects, evaluate ongoing work, revise workflow and logistics, and provide input for coordinated efforts among divisions of the company, as well as with clients and subcontractors.

I felt like a fool, now that I saw the bigger picture.

I began to doubt my work and my assumptions. I wondered if my anger or my push for progress had clouded my judgment. Looking at the predominance of the light blue, I knew the data didn't fit a normal analysis result. With forty-seven real possibilities of trucks that fit the search criteria, the probability of finding the one that the killers had used in the last ten percent of possibilities was not realistic. It should have shown up somewhere in the middle of the pack. It was not impossible that it was one of the last four left to verify, but it was highly improbable. Simply put, I should have found it by now.

I questioned my early analysis. I questioned my philosophy of eliminating trucks based on certain features that I could not prove were not in the truck I wanted to find. My thoughts went astray to areas where I questioned whether the owner had removed the hitch or changed some other feature on the truck to throw off any search. I even wondered if I had taken accurate notes. Beauchamp's pudgy face came to mind, and I heard him telling me it was too far-fetched to try.

I resolved to recheck my notes against the spreadsheet and make a plan to follow up on the four trucks that needed verification. That resolve and four aspirin got me to sleep that night.

I woke in the dead of night, crying from a nightmare about Lee, and did not get back to sleep for a couple hours.

# Chapter 16

**Sunday, July 8**

I knew it was a mistake that I hadn't kept accurate notes on the specific features I'd used to set up my original list of trucks. A printout of the spreadsheet with the forty-seven trucks sat next to my laptop on the dining room table, where midday sun streamed past the curtains. The page full of blue-filled lines confirmed my mistake. I rubbed my hand over my unshaven jaw and wondered if I could trust my own judgment. I should have known that I couldn't boil down the original list of thousands of trucks to a mere forty-seven possibilities. I was better than that. I knew I had to start over, carefully select and note my setup parameters, and take it one step at a time. I was close; at least, that was how I'd felt. Now, it was back to square one.

My cell phone rang. I flipped for it through the clutter of papers. On the fifth ring I picked it up and saw Sue MacKenzie's name. My first reaction was to let it go to voicemail, but I answered on the last ring with a reluctant hello.

"Hi, Mark. I hope I'm not calling at a bad time." She must have sensed my mood.

"No, it's fine. I'm irritated at myself. I've made a big mistake and wasted a lot of time."

"Is there anything I can do to help?"

Her offer surprised me. "No, I just have a lot of work to start over."

"How about lunch? Seems like you could use a little recharging."

Her second offer surprised me again. I didn't know when I had met someone so considerate. "No, thanks, I…"

"Wait a minute. You don't even know what you're passing up. A couple friends and I usually go out for a nice lunch after church. We're on our way and would like the chance to cheer you up and buy you a nice meal."

I knew immediately what that meant. I was in no mood to put up with some busybody women or patronizing husbands. I was sure my tone was clear. "No, thanks. Maybe some other time. I've got to get back to work."

The line was quiet for a few seconds. "Okay, I understand." Yet the tone of her voice didn't sound like she did; it was soft and unsure. I hoped she would say goodbye, but instead she said, "Mark, how about just the two of us have lunch?"

When I didn't answer, she said, "Maybe you need someone who will just listen."

"I think I know what the problem is." My voice didn't carry conviction.

"It can't hurt to talk it out. And, I bet you haven't eaten anything today."

She connected with both statements. "Okay, but I'll need some time to clean up."

"Really?" In her one-word reply I heard a playful note, and I suddenly felt glad that I'd agreed to lunch. We set a time and a place, and I went to take a shower.

\*\*\*

She was at a table for four in the back corner of the restaurant, a chain that served Italian-style food.

She smiled when I sat. "It's good we came a little later. The crowd from church has thinned out."

"I could use some good news." I laid the color printout of my spreadsheet on the table.

She picked it up. "This is impressive."

"It may be impressive, but I am afraid my approach was a failure."

A waiter stopped at our table, and we ordered.

"Why do you say your approach failed?" she said. "It looks like you've eliminated quite a few real possibilities."

"But, if they were the most reasonable suspects, I should have found the killers' vehicle in that bunch."

She scanned the page again. "I see you have four vehicles that need to be investigated. Surely, it's one of those."

"Very unlikely."

"To me, you've done all the hard work. Why don't you take your results to the police? If the killer is one of the last four, it would be much safer for them to make the approach."

I grabbed the printout and waved it at her. "Don't you see what this means?" My voice rose. "I made a huge mistake in my assumptions, and I've wasted all this time." I slapped the sheet on the table, breathing hard. "I really doubt the killers' vehicle is on this list."

Sue gently laid her hand on mine. An electric shock coursed up my arm to my chest. I flinched, but didn't pull my hand away. Her gaze held me. "Mark, I'm only offering my suggestion." Her voice echoed the sincerity in her eyes, and I knew I'd hurt her. I'd done the same with Lee when she'd tried to help me work through problems.

"Sue, I'm sorry."

"It's okay. I know what you're going through."

"The past few weeks have been intense, and I thought I'd made real progress. Now, all I can think is that it's been for nothing, and worse, that I didn't think it through and approach it the right way. I'm worried I won't get it right again."

"Stop worrying. Of course you make mistakes. Are you a professional investigator? What you've done is extraordinary." She squeezed my hand.

"I wouldn't call it extraordinary. But, I do know what to do next. I'll restructure my analysis. Then I'll start over." I tried to smile.

"That's great, but isn't it true that the killers' truck could actually be one of the four you haven't been able to investigate fully?"

"Sure, it could be one of those. I've tried to locate each one of them. A couple of them I've even tried to investigate twice. But, I doubt one of them is the killers' truck."

She waited until the server set our lunch on the table. "Oh, this smells good." We both started in on our meals. She had something alfredo and I had spaghetti with meat sauce.

After a petite bite, she said, "Back to the four that are left to find, doesn't it make sense that the killers' truck would be hard to find? I mean, if they're trying to keep a low profile, wouldn't they hide it or keep it out of circulation?"

She was sharp. She had a clear grasp of my plan and how I'd executed it. She amazed me, and I had to smile. "You may be right. I hadn't thought of it that way. Maybe I should focus on these last four before I start over."

"I think that's the way to go. But, Mark, I'm worried about you. You think it's possible that in looking for the killers you may have tipped them off?"

"How?" I shook my head, trying to think what I'd done that could have been a tip-off. "No, I can't imagine how that could happen."

"I'm still concerned. Why don't you take your notes and results of your investigation to the police? Just lay it out for them, and get them to investigate the last four. I have a feeling that it's one of last four, and I don't want you to get hurt."

"What about the information I got from the motor vehicle department?"

She looked up. "You've got to keep me out of it."

"How do I do that?"

"I've thought about it quite a bit, and I think there's a way. You know, at the DMV, we have direct network connections to the state computer and the database. But, there are other agencies that need the information, especially for security purposes. In the past, they would work through our division, but with interagency cooperation, there is such a huge demand that a secure website was established. I can give you the web address, but I don't have the password."

"That's great, but I still have a problem. Where did I supposedly get the secret web address?"

"As I understand, with the right keywords and a dedicated search, you can find it. I can give you the keywords. You don't have to do the actual search, but if questioned, you can provide them the keywords."

"What about the password?"

She shook her head. "I don't know. If they ask, just tell them that you can't say."

What she offered was a way out for her and maybe a chance for success on the part of the cops. It would take the pressure off me, especially if the cops could solve it with what I gave them. Of course, it only made sense if the killers' truck was one of the last four trucks on the list. "It could work. But, you know, I have little confidence in the detective on the case."

"Mark, I would feel much better with the cops taking it from here. You've already done so much."

"I'll give your approach a try. I have to say that your understanding is remarkable. I just hope that the web address thing will convince them."

"For your sake, I hope they follow up on the investigation."

# Chapter 17

**Monday, July 9**

Detectives worked at most of the desks in the department. Beauchamp stood as I approached his and said, "Let's move to the conference room."

I followed him across the room, and he pulled the door open, motioning for me to go ahead. He took the chair across from mine. "Mr. Stone, I hope this isn't about the getaway truck again."

"Detective, until we deal with the truck, Lee's murder will never be solved."

"Then this conversation is over." Beauchamp pushed his chair back.

I flipped open the manila folder and slid the colorful spreadsheet across the table. It stopped between his two hands. He bent to look at it. "What's this?" He scanned it for a few moments. His eyes grew wide, and he dropped back into the seat. "Where did you get this?"

"I'm glad you asked. Now I know that you know it's real."

"I asked you where you got this information."

"It took a great deal of work, but you can thank Homeland Security for letting me have it."

Beauchamp's face began to redden. His expression told me to quit playing with him. "It is against the law for you to have this information. And, worse, it's dangerous for you to have it. For the last time, how did you get access to personal information on decent citizens?"

I opened the folder and slid another sheet across to him. It had one line on it with the address of the secure interagency website that provided access to vehicle registration data. He glanced at it and grimaced. "Mr. Stone, you're…"

"Detective, you're way off track. I've done a lot of work that the police don't have to do. Hold off with the threats for a moment, and listen to what I have accomplished."

He held the sheet but looked at me. I took that as a sign that he would listen. I explained what trucks were on the list and why. I told him how I had set it up to provide only the trucks that fit my criteria and how I had personally investigated each one and eliminated the ones highlighted with the light blue background. "I haven't been able to investigate the last four entries that are highlighted in yellow. The killers' truck is one of those, and I think you should investigate them."

"And why is that?"

"First, either I can't seem to find them, or I can't get close enough to verify them. Second, if I snoop around too much, the killers may recognize me."

Beauchamp didn't hide his contempt. "You weren't concerned about the killers recognizing you on the other forty-three trucks on this list?" He laid the sheet on the table and pulled a pen from his inside jacket pocket. He drew a line through one entry on the page, saying, "This one is a very well-respected and extremely wealthy businessman in Windermere Oaks. He is not a killer or burglar." He crossed out another line. "This one is a construction company. I know the owner personally. Likewise, he is not a murderer or burglar." He tapped the point of his pen on the two other entries. "These other two aren't worth looking at. You haven't done a rigorous or thorough investigation. Your data isn't reliable and can't be trusted."

I looked him in the eye but kept my mouth shut.

He flared his nostrils. "And, if you keep this up, I am going to charge you with obstruction of justice for interfering with an ongoing murder investigation. Good day, Mr. Stone."

# Chapter 18

Before I reached the creaking stairs, I clamped control on my anger. Beauchamp hadn't given my work a chance. As soon as he'd seen that I had used illegal information, he'd made up his mind to shut me down. His threat meant nothing to me.

When I got to the car, I flipped open the folder on the hood and pulled out a copy of my data. I found the first address of one of the four remaining truck addresses that I needed to investigate. I jumped into the Stratus and cranked up the air conditioning before my sweat had a chance to drip on the folder.

Beauchamp had convinced me. I'd expected the cops to do their job. Maybe he thought he was doing his job, but it was clear to me that he wasn't. I'd hoped for some progress, something I could hold onto as a ray of hope. Lee deserved justice, and I the killers needed to pay.

I wouldn't depend on Beauchamp or the cops again, and I wouldn't give up.

Twenty minutes later, I pulled onto the street where I hoped to find the first of the last four trucks. I remembered this street from my two previous attempts. The address was in a mature neighborhood on the north of Orlando.

The neighborhood streets were just wide enough for two cars to pass. Many of the residents parked on the street, and I would have to pull behind a parked car so a car approaching from the opposite direction could go past. The house had been renovated; the original garage had been made into living space, and the driveway ran along the side of the house to a detached garage in the back. I drove past it slowly. I looked down the driveway but didn't see a truck anywhere.

I circled the block and made another deliberate pass with no success. I considered circling the block all day, just in case. My anger simmered, but I was not about to give up. I couldn't tell if anyone was home and briefly thought about parking down the street and snooping around the garage in back. Instead, I headed for a coffee shop nearby.

An hour later, I drove toward the house from the opposite direction. From four blocks away I spotted a white Dodge pickup pull from the driveway and head down the street away from me. My first impression was that it was a match to the killer's truck. I sped up but had to drop behind a parked car to let another car pass from the opposite direction. When I pulled out, the white pickup turned left onto a broad avenue. It was a busy avenue, and I hurried to follow. By the time I made it to the stop sign at the avenue, I couldn't see the truck. I turned left, accelerated, and saw the truck six blocks ahead, easing onto I-4 heading south.

I made it to the on ramp and fit into the highway traffic. I drove recklessly and caught up, pulling in directly behind it. I took a good look. I pulled into the lane next to it and eased up along the bed of the truck, but stayed behind the cab. I made out a young man at the wheel. I dropped back. It was a match to the killers' truck. The hitch was the clincher. I slowed and took a position six car-lengths behind the pickup. There was no way I was going to let him out of my sight. He drove conservatively, and I had no trouble following. Ten minutes later, he took an off-ramp and made his way to Orange Avenue, heading south. He turned into a massive hospital complex where ongoing construction disrupted the normal routing of the streets around it. It came to me that he might be a construction worker, and I needed to be careful.

The truck turned into a small parking lot packed with cars. It seemed like an overflow lot due to the construction. When I got to the mouth of the lot, I hesitated to pull in. The pickup had pulled straight in and taken the last open parking slot. I stopped with the nose of the Stratus in the lot and the trunk sticking out into the street. The man got out of the truck and walked around the back to the passenger door without looking at me. He opened the door and lifted a small boy out, set him on the ground, and leaned back into the cab.

The little boy had a ball that popped out of his hands as he lifted it toward the man. The ball bounced and rolled down the parking lot right toward me. I could see the alarm on the boy's face and he ran after it. I jammed the gear shifter into park and jumped out of the car. I moved around the front, grabbed the ball three feet from the bumper, and turned toward the oncoming child. As I stood, the man yelled, "Petey!" The little boy came to a stop five feet from me. For a moment he looked at me, terror flashing across his face. He turned and ran back, and I looked at the man. He held a small baby in one arm and stretched the other out to the little boy.

I walked across the small lot. When I approached the man and boy, I crouched down and tried to hand the ball to the little boy. "Here you go, buddy. I found your ball."

He buried his head in the man's pant leg.

The man said, "Petey, can you take your ball?"

The little boy made a muffled noise and clung tighter to the man's leg.

As I stood, the man said, "Thanks, I'll take it."

A car horn blared from behind me. I handed the man Petey's ball, and he said, "It's like this every day." I told him to take care and turned back to my car.

I pulled away from the lot, knowing that this father couldn't be the killer. And meeting Petey had dissolved my anger.

# Chapter 19

I found a gas station, pulled in, and parked away from the pumps. I checked my list of three remaining trucks and checked my notes. I decided on the estate in Windermere Oaks. It took me almost an hour to work my way through traffic to the outskirts of the little town. The area mixed old Florida small town with million-dollar homes and estates. To me, the combination now seemed forced. I followed a county road south, threading between lakes on either side, and I spotted the mansion behind its tall perimeter wall.

I drove past the estate slowly. It was difficult to learn anything from the roadway except that the grounds inside the wall must have been gorgeous, based on the landscaping outside the wall, which sat fifty feet from the road. I turned around at the next intersection and drove back to the entrance, pulling in. A pair of wrought iron gates blocked the road, and the end of the right wall bumped out to become a small guard shack.

A man in uniform came around the front of the car. "Good afternoon, sir. How may I help you?"

"I'm investigating an accident, and there is a truck registered to this address that matches the description of one of the vehicles. I would like to verify that it wasn't involved."

"Are you with the police?"

"The insurance company."

"I'm sorry, sir, but I cannot help you today."

I looked at him sharply, but before I said anything, he turned and went back into the guard shack.

I backed up and turned out at the county road, headed north, and scanned the area around the estate. I looked for a cross street to find a way around the back of the estate, but the lakes on either side of the road didn't allow for any cross streets. When I drove south again, I didn't find a way around to the back of the estate for the same reason. It didn't sit well with me, and I drove home.

I found out all about the estate using the Internet. It turned out to be a twelve- or fifteen-acre peninsula on a lake maybe five or six miles wide. I used the satellite photo of the place and zoomed in until it was displayed at the fifty-foot scale. I studied it and learned that the wall enclosed about five acres that included the mansion, a couple pools, a tennis court, a putting green, and a few detached bungalows at the backside of the compound. Beyond the back wall, a gravel road led northwest to the far tip of the peninsula and a small building. A road branching south led to a white beach and a long dock that pointed to the middle of the lake. The dock incorporated a boathouse three-quarters of the way along it. There were also a couple large utility buildings outside the wall. The entire peninsula outside the wall was thick with natural growth except for the beach area. A few hundred feet of water separated the peninsula from a bulge of land to the south side, whereas the north side of the peninsula tapered to about a hundred feet of water between it and the mainland. The property on the mainland to the south, bulging into the lake, held a housing community of large lots and expensive homes. A swampy area seemed to fill the lake area to the north, and the mainland there didn't have any homes or other developed properties for quite a way inland. I zoomed into both areas and spent quite a bit of time studying them and the compound.

I finally killed the computer and went out for a run. I took it easy and was back, logging my nineteenth run in Lee's notebook, in less than a half-hour.

***

The dash clock showed 3:17 AM when I drove past the mansion. I turned in through massive brick pillars that decorated the entrance to the community to the south of the estate. I searched for ten minutes before finding a house with a lot that would provide easy access to the lake. It took another ten minutes to find a place to park the BMW and get back to the lot after I left my shoes in the car.

In shorts and a tee shirt, I eased into the warm lake slowly until the water was up to my thighs and then slid forward to swim quietly. The dock and boathouse from the peninsula estate floated on the dark water hundreds of feet ahead of me. The water temperature barely dropped as I headed into the deeper part of the lake. I knew it wouldn't drop enough to keep me from sweating. The boathouse was dark, but a light showed through a porthole on the biggest boat tied to the dock. Halfway to the dock, I spotted two other boats tied there: a ski boat and a flat-bottom boat with an outboard motor. My goal was the sandy beach to the south of the dock, where I could make it to the thick underbrush near the water. I only wanted a look inside the compound to see the truck. I made a course correction and concentrated on smooth strokes. As I swam, I was aware of the muscles around my healed bullet wound, but it was only a minor pain.

When I neared the beach, I felt the sandy bottom with my outstretched hands and pulled myself along until I floated in the water with my chest touching the sand. I made a lot of noise breathing hard, but crickets, cicadas, and frogs filled the air with a thrumming that covered it completely. As I rested, I was grateful for the physical therapy and running routine, even with the light burning in my healed shoulder. When I had my breathing under some control I crawled up the beach to the scrub brush. I saw my location in my mental map of the peninsula and knew to make my way north along the general direction of the wall. I didn't want to approach the gate at the backside of the compound, because I didn't know if they had dogs, cameras, or other security sensors.

Sweat began to mix with the lake water, and neither one smelled good. I stood in the shadow of a small tree and studied the length of the wall. I needed to find a large tree I could use to look down into the estate. The best choice was a large oak growing on the far side of the gravel road that led out the wall. Getting to it meant crossing the road. I worked my way along the scrub line and crossed the road quickly when I came upon it. The crushed shell was packed hard so I made no sound as I trod it.

The lowest branch on the oak tree grew at ten feet above the ground. I had to hug the massive trunk and inch my way up. From the first branch, I climbed to a second and a third branch and settled in at about twenty feet above the ground. For a few minutes I rested, sweat pouring off my face and my breathing hard again. When I looked into the property, the bushes and trees blocked a great deal of my view. I didn't care about the main building or pools. I bobbed my head to see past the branches and other foliage in trying to spot the pickup truck. I moved out farther on the branch, hanging onto other branches to steady myself. Seeing the accent lighting, lush foliage, flowering bushes, and manicured lawn, I began to doubt the success of my plan. There were no vehicles in sight, even though a concrete roadway wound through the estate.

I climbed back to the main trunk of the tree and found another large branch above and at a different angle. I crawled up to it and worked my way out along it until I clung to a spot just above the wall. Three bungalows sat along the north wall, and each had a carport and driveway leading to the main roadway in the estate. Under the carport at the middle bungalow I saw the tail end of a Dodge pickup truck. Jutting out under the bumper was the frame of a heavy-duty tow hitch. From my angle, I could only see the left rear quarter and backside of the truck. I needed a better view. I tried climbing to two different locations, but still could not see it. Glancing between the truck and the back gate, I realized that seeing it from the back gate, I could see more than half the truck.

When I made it to the ground, I had to stop and catch my breath. I sat with my back to the tree. I would be glad when this night was over; fatigue gripped my body. I worked my way away from the tree and wall, keeping to whatever cover I could use. Palmetto plant leaves had razor-sharp edges, and I had brushed against a few of them. I dropped behind one and studied the corner of the wall. A wrought iron gate like the one in front closed off the opening in the back wall. Inside the gate a wide concrete courtyard filled the area. The crushed shell road outside the wall met the courtyard at the gate. The gate was made of pickets about four inches on center that spanned from a horizontal lower frame to an arched upper frame.

The back gate didn't have a guard shack, and I could see no activity inside the estate from where I lay, fifty feet from it. When I got up, my cheek brushed the palmetto, and I slapped my hand over the wound.

I crossed the crushed shell road and hunched my way up toward the right-hand side of the gate. With my hand pressed against my cheek, I stopped, facing the wall, and rested. This wasn't worth it, and I regretted coming tonight. I needed a quick look at the truck, and then I would ease back out and get home to my bed. I wiped my cheek on my left shirtsleeve and inched toward the edge of the wall. My tee shirt was soaked and wouldn't dry in ninety-percent humidity.

Before peeking around the edge of the wall, I squatted to be out of eye-level line of sight. I pressed my palms against the wall and peered around the edge and between the pickets of the gate. The truck sat in a deep shadow. I was able to make out most of it along the driver's side, including the exact match to the towing hitch. I leaned back behind the wall, taking a couple slow breaths. I shuffled closer to the edge and tilted out, grabbing one of the gate pickets with my left hand. The courtyard area instantly flooded with light, and I jerked back, falling on my butt. An electronic siren began to wail.

I started to scramble up but froze in shock on my hands and knees. The perfect Dodge truck, illuminated as if by daylight, was blue, not white.

I jumped up, slipped on the crushed shell roadway, and went to a knee. I saw a man rush out of the end bungalow. The gate began to open outward. I ran. I heard a yell and another, but I focused on running.

I headed toward the dock. There was no way of cutting across the property with the palmettos and low wild brush, so I stayed on the crushed shell roadway until it branched and headed for the dock. I heard at least one person behind me, maybe more, but I didn't look back. I hit the dock. My loud, pounding footfalls echoed off the wood. Six, eight, ten strides, and then I launched off the end of the dock… a violent splash, and then all was quiet as I stroked under water.

I had taken a deep breath as I'd flown through the air, but there was no way of holding it long. My lungs hurt from the sprint, and I needed air. I struggled to the surface, panic racing toward me as I realized I was much deeper than I thought. I broke the surface with as violent a splash as I had made diving in. I gulped the air deep and fast, knowing that I made too much noise. I tried to listen between breaths and heard yelling a short way away on the dock. I turned and began to flail through the water directly away from the dock.

I found a rhythm and kept at it for two or three minutes. My breathing raced, and I knew I couldn't keep it up for much longer. The sound of a motor came across the water, and I stopped. I tread water and turned until I could see the lights of the estate and boathouse. A small boat pulled away from the dock. It was the flat-bottomed boat, and a man with a powerful searchlight stood in the bow, swinging the beam in a wide arc.

The boat came about halfway to me and began to curve to the right. I could tell that they expected to find me closer to the dock. With the motor running, I knew they couldn't hear my panting. I concentrated on relaxing and tried to slow my breathing. I needed the rest and watched the boat for a few minutes. It did ever-larger circles away from the dock. I headed toward the shore where I had come across earlier. I used a sidestroke to keep my eye on the boat and to conserve my strength.

I was about halfway to shore when the boat turned

directly toward me.

I stopped again and watched. I was sure they hadn't seen me. But, the boat made a direct line toward the bulging shoreline. It was clear they knew it was the only way to get away, the only land where a swimmer could get out of the water. The boat made a turn directly toward land to the south, and I realized that they were going to come between the shore and me. They would probably cruise slowly along the shore to cut off any approach. I decided to go directly east, behind them in the opposite direction. Sooner or later I would hit the land that held the county road running north and south.

I swam a sidestroke parallel to the shore while the search boat passed between the shore and me. The searchlight never swung back out toward me; it flicked over the shore and the water in front of the boat. I kept up the slow pattern of the sidestroke. My body didn't want to do it, and the healed wound in my right shoulder burned with real pain. The boat finally disappeared around the far side of the bulging land, but I occasionally saw a flicker of light in its direction. I looked ahead and concentrated on the black strip of land as my goal.

A few minutes later, I glanced back and was shocked to see the boat headed toward me. It was not close, but it was now clear that the searchers had come to the same conclusion as I had. I maintained my sidestroke rhythm and glanced ahead. The shoreline was choked with lily pads. There was no way to make my way through them without being spotted, especially since they grew in muddy-bottomed areas, very difficult to get through on foot. I visually followed the shoreline and saw where it curved around to intersect a small concrete bridge supporting the county road. A square block of lighter gloom illuminated the opening under the bridge. North of the bridge, the shoreline became the manicured lawn of the estate, wide open, providing no way out. I changed direction and headed for the bridge.

I picked up the pace. Glancing at the boat and estimating the distance to the bridge, I knew it was going to be close. I dared not switch to a faster swimming stroke; it would give me away easily. I recalled when I had been hired as a lifeguard when I was sixteen. One of the prerequisites was to swim a mile. I had made it, mostly on the strength of my leisurely sidestroke. For some reason I sank in the water and couldn't use a floating backstroke. I had switched to the freestyle occasionally, but that takes a lot of strength and endurance. I doubted that I had done a mile in the water tonight, but it felt like ten.

I glided under the entrance to the bridge, took a deep breath, and swam underwater as far as I could. If the guy with the searchlight had shone it on the water under the bridge while I swam on the surface, I would have been caught. When I surfaced on the other side of the bridge, the boat concentrated on the bank where the lily pads grew, and I knew I was safe for the moment. I crawled up the bank on the south side of the bridge, out of sight of the boat. The bank inclined from the water to the roadway about ten feet high. I didn't want to be seen above the roadway from the search boat, and I lay back on the bank, resting.

I heard an ominous change in the pitch of the motor as the boat entered under the bridge. I was dead if they came through and shone the light on the bank. The motor dropped to an idle, and I heard the crackle of a walkie-talkie radio. I inched up the bank and heard them give their position and ask for directions. The reply was hard to make out.

The boat nosed out from under the bridge, and I

jumped up onto the county road and lay flat, my head turned toward them. The light swept the bank where I had lain and then swept the opposite side. The boat made a U-turn, light sweeping both banks, and headed back under the bridge. I got up and ran for a few seconds down the road to the south. I dropped down on the east side shoulder and lay panting. From the corner of my eye I saw the search boat putter out into the lake, search light swinging back and forth. I hoped that no traffic came my way while I waited for the boat to get farther away.

When I finally got to my hands and knees, the eastern sky was pink and gray. The search boat crept along the shore far enough away that I knew the searchlight couldn't reach me. I made my way past the massive brick pillars into the community where I had parked, found my car, and headed home.

# Chapter 20

## Tuesday, July 10

I woke hot and sticky. Daylight flooded the room. My eyes were blurry, and I squinted to make out the clock at 1:13 PM. As soon as I moved, my shoulders, back, and legs shot with pain. I crawled out of the bed straightening up slowly. When I felt stable, I hobbled into the bathroom and splashed cold water on my face. I breathed in the odor of the lake and didn't like it. I regretted trying to spy on the estate last night and felt foolish. I was no better than the criminals who had broken into my house. I slipped on my running shorts and shoes, knowing a run would be painful. But, as I went out the front door, I hoped the pain would grind up my anger and get me thinking straight.

I ran for seven minutes and quit. The heat sapped my strength quickly, and I had no reserves. An hour after I dropped onto the couch, sweat continued to trickle off my face and body into the big towel under me. I took a cold shower and dressed.

I kept coming back to Beauchamp's comments from the day before. I sat at the laptop on the dining room table to research the pickup he had told me belonged to a construction company. I started with the registered owner and quickly found that he had been right. The construction company was one I recognized from projects I had done at J & K. I had no specific memories of the company, but I knew of them. I mapped its location and headed out in the Stratus.

The construction company yard and offices took up half a city block in an industrial area. Across the street, a construction materials yard fed a haze of dust into the air as large trucks were filled with sand, rock, and gravel. I parked in the construction company lot near a cluster of vehicles and waved at a guy washing down a portable cement mixer. He turned the hose into the barrel of the machine when I approached.

I said, "Are you the yard supervisor?"

"Nah, he's inside where it's cool."

"I'd like to talk to him. Do I head in that way?"

He twisted the hose off. "I'll get him for you. What's your name?"

My phone clipped at my belt made an urgent noise. It wasn't a call but an alarm I had set for the perimeter security system at my house. I unclipped it but looked at the guy. "Thanks, I'm Mark Stone."

He shuffled away and said over his shoulder, "Back in a minute."

I walked under the shade of a metal overhang on the building and looked at the alert. Something or someone had entered my yard. As I unlocked the phone to go to the web page with the detail information on the alert, it went off again. On the detail page, I found that something the size of a car had set off the system in the driveway and then a few seconds later had done the reverse. By the way the system classified the security breach, it indicated that a car or truck had used my driveway. I saved the data and clipped the phone back in place. A few minutes later, the guy cleaning the mixer and another guy came out of the building. The first one went back to his work, and the other walked up to me. He stuck out his hand and said, "I'm Jason Wheeler, shop supervisor.

How can I help you?"

"Jason, my name's Mark Stone. I'm looking for a truck that may have been involved in an accident, and I have information that a truck that matches its description is registered at this address."

"What kind of truck are you looking for?"

"A 2002 Dodge Ram 1500, white."

"Yep, we have one. If that truck has been in an accident, I need to know about it."

He tilted his head, walking away. "This way."

I followed him around the end of the building and spotted the truck parked with a half-dozen other pickups. It seemed to be the oldest and most beaten-up. A rusty dent caved in the tailgate, and the rest of the truck looked pretty sad. It had the right hitch, but nothing else matched.

Wheeler stopped a car length away and turned toward me. "Here she is, Mr. Stone. What kind of accident was it?"

"Sorry to waste your time, Mr. Wheeler, this isn't the truck. The one we're looking for was in much better condition, according to the witness' statement."

"Oh, no problem, Mr. Stone. It's a load off my mind, anyway. I hate dealing with the employees, cops, and insurance when we have an accident."

I stuck out my hand. "Thanks for your time. Sorry to bother you."

The Stratus was a sauna, and I kicked on the air. Thirty-five minutes later, it had cooled enough, and I was ten minutes from home. The security alert troubled me. It seemed a car might have used my driveway to turn around, but that never happened. I'd had false alarms in the past months, but I couldn't let it go.

I pulled into the parking lot of an insurance agency and parked in the shade of some trees with the engine and air running. My home security system had a feature for viewing two areas inside from miniature cameras, but it cost extra to access it each time, and I'd never used it. But, I logged onto it from my cell phone and accessed the security camera in the master bedroom. I didn't see anything there and switched to the living room camera. A man sat on my couch, leaning back with his arms across the top of the seat. Another man walked in front of the coffee table. A pistol sat on it.

I slammed the steering wheel. My first thought was that they were there to rob me again. But, with the next thought, I gripped the wheel. Maybe these guys were the killers, back to take care of me. I gritted my teeth and imagined crashing in the front door and opening fire. I reached for the Walther in the door pocket and wrapped my hand around its grip. I watched the screen for a minute. As my thoughts evolved, I let the pistol slip back into the door pouch. No matter how I imagined it, there was no way I would be able to go in the front door without getting shot. I put the phone on the center console and dropped my head onto my hands on the steering wheel, thinking of a way to get the upper hand on the guys in my house. There was one thing I knew for sure: if I called the cops, they would arrest these criminals, and I would learn nothing about Lee's murder.

Five minutes later, I pulled out of the lot and headed to my house.

# Chapter 21

I drove past my house, taking a quick glance, but saw nothing. I went to the next block, turned left, and parked in the shade of an old tree.

I'd figured out how to get into my house without alerting the killers.

Lee and I suffered through four hurricanes that struck central Florida in the summer of 2004. Hurricane Charley hit in the middle of August, followed by Frances, Ivan, and Jeanne. Hurricanes generally threatened central Florida once every ten years, but that year it was off the charts. Some people lost everything. We were fortunate. The hurricanes blew down a handful of trees from our yard; our roof was seriously damaged; and four windows were smashed.

We'd survived without electrical power for a week at a time with each of the four hurricanes. Afterward, we'd made repairs as we could afford them. It was three years before we could replace the roof. The house had been built in the early 1970s and had aluminum-framed windows set in concrete block walls. When we finally got the glass company to come out to repair the windows, both Lee and I had watched them do the work from the outside of the house.

Using his finger, the installation technician had pushed on a lightweight clip that ran along the edge of the frame holding the glass pane. This made a depression for him to slip a screwdriver under the clip. He'd slid the screwdriver down the length of clip and popped it out, freeing one edge of the glass. He repeated the technique on the other three sides of the frame and popped out those clips. The cracked pane of glass almost fell out, but the tech removed it carefully. Lee and I were stunned. In less than thirty seconds, the tech had totally removed a pane of glass from outside the house, leaving a hole for easy access into our house. Lee became very uneasy. We'd mentioned to the tech the ease of removal and how insecure it was, and he'd said that most people didn't know about it. In fact, it was really secure, because the window appeared quite solid since the clip appeared as though it were sealed in place.

Later, Lee and I had discussed it many times. We had always hoped to replace the windows with ones that were more secure. It came up a couple times a year, whenever Lee thought about it and we discussed how easy it was for someone to break into our house. I had even thought about it when I'd installed the new security system a few months back. I'd learned that the system used wireless sensors mounted next to a magnet to determine when a window or door was opened. In most cases, the sensor was mounted on the wall next to a window or door. The magnet mounted on the window or the door itself so that when the window or door opened, the magnet no longer activated the sensor.

However, if the glass were removed from its frame, leaving the actual window closed, the system wouldn't recognize it as an intrusion and wouldn't send out an alarm.

I got out of the car and slipped the Walther into my right pocket. I made my way around the block to our backyard and surveyed the house from behind the trunk of a huge oak at the corner of our lot. The house was quiet, and I didn't see any motion in the back windows. Two bedrooms made up the back of the house. Lee and I had kept one set up as a guestroom, where I normally slept now. The other didn't quite make it as a guestroom, and we'd used it for storage. I went across the backyard to the corner of the house and slid along the wall to a window in the storage guestroom. The central air conditioning unit sat on a concrete slab below the left corner of the window, which was about chest-high from the ground.

I peeked in the corner of the window to a dark room. I listened for a half a minute and looked in again. I pried out the lightweight screen with a car key and set it aside. Every move was slow and quiet. I pressed on one clip holding the pane of glass and slid the key along its length. I didn't let the clip snap out but eased it away from the glass. Slowly, I did the same for the other three clips and held the pane in place with one hand while I dropped each clip away from the window. I slipped my keys back in my pocket and used two hands to remove the pane of glass. I pulled the top edge out, gripped it with both hands, and gently lowered it to the ground away from the window.

I climbed on the air conditioning unit and stood with my back to the wall next to the open window, listening for any sound from inside. After a few seconds, I reached in and pulled on the cord to raise the mini blinds. I inched them up, taking a full minute to raise them out of my way. I took a quick look inside and raised one leg over the edge of the opening, then brought my head and chest in the window. I stretched my hands toward the floor and slid over the edge. I held my weight with my arms and lowered my body to the floor. I thought I'd made too much noise so I froze, listening for at least a minute while lying on the floor.

It seemed clear. I stood and moved to the bedroom door, stepped into the hallway, and at once moved back into the bedroom with a stab of fear. I could be walking to my death. I could also be on the verge of catching Lee's killers. The thought hardened my resolve. I couldn't go forward with my normal nice-guy attitude. They would take advantage, and I would probably get killed. I had to be totally committed to taking charge. I had to be ruthless and determined. If it came to it, I had to pull the trigger, or they would.

I pulled the pistol from my pocket and moved to the bed. I slid both hands under the pillow and pressed it down with my chin. I racked the slide, chambering a round and cocking the pistol soundlessly. I kept my finger along the side of the trigger guard. The gun was hot; a twitch on the trigger, and someone could get shot. I caught my breath, feeling my heartbeat ramp up.

I moved to the door, checked the hallway, and eased toward the kitchen. I checked the kitchen and heard voices in the living room. I crossed to the corner that fed to the dining room and crouched. I couldn't make out the conversation between the two in the living room, but I heard one of the men pacing.

I took a quick glance around the corner. The dining room and living room were one big space with a vaulted ceiling. One man walked away from the dining room while the other sat on the couch. The guy on the couch wore an empty shoulder holster that puckered his white shirt. A dark tie matched his trousers. The pistol remained on the coffee table. The other guy wore jeans and a dark tee shirt. I assumed the guy pacing carried a gun.

The crouching hurt my knees, and I eased to a standing position with my back to the wall, a couple feet from the corner to the dining room. I suddenly felt in grave danger. I couldn't rush around the corner; one or the other of the men would shoot me before I could take control. Then, it got much worse. I heard one of them cross into the dining room, heading toward the kitchen. I looked left and right trying to find a place to hide, knowing I only had seconds. I began to move back toward the hallway when I heard a cell phone ring. The voice in the living room answered it, and I heard the one heading toward the kitchen stop.

"Well?" said the voice near the kitchen.

The guy in the living room said something I couldn't hear clearly, but I got the impression the conversation on the phone had been brief. Then I heard the guy in the living room clearly tell the other to go in there. I knew it was my cue. I slipped my finger onto the trigger, moved to the corner of the kitchen again, and glanced around the corner. The man in the tee shirt had turned back toward living room, and I rushed around the corner and slammed him in the back of the head with my fist, grip end of the pistol leading the way. The solid contact between the gun and his head jarred my finger wrapped around the trigger; the gun roared, and a bullet flew into the ceiling. The guy stumbled and fell forward. The man on the couch jerked up and stared at me with wide eyes.

I yelled, "Hey!" and squeezed off a round at him, deliberately over his head. He flattened against the back of the couch. I kept walking toward him.

"Get on the floor!" I pointed at the guy on the couch, and he slid a few inches toward the far end of the couch. "You don't think I'll use this? I said get on the floor." I growled at him, and he took a quick glance at the pistol on the table. He and I knew he wouldn't make it to the gun before I shot him. He lifted both hands and slid to the floor on the far side of the coffee table.

"Face-down!"

He complied.

The man in the tee shirt at my feet moaned and moved to get up. I pointed the Walther at a spot a few feet from his head and pulled the trigger. Chips of ceramic tile spewed from the bullet hole. He cried out and grabbed his face.

"I'm telling you guys, I'm dead serious. If you don't want to die, do exactly as I say." I took a step toward the coffee table and snatched the pistol. I kicked the table up, flipping it toward the couch and on its side, giving me direct sight of both men on the floor.

I knew I wasn't in the clear yet. "You with the tie, slide over this way. On your stomach." He slid on the tile closer to his partner until I told him to stop.

"Both of you, turn your head away." They both did. "Okay, you with the tee shirt, I want your gun. Pull it out slowly, and put it on your butt. If you move a fraction faster than I want, I'll put a bullet in your head, and you won't even know it's coming." The Walther shook, and I was glad they couldn't see it. The man in the tee shirt pulled his right arm up deliberately to his waist and withdrew a semiautomatic pistol from a concealed holster inside the belt at his hip. He placed it on his butt and moved his hand away slowly. I glanced between the two men. I was glad I had made them look away. I stepped closer to the man and flicked the gun off his butt with my right foot. It skittered across the tile ten feet away. I stepped between the two again.

"Okay, Mr. Tie, I want your gun now."

His voice muffled by the floor, he said, "You already have it."

I thought so, too, but something told me to keep pressing. "A professional like you? If I have to kill you to get it, I will. Move slowly, and pull it out."

He hesitated. I took a small step toward him as he began to stretch his left hand toward his left ankle. He pulled his pant leg up, exposing a holster and a small pistol. I flicked my eyes to the other man and back. "Pull it slowly, and hold it with a finger and a thumb only."

He did.

"Now, you move a muscle more than I tell you, you're dead. Got it?"

"Yeah."

"Flip it toward me."

It was a pitiful flip, but it skittered on the tile to my feet. I watched both of them for a few seconds. Neither moved, and I picked up the gun. It seemed to be a smaller version of the 1911 Chief Mackey owned. I stepped back and said, "Either of you twitches, and I'll shoot." Neither moved. I jammed the Walther in my belt and pressed the clip release on the other gun, dropping its clip into my palm. It was full, and I jammed it back in place and worked the slide, which loaded and cocked it. I pulled the Walther from my waistband. The odds seemed to be turning in my favor.

"I don't trust you two, so, we're going to the next level. As you heard, I now have two loaded and cocked pistols, one in each hand, one for each of you." The one in the tie shifted, and I said, "Since you're so impatient, you go first. Take off your shoes. But keep your face turned away."

He reached down and removed his shoes, moving slowly.

"Kick them away, not toward me." He did, and I said, "Now, take off your pants."

His muffled voice came back, "I can't, lying like this."

I growled between clenched teeth, "Try."

A few seconds passed, and he struggled with his belt buckle. A few minutes later, he pulled his pants over his hips. He worked them down around his ankles and finally pulled one leg free, then the other. "Good job. Now kick them away." When he did, I said, "Okay, now the tie, shoulder holster, and the shirt." When they finally came off, he tossed them aside.

"Now, you lay still, and we get your pal to do the same."

Over a few minutes, the man in the tee shirt struggled out of his clothes, and both men lay on their stomachs in boxer shorts and socks.

"Okay, guys, now that I know you are completely free of any weapons, you can roll over on your back. Oh, but only one at a time. Mr. Tie, roll over slowly onto your back." He turned over. "Tee Shirt Guy, your turn."

I stepped closer, a pistol in each hand, looking down at them. "So, let's talk."

# Chapter 22

"Put your hands behind your heads." I smiled. "You may be more comfortable that way." I looked down over the gun barrels one at a time at each of the men. "Let's get down to business. You killed my wife, and now you're here to finish the job."

They each denied it and the one who had worn the tie said, "Let me do the talking."

I looked at him. "Is your name Liam, or is Liam this one over here?" I flicked the gun in my right hand.

"Neither one of us is named Liam."

"We'll find out soon enough." I could feel my pulse pounding in the grip I had on each pistol. "You robbed my house and killed my wife, and now you're here because you know I'm closing in on you."

"That wasn't us."

"How about I call the cops? I've got them on speed dial."

"No, we're here for another reason."

"Who are you?"

"Can you let me up? I'll get you my ID from my jacket."

"Not a chance. Either of you moves, and I'll shoot you both." I glared at one, then the other. His jacket was on the back of the couch. I moved away from the two and circled around to the couch. Both men's eyes followed my movements. I lifted the jacket slowly with the tip of the Walther. I backed away and moved close to where I had been standing. I stepped back and draped the jacket over an armchair.

I looked from one man to the other for a few seconds, then thumbed the safety on the Walther and slipped it inside my belt. I moved the larger gun in my right hand back and forth as I aimed it for a few seconds at each of the men. I kept my eyes on them while I patted the jacket, feeling a bulge in an inside chest pocket. I worked my hand inside and pulled out a wallet with two folded sheets of paper. I flipped the wallet open on the back of the armchair but didn't look at it for ten seconds. When I did, I glanced at a Florida drivers' license on one side. The photo matched the tie guy on the floor, and his name was Anthony Marino. On the opposite side of the open wallet was a Florida Class C investigator license. I kept an impassive face and over a few slow seconds pulled a few cards from the wallet. I found a Florida Class M security license, a Class G firearm license, and a business card showing his title as Chief of Security, International Group, LLC, Windermere Oaks, Florida. I let the cards and wallet drop into the armchair seat and opened the folded papers, but again didn't look at them for a few seconds as I swung the pistol between the two. I expected one of them to try something.

When I took quick look down at the top paper, I saw a photo of me behind the wheel of my car. The second paper showed me on my butt, in the dead of night, outside the gate of the estate. "Okay, Marino, where did you get the photos?"

"They were taken at the estate of International Group, LLC. The one of you in the car was taken yesterday afternoon when you pulled up to our security gate. The other photo was taken this morning around 4 AM. My partner here chased you all over the lake."

My stomach fell. "Why are you here?"

"We wanted to interview you about your activities."

My voice rose. "So, you broke into my house?"

"This was a serious matter."

I thought for a few moments. "You wanted to scare me."

"Mr. Stone, I'm charged with maintaining absolute security for IGL. We needed to know why you wanted to break in and what your intentions were once you did break in."

"Mr. Marino, I'm in charge of maintaining security around here. I've already been on the wrong end of a break-in, and I won't let that happen again." I pulled the Walther from my belt, pointed it at Marino, and aimed the other gun at his partner. "Now, I need to see your ID. You can use one hand, but move slowly and pull it out."

He inched toward his trousers, fumbled with them, and held up a wallet. I told him to flip it to my feet, and he did. When I looked at it I found him to be Miles Bowman, with an IGL business card and a title of Technology Engineer. I let all of it drop into the seat of the armchair. I lowered both pistols so that my wrists rested on the back of the chair. I stretched my back, realizing muscles ached throughout my body.

"Marino, how'd you find me so quickly?"

"That's part of my job."

"Okay, how'd you break in here without setting off my alarm system?"

Miles flashed a smile. "That's my job."

I was inclined to believe them. "What can you do to prove you aren't my wife's killers?"

"Mr. Stone, I'm sure I can prove that neither of us broke in here before and killed your wife."

"That's the only thing that will keep you from

getting shot or turned over to the police. How are you going to prove it?"

He stared at me and compressed his lips. After ten seconds, he broke his eyes away a moment and then looked back. "As part of our tight security at IGL, we keep accurate records of our own activities on and off the job. We have a record for each of us on the security team for the night your wife was killed. I would need to take you to our offices and show you the records."

"You're not going anywhere. You have someone at the IGL you can call?"

He hesitated again. "Of course."

"You're going to call them and have them e-mail the records to your cell phone, for you and your partner for the night of May 9th. I'll keep the guns on both of you, and we'll see what shows up."

I found Marino's cell phone in his trouser pocket, and I made him call using the speakerphone. A woman named Gloria answered and Marino handled it very calmly. She told him it would take a couple minutes. I had him mute the phone. "While we're waiting, I want to know about your staff."

Marino explained that they had four gate guards; Gloria, the facilities business manager; himself; Miles; and another security officer named Jake. Gloria and the four gate guards didn't live on the estate, and came in for their shifts. He, Miles, and Jake lived on the estate.

I gave it some thought. "What about these gate guards? Do you have records on them?"

"We keep a log of everyone on duty. That means that there are two guards who didn't work that night and were not logged in during the night of your wife's murder. But, we are a tight group, and we can find out about their activities for that night."

Gloria's voice came over the phone. Marino cancelled the mute, and she told him the records had been sent. He thanked her and signed off.

I had Marino bring up the first record and slide the phone across the tile floor to me. I put the Walther in my belt again and took my time, mostly keeping my eyes on the two men on the floor and taking quick glances at the first record. Marino had been on duty and had not left the estate all night. I scrolled down the page and looked at Bowman's log, which showed the same as Marino's. I put down the phone. "Who else lives at the estate?"

Marino leaned up on his elbows. "Look, I understand you want to find the killers. It should be obvious by now that we aren't the killers. Let us up and get dressed. We'll cooperate and answer any questions you have."

I still felt uneasy. "You know, it's well within my rights to shoot both of you for breaking in. I…"

"No, Mr. Stone, you're a very resourceful and level-headed guy. I think you'll do the right thing."

"You broke in. I should just call the cops."

"You could." He nodded twice. "But, don't forget, we have proof of you breaking in to IGL. You call the cops on us, we'll call them on you. This whole thing would turn into a mess."

He was right.

Marino said, "Look, you have questions. I'll answer whatever questions you have. But, I also have questions. How about we talk this out, and perhaps we can find a way to help you?"

I knew that there was only the slightest possibility that Marino and Bowman were the killers or had played some part in it. There was also his cooperation, his willingness to help. It just didn't point to them.

"Okay, but I have some ground rules. First, you

can both get up and dress, but I keep the guns for now. You don't prosecute me for breaking in at the estate, and I don't prosecute you for breaking in here. When we finish today, there won't be any fallout from what has gone on so far; you don't bother me, and I don't bother you. Agreed?"

Marino looked at me with pursed lips and nodded. He got up and sat on the edge of the couch with his trousers in his hands. While he was pulling on the pants, I said, "Back to my question: who else lives at the estate?"

Without pausing, Marino said, "We have the groundskeeper and three housekeepers. I have a suite in the main house, and each of the other two security staff live in a bungalow. The groundskeeper also has a bungalow. The housekeepers have rooms in the main house. Of course, the owner and his wife often live in the main house. All the other staff come in on a scheduled basis."

"Who drives the blue Dodge pickup truck?"

"The truck is only used by the groundskeeper."

"Do you maintain records on his time?"

"No, he is a salaried employee and reports directly to Gloria."

"How long have you known the groundskeeper?"

Marino hesitated. "Three years."

"How long has the truck been blue?"

Marino looked at Bowman, who turned away. "Maybe a month."

"I need to talk to the groundskeeper."

Marino raised his eyebrows and nodded. "I can arrange that."

"Good. Until I talk to the groundskeeper, I don't have any more questions."

"Mr. Stone…"

"Mark."

"Mark, you mind if we ask you some questions?"

"Go ahead." I released the hammer on the Walther and slipped it in my pocket.

"How did you get in the house without alerting us? Your security system didn't make a peep, and you were on top of us."

I released the hammer on the other pistol and looked at it. "Before I answer that, how about you tell me how you got in without setting off the alarm?"

Miles spoke up. "My specialty. I used an electronic garage door opener that reads your code and opens the door like you did it yourself. I also have an electronic device that scans your security keypad and returns your password in about three seconds. I punched it in, and it shut down. As far as your security system was concerned, it was as if you came home using your own garage door opener and used your own password. These security systems aren't really that good."

Marino nodded at me. "Your turn. How'd you get in?"

"I guess Bowman is right, the system isn't that good. I removed a pane of glass from the back bedroom window. The window frame is still in place, and the security sensor on that particular window thinks it's still closed. I guess you shouldn't trust the security system for your own security."

Marino nodded thoughtfully. "But, how did you know we were here?"

"Mr. Marino…"

"Tony."

"Tony, I know a little about technology myself. After the break-in and murder of my wife, I installed a second layer of security on this house. It's a new product and not readily available on the consumer market. The system passively monitors the entire perimeter of my property and alerts me when it is disturbed, which you guys did when someone dropped you off here. Once I knew a car had pulled in, I logged into the normal security system and accessed the cameras in the house." I turned and pointed my thumb at the small camera mounted near the ceiling in the corner of the room.

Tony shook his head. "Impressive. We took a chance and thought you wouldn't have any reason to access the video feed if your alarm hadn't tripped."

"That was the first time I accessed it since it was installed."

"You're a man of considerable resources. How did you know the Dodge pickup was recently painted?"

"The DMV lists it as white, which is what I am looking for."

"Your wife's killers drove a white Dodge truck?"

I nodded.

"If that truck was involved in any way with your wife's murder, it falls in my area of responsibility to protect my employer." He hesitated, nodding absently. "Look, I'll help you as much as possible, as long as it doesn't conflict with my duties at IGL."

"Great. I want to interview the groundskeeper."

"Come over tomorrow, and I'll set it up." He stood. "If you'll give us back our guns, we'll leave."

"I'll give them back tomorrow when I come to the estate, but only after you provide me some information on the two gate guards you mentioned earlier. I also want to take a look at the personnel logbook you mentioned. You know, the one from which your secretary pulled your records. I don't want any loose ends. That okay with you?"

Tony shook his head. "I told you I'd help you. If this is how you want to handle it, that's what we'll do."

I nodded. "Thanks. How about nine tomorrow morning?"

"Fine." He slipped his phone from his pocket, hit one number, and said a couple words. When he opened the front door, a dark sedan pulled into my driveway.

# Chapter 23

**Wednesday, July 11**

I stopped the car just far enough ahead of the guard shack at IGL that the guard had to step out and approach my open window. I looked up at him and said, "One of IGL's finest. I have an appointment with Anthony Marino."

"Hold on a minute." He went back into his shack. I closed the window and watched the gate until it swung open.

The driveway changed to stone paving blocks as it passed through the gate and wound into a scene from paradise. A perfect carpet of deep green grass rolled over gentle mounds like a links-style golf course. Lush foliage and trees seemed perfectly placed, hiding some of the details and edges of the mansion to my left. The ground level rose as it approached the house, which seemed to be built on three layers. The roadway curved away from the house through trees and then back toward it. On the back side of the mansion I glimpsed a large, elevated swimming pool at level two, where I saw an edge of clear water spilling eight feet into a lower pool that I could see. The roadway expanded into a well-shaded, rectangular parking area that may have been as big as an acre. In addition to the huge trees around it, the parking area had islands of old oaks throughout. On the far end, the three cottages I had seen on my overnight visit hugged the property's back wall. The blue pickup sat in the carport of the last bungalow. I turned and saw Tony standing on a walkway that wound its way through the trees and up to the back of the mansion. He held up his hand and motioned me over. I parked near him and got out.

"So, this is what it's like to live in paradise."

He gave a tight-lipped smile and said, "It takes a lot of work to make it and keep it a paradise. Maybe that doesn't make it much of a paradise, then, does it? Let's go to my office."

We followed a path through the trees and bushes to the mansion and came to a solid wooden door with an electronic lock. It was cool inside, and we passed through a second electronically locked door ten feet inside the outer door. It opened up to a beautiful lobby area with business offices around its perimeter. We headed straight across to a glass door, and Tony tapped on it. A brunette in a business suit looked up from a desk that may have been used by King Arthur himself. She waved us in, and Tony introduced us. She was Gloria, the facilities business manager. We left and headed for Tony's office, which wasn't so elaborate; the desk must have only belonged to one of the Knights of the Round Table. He went behind it and asked me to sit for a minute.

I didn't sit. "These are yours." I pulled his two pistols from my rear pockets and placed them on his desk. I pulled Bowman's pistol from my front pocket and laid it next to his.

"Thanks. You carrying?"

"No."

His eyebrows went up, but he didn't say anything. I took a seat in a leather chair at the corner of his desk. He picked up a binder and handed it to me. "This is the past forty-five days of our security personnel log.

Each person is filed under his own tab. Feel free to browse through. I've redacted some sensitive issues, but there were none on the day of your wife's murder, so those records are clear."

I thumbed through it and checked each person's log for May ninth, including the afternoon and overnight shifts for the gate guards on duty that night.

Tony turned a big flat-screen monitor so that I could see it. "Here is my daily log on screen for today. I will update it throughout the day and then save it. It's all part of our normal procedures, and it's stored on our facility network here."

I slid the binder onto Tony's desk. He handed me two sheets of paper. "These are summaries of the whereabouts of the two gate guards who weren't on duty the night of May ninth. I interviewed both of them yesterday evening. I would say they both have solid alibis and were not involved."

I scanned both sheets. Tony was a professional, and I felt foolish for what I had done to him yesterday. I slid the papers on his desk and leaned back.

He leaned forward. "Now, how do you want to handle the interview with the groundskeeper?"

"First, if he's one of the killers, I'm worried he might recognize me. If not, he may just know my name."

"Do you want me to interview him?"

"No, I need to look him in the eye. I think I'll know if he's one of them."

"You need to be careful how you approach him. If he recognizes you, he may get violent."

"If he knows who I am, it'll be pretty conclusive that he's one of the killers. In that case, let him get violent."

Tony cocked his head. "If he doesn't recognize

you, you may tip him off if you go at it the wrong way. Somehow, you need to get a clear indication if he was involved without him catching onto what you're after."

"I want to know why the truck was painted a different color. Also, I think if we stand around it or lean against it as we are discussing it, he may give something away."

"Good idea. It may also help if I stay out of the conversation initially. I don't want to spook him."

"How about when we approach him, you hang around until it's clear he doesn't recognize me?"

"Okay, I'll follow your lead. I'll ease out of the conversation, but I won't go far."

We left the main house and walked to the groundskeeper's cottage. I stared at the truck as we walked. At the door, Tony knocked with no result. We hadn't expected him to be there, and Tony called him on a handheld radio. I walked around the truck, and it gave me a queasy feeling. I could see it fishtailing away into the night as I bled through my hand.

The groundskeeper came around the corner. He was a middle-aged man in khaki pants and a work shirt wet with sweat to the second button from his neck. He held work gloves in his left hand and pulled off a ball cap as he came into the shade.

Tony looked at me. "Mark, I want you to meet Gary Shacklee. Gary, this is Mark, a business associate. He is investigating an incident and would like to ask you a few questions."

Shacklee looked from Tony to me a few times. I could see his mind at work. Finally, he wiped a palm on his pants and held it out, a broad smile on his face. "Any friend of Tony's is a friend of mine. Let's step inside, where it's cooler."

I looked at Tony, who kept his face blank. I turned

back and said, "It's okay, we can take care of it right here. It will only take a few minutes."

Shacklee turned and pulled open the screen door. "Come on in. I've got to get out of this heat." He pushed the main door open and went in.

I slapped the top of the bed rail and followed him. Inside, Shacklee had the refrigerator open and pulled out two beers. He waved one at me, and I said, "No, thanks, can't." He put one back and sat at the kitchen table. I pulled a chair and sat across from him. Tony stood behind a chair between us. We both looked up at him, and I gave him a faint nod. He said, "Gary, I'm going to give you two a little privacy and wait outside. If Mark's issue turns out to involve security at IGL, I'll get involved at that point." He pulled the door closed on his way out.

# Chapter 24

Shacklee swallowed a mouthful of beer. "What's this all about?"

"When did you get the truck painted?"

He drew his eyebrows together for an instant and as quickly relaxed his composure. "Is there a law against painting a vehicle?"

"Did you pay for it?"

"No, IGL agreed with me that it was looking pretty shabby and needed it."

"So, when did you get it painted?"

Shacklee took another swig, but he kept his eyes on me over the can. "Maybe a month. Why?"

"You know a guy named Liam?"

I could tell he tried to keep the reaction off his face, but his eyes widened for a fleeting instant. He grabbed the beer and tipped the can up, holding it there until it was drained. "I don't know anyone named Liam. What kind of name is that?"

He knew something.

The broad smile was back, and he pushed back from the table. "I need another one of those. Sure you don't want one?"

I shook my head and held up a hand.

He went to the refrigerator, and I tried to think of what I could ask to get something concrete out of him. I knew he was playing me. He might or might not be one of the killers. I couldn't tell. I looked around absently and thought of how I could trip him up. The kitchen opened to a living room, and I noticed a shelf running the length of all three walls about a foot and a half below the ceiling. It was filled with all kinds of sports memorabilia. It intrigued me. To buy some time I said, "You have a nice collection." Shacklee followed my line of sight.

"Yeah, that's a lifetime of collecting."

I stood and shoved my hands in my pockets as I stepped toward the living room. "You mind?"

"Not at all."

I wandered around the room and saw autographed footballs, basketballs, pennants, ball gloves, hockey sticks, trophies, ball caps, and the like. I thought hard on how I could get him to trip up and tell me something I could use. He pointed out some of his key items, but I didn't pay any attention. Finally, I turned to him and asked, "Can you prove your whereabouts on May ninth of this year?"

"What? You kidding me? What's this about?"

"It's a simple question. Where were you on the night of May ninth?"

"You a cop? You have a warrant?"

"This is a private investigation."

"Sorry, man, I'm only talking to you because Tony asked. But, I'm done. You're going to have to leave. I got work to do." He went to the door and opened it, holding it for me to leave.

I stood in his living room, my hands in my pockets balled up in tight fists. I'd blown it. He was involved with Lee's murder, and I needed proof, but all I could do was fume.

"I said, it's time for you to go." I heard the menace and stepped toward the door.

Tony appeared in the door. "Everything okay here?"

"Your friend here is just leaving."

"Mark, was Shacklee able to help you?"

"No. Maybe you can get him to tell you where he was on the night of May ninth."

Shacklee's voice rose. "I don't have anything to say to either of you."

Tony held widely open hands chest high. "Look, Gary, if you just tell him what he needs to know, this could be all over and forgotten."

"I got nothing to hide, but I don't have to tell some stranger my personal life." He tugged his cap on. "I got work to do." He moved toward the door. Tony and I moved out, and Shacklee pulled it closed behind him. He walked away without another word.

I watched him cross the large parking area and turned to Tony. "He was involved. If not directly, then he knows something about it."

"How do you know?"

"He didn't say anything, but he gave it away. It came so quickly. I didn't have a chance to get anything substantial. I was stuck and asked him point-blank where he was."

Tony leaned against the bed of the blue truck and pinched his chin. "So, now he knows you know."

"Right, and he's not saying anything."

"You think it's time to take this to the cops?"

I put my hands on my hips. "Take what to the cops? Tell them about a truck that was repainted shortly after my wife's murder? Tell them I know a guy who knows something about it but won't say? It's all conjecture at this point."

"They could get a warrant."

"Based on what?"

"Suspicion of murder. There seems to be probable cause to me."

"They can't get a warrant based on my suspicions."

"Maybe you can lay it out for them and see if they

come to the same conclusions."

I walked out from under the carport, and Tony followed. "I doubt it." We made it halfway across the parking area and I said, "Hold on a second." I pulled out my phone, focused on the truck, and took a few pictures. I backed up and shot some more.

Tony held out a hand. "Let me know if I can do anything else."

I shook it. "Can you put the pressure on Shacklee? Get him alone and see if he'll spill something?"

Tony shook his head. "I can't do anything at this point. I'm convinced, but without any kind of proof, I'd be stepping over the line."

I let the hand drop. "Thanks for your help. I don't know what to do next, but I'll try not to bother you anymore."

I drove to a high school that had a rubber track and ran laps until I lost count.

# Chapter 25

Sweat soaked into the car seat as I drove home. Fatigue made my muscles vibrate. I had no idea how long I had run, but I was sure it was longer than any run I had done since starting. I stumbled into the house, drank a Gatorade in one long pull, and headed for the shower. I could only concentrate on the specific thing that I was doing; otherwise my mind was a blank. I dried myself, slipped on shorts and a tee shirt, and flopped onto the couch.

I woke to darkness and the caress of the overhead fan. I couldn't remember where I was, and it took me a few minutes to get oriented. I remembered the devastating run and then what had prompted it: the meeting with Shacklee. He knew something about Lee's murder. He'd taken part in it as one of the killers or in some way had something to do with it. I knew it. I'd seen it in his eyes, in his reaction to my blunt question. I realized that if he was one of the killers, he knew I was onto him. If he wasn't one of the killers, but still connected somehow, then the killers would know I was onto them. Either way, they would know I had made the connection. I needed a break, and when I got it, I would make them pay.

I sat up, stretching. The room came into focus, and I felt a stab of doubt. How sure was I that Shacklee's truck really was the one the killers had used? The actual one was only a memory, one that grew dimmer by the day. I had seen other trucks that had seemed like the right one and hadn't been. The doubt badgered me, until I had an idea to try.

I went to the dining room and made notes in my running log. I picked up my phone and saw that Sue had called and left a message. I put it down and went to the front door. I opened the door and looked down the street where I had seen the truck make its getaway. The street was empty except for the cone of light from the nearby street light. I adjusted the camera settings on the phone and took a picture. It didn't turn out well, and I tried again. I worked through the menus for the camera function and found settings for nighttime photos. I took a few more photos before I started to get something acceptable. After ten minutes, I finally had a couple shots that looked good and seemed to duplicate the vision of the street from my memory of the night of Lee's murder.

At the computer on the dining room table, I downloaded all the photos of the street and of the photos of Shacklee's truck. I studied them and picked a few to work with. I loaded the photo of the blue truck into an image-editing program and painted the truck white. I carefully cut it out and pasted it into the shot from the street. It wasn't quite right, and I played with the scale of the truck and finally got it right. I played with the light source, contrast, and brightness, until I finally had an exact photo of the truck in the exact position where it had been on the night of May ninth.

I printed the photo on a letter-sized sheet, in full color. I knew it was the truck. I pressed my hand against my healed wound and shuddered. I was sure of it. I took it to the front door and opened it to the night. I held it up, matching the edges of the photo to the street, trees, and other items around it. I had found the truck, but I needed to find the killers - or somehow prove that Shacklee was one of the killers. I closed the door and dropped the photo on the dining room table. My cell phone sat next to the computer, and I remembered the call from Sue.

I played her message. She'd called to see how I was doing and was concerned that she hadn't heard from me in a while. It was like her to call; she was such a considerate woman. I wondered if she might be able to give me some feedback on finding the truck, the doctored photo, and Shacklee himself. I would call her in the morning to see about getting together.

I knew I had made real progress, but somehow it didn't feel like it.

# Chapter 26

I left a message for Sue at mid-morning, and she called back on her lunch break. She had some things to do after work but said she would come by for coffee in the evening. In the heat of late afternoon, I did a short run around our neighborhood. It was easy and I made a mental note to map out some longer routes. I felt I was getting in shape more quickly than I had expected. But then, maybe the run went by quickly because instead of thinking about the effort of running, I concentrated on trying to solve the standoff with Shacklee and how to get real evidence.

After showering and dressing, I used my subscription to the online research software and looked up Gary Shacklee. When I sorted through to the right one, it listed all the information I already had on him, which wasn't much. No help there.

Sue showed up a few minutes after 8:00 PM with a store-bought apple pie. I made coffee, and we had pie and coffee in the living room. She was interested in my progress, and I told her about my late-night investigation at the IGL estate, my near-capture, and marathon swim to get away. She didn't seem entertained as I had expected. However, she suspected something about the truck being blue and asked if it could have been the right one.

"I had the same feeling, but I couldn't figure out

152

how to dig deeper, so the next day I found one more of the four remaining on the list and eliminated it. That's when things got interesting."

She gave me an expression of concern and asked what I meant. When I described how I'd found Marino and Bowman in my house, her expression turned to horror. I told her how I had broken in and caught them by surprise, showed her the chipped tile and bullet hole in the wall behind the couch. She became upset and started to get up. I calmed her down and told her that things were okay, that no one had gotten hurt. Yet I think I saw a change in her. I finally finished the story about Tony and Miles and how Tony had become an ally. She brightened when I told her about Tony helping me and verifying that the truck had been white but recently painted blue.

"Did you get a chance to look at the blue truck?"

"Yes, but even better, I got to talk to the guy who drives it."

"But, what if he's one of the killers?" Her voice rose, and she put a hand on my forearm.

"He could be, but didn't give me any indication that he knew who I was." I told her about talking with him and his reaction to what I'd said. She nodded when I described how he'd reacted to my blunt question about May ninth and how he'd become uncooperative.

"From what you describe, if he's not one of the killers, there's no doubt he knows something about the night of the break-in," she said.

"Yes, I'm convinced of it. I just need some evidence to connect him."

"I think the police can find that evidence. You should go to them with what you now know."

"I've got something to show you." I stood and went into the dining room. When I grabbed the doctored photo, I said, "Come take a look at this." She met me at the front door, and I flipped off the lights. I had her stand where I'd stood on the night Lee was killed. I held up the photo at her eye level and an arm length away.

Sue sucked in a quick breath and put a hand to her throat. "That is incredible! How did you get that?"

"This is a photo of the blue truck superimposed on the spot where it was on the night of May ninth."

"Mark, you have to take this to the police." Excitement came through in her voice. "You've got what you need to get them to finish this investigation and arrest your wife's killers. What you've told me is absolutely amazing."

"No. I'm going to follow this to the end. They need to pay for killing Lee."

She looked at me sharply. "I'm amazed and proud of you for what you have accomplished, but it's too dangerous, and I'm worried about you."

That made me feel good, but the truth washed it away quickly "All I have is conjecture, no hard evidence. If I go to them with this, regardless of how true it may be, they'll just tell me to stay out of police business again."

She searched my face. "What you have now is at least enough to interview Shacklee. When my husband was killed, I remember them interviewing people from shops a block away from the murder scene."

I felt the anger constrict my throat. "Maybe that's because you're a woman. The detective is either lazy or incompetent, and he doesn't care a bit about my wife's murder."

She drew back, a flash of fear crossing her face. I was too angry to care.

"Mark, I'm worried about you, especially your need for vengeance. You may cross the line, and you'll be the one to go to jail, or worse - you could get hurt or killed."

"I'm not letting go of this. It's all I have and all I want." My hands clenched to fists, wrinkling the photo.

Her chin quivered, and she quietly said, "It's time for me to go."

# Chapter 27

**Friday, July 13**

I woke with the feeling I had slept soundly. I kept thinking that I was closing in on the killers. I threw on my running shorts and shoes and headed out the front door. As I ran, a memory of Lee surfaced, and I saw a look of fear on her face similar to the one I had seen on Sue's last night. But, I was too angry and had brushed it aside, too full of my own convictions to see what I had done to Sue. I recalled doing the same thing to Lee and saw the hurt it had caused. With Lee, I had always come to my senses and taken time to see it her way. I'd apologized and tried to make it up to her. I was always amazed to regain her trust and realize the she never loved me less.

I was afraid that I wouldn't have the same chance to apologize to Sue. It wasn't the same kind of situation, but I knew I'd been wrong. I didn't have to take it out on her. That got me to reconsider her suggestion. She was right that it was the most compelling information, if not evidence, that I had dug up so far. What I knew now could be independently verified by the cops. I didn't think I had broken the law, and Tony would probably back up anything I told the police. I remembered that Tony had also suggested taking all of the information to the police and letting them take it from here.

I realized I'd missed my turnaround point and

came to a stop. I didn't mind, because it was one of the benefits of running that my thoughts could roam free; I often worked out problems mentally when I ran. Now, this would be a longer run than normal, which was okay; more was always better. I headed back.

Halfway home, a cramp ripped through my right calf, and I nearly fell. I cried out, hopping and stumbling. I fell over on a bank of grass and grabbed my leg, massaging it even as the pain intensified. I moaned through clenched teeth and writhed on the ground. The muscle tightened in waves of torment. Sweat burned in my eyes and dripped off my nose and chin. I massaged my calf for ten minutes as I lay in the direct sun. The cramp gradually relaxed as I worked on it, and when I thought I could move, I inched on my butt up the grassy incline to the trunk of a tree and shade. I worked on the leg for another ten minutes, until I could move my foot without fear of the cramp grabbing my calf again.

As I sat in the shade, I thought about laying it all out for Lt. Beauchamp, wondering what action he might take. If he found evidence that Shacklee was involved, it could lead to an arrest and probably a conviction. If he didn't take action, what did I have to lose? I didn't have anything to go on now, and I wouldn't be any worse off, I hoped.

With the cramp and my speculation on Beauchamp both seeming to head in a positive direction, I got up and tested my leg while leaning on the tree. The cramp had left an ache in the muscle, but it worked okay. I made my way gingerly down the grassy bank to the sidewalk and started off at a leisurely walk.

At home, I used a towel as I walked around for ten minutes, cooling down. I made a note in Lee's notebook about the run, the cramp, and my fear of it happening again, then jumped in the shower. As I dried and dressed, I decided to go to Beauchamp. I would somehow make my apology to Sue and let her know if and when Beauchamp made progress.

*\*\**

When I pulled open the door to the police station, it sucked cold air out with it, and I was glad to get out of the midday steam bath. The old receptionist happened to be looking my way and gave me a flip of a limp hand, which I took to be a signal to head to Beauchamp's office. I raised a manila folder at her as a form of acknowledgment. She picked up the phone, and I headed toward the doorway leading to the wooden stairway.

Beauchamp set down his phone when I came through the door. He stood and motioned to me while looking down at his desk over the bulge of his belly. As I approached, he tugged on the lower edges of his vest and continued to avoid looking at me. He motioned to the old wooden chair next to his desk and dropped into his own chair.

I sat and said, "I found the truck the killers used when they broke into my house and killed my wife."

"Oh?" He glanced up with feigned interest.

I'd known it was a mistake to come. I thought about leaving, and fifteen seconds ticked by before I decided to plow ahead. I opened the folder and pulled out the photo I had made of the white truck. I took a deep breath and said, "This is exactly the truck and exactly where it was parked when they broke in and killed Lee."

Beauchamp leaned forward and raised his chin to look through his bifocals at the photo. "Okay, where is the real truck?"

I slid the next photo from the folder on top of the first photo. It was a shot I'd taken of the blue truck that Shacklee drove. Beauchamp considered the photo for a few moments.

"Well, Mr. Stone, I happen to have seen that very truck, parked in that very spot earlier this week. I can tell you with certainty that isn't the killers' getaway vehicle."

His words were a kick in the gut. "What do you mean?"

"Just what I said. You gave me a list of four trucks on your last visit here, and I investigated each one of them. You see, that truck is owned by a well-respected local company - International Group, LLC - and is assigned to a Mr. Shacklee, a direct employee of the company. I interviewed Mr. Shacklee yesterday. Neither he nor the truck was involved with the break-in and subsequent death of your wife."

I straightened. "You mean murder of my wife."

"Yes, murder."

"I also talked to him. He didn't admit his involvement, but his reactions clearly told me he was involved."

"Yes, I know you talked to him, in direct violation of my advice. You need to be very careful that he or the company doesn't bring a suit against you."

"He was involved, and the paint job was a half-baked idea to throw off any investigation." My neck and face burned, and I gripped the armrests with both hands.

Beauchamp pushed a few papers around his desk, found a note, and scanned it. "Likewise, Mr. Stone, the other three trucks on your list also checked out. None of them was involved either. Now, I've told you in the past that this line of investigation wasn't reliable, and this proves it."

I jerked to my feet, and the wheeled chair flew back and slammed into the filing cabinet. I pointed at Beauchamp and yelled, "You're the one who's unreliable!"

He pulled back in his chair with a look of annoyance. My breathing came short and quick. Behind him, the door to the Detective Chief's office swung open and a man appeared taking in the scene.

I felt the blood pound at my temples. "Detective, you're not just unreliable, you're incompetent."

He stood, unruffled, pulled his vest down, and said, "Mr. Stone, you're out of line."

A chair scraped, and a voice came from across the room behind me. "Detective, do you need any help?"

I stared at Beauchamp. The Chief of Detectives worked his way from his office toward us.

Beauchamp looked beyond me toward the voice. "No, I was just about to educate this civilian on law enforcement matters before he leaves." He sneered at me. "Mr. Stone, you have no idea how many things can come up to bury your wife's file, so that it would never see the light of day."

I sucked in a quick breath. My right fist shot out and piled into Beauchamp's fat cheek, sounding like the crack of a whip. His head snapped back, and he tumbled back into his chair. I stepped toward him with clenched fists. The Chief of Detectives skipped around a desk and came up to me as Beauchamp whined through pudgy hands, cradling his face.

"That's felony assault."

My ears rang, and my arms shook.

"Take it easy, Mr. Stone." The Chief of Detectives stepped between us, forcing me to move back. He glanced over my shoulder and called out, "Detective."

I looked at the Chief. He meant business. I heard the other detective come up behind me. I relaxed my arms.

The Chief turned toward Beauchamp, who was sprawled in his chair, holding his face. "Detective, I'm taking charge of this situation. You stand down." He turned to me and said, "He's right, and a conviction for felony assault carries a minimum sentence of a year in jail."

The other detective came up beside me, and the Chief said, "Cuff him, detective."

I sagged and almost fell.

The detective jingled a set of cuffs from his belt and looked me in the face. He gave a sad, nearly imperceptible shake of his head. He took each hand and snapped the cuffs on.

The Chief grabbed the center of the cuffs and pulled me a step away. He turned to the two detectives. "Detective, see what you can do for Detective Beauchamp. I'm taking Mr. Stone down to processing personally."

He put a hand on my back and guided me toward the exit to the wooden stairs. I went down the steps slowly and stopped at the bottom. I shook my head absently.

The Chief looked at me. "You okay?"

"That was stupid."

"Most crimes are."

"I just want some progress on Lee's murder. I didn't mean to…" My voice trailed off and I shook my head again.

The Chief gave me a tight-lipped look and a shrug. "Let's go."

We went down a long hallway to the back of the building and across a short, covered walkway to a new building. We came into a lobby area through a single door from what appeared to be the back. A set of wide double doors fed it from our right and a cop sat at a desk on a raised platform.

We walked up to him and the Chief said, "Hey, Sergeant."

He looked up and chuckled. "Well, Chief, it's a rare honor to see you bringing in your own man."

"Yeah, it seems as though they're just walking in and committing the crime under our noses, just to make it convenient for us."

"How nice. What do you have for me today?"

The Chief paused and looked at me from the corner of his eye for a few seconds. "Tell you what, Sergeant, I'll take him back for processing. I gotta do something to earn this collar."

"Be my guest." The Sergeant waved us down the hall behind him.

I went with the Chief of Detectives, head down, and unaware of anything around us. We turned into a room and the Chief told me to sit. The room was bare, with a small table in the middle and a wooden chair on either side of it. I moved to the table and pulled a chair. A mirror spanned four feet of the opposite wall, and it came to me that we were in an interrogation room. I dropped into the chair and laid my cuffed hands on the table.

The Chief of Detectives stood with his hand on the doorknob while another officer entered the room. Carrying a small plastic bin and a clipboard, he came to the table.

The officer said, "I need you to empty your pockets, please." He placed the bin on the table and nodded at it.

I struggled to empty my pockets while wearing the cuffs, and when I was done, the officer frisked me. He made notes on the clipboard and tore off a strip at the bottom, placing it in the bin. He took the bin and went out the door.

The Chief of Detectives called after him. "Thanks." He turned to me. "Have a seat and relax a few minutes, Mr. Stone." He pulled the door behind him and I heard its lock snap in place.

When it became too uncomfortable to sit on the wooden chair, I stood and stretched. I walked around the table a few times and then walked the perimeter of the small room. I couldn't estimate time very well, but I knew it had been much more than a few minutes. When I got tired of walking around, I sat at the opposite chair. It was no more comfortable than the first one. I studied the cuffs and admired their polish. They seemed heavier than I would have expected. After a while, I stood again and paced the room. Taking one step every second, I found I could make it around the room in thirty seconds. I performed some mental arithmetic and estimated that I had been in the room for at least an hour, then admitted it could have been two hours. I sat and laid my head on my arms on the table. I felt numb and didn't want to think about what I had done.

It had to be another couple hours before the door rattled. When it opened a corrections officer stepped in with a plastic bin holding a folded jumpsuit with a pair of white socks on top. He dropped them on the table and told me to stand. He unlocked the cuffs and clipped them to his belt.

"Mr. Stone, please, change your clothes. You can keep your shoes, but remove the laces. I'll be back in a few minutes."

When he left, I stripped to my under shorts and wiggled into the faded red jumpsuit. I put on the white socks and pulled the laces from my shoes. I sat and waited again.

After a half-hour, I tried pacing again, but the laceless shoes made it difficult. My wait stretched into at least an hour.

The same officer came in. He put a different set of cuffs on me and had me pick up the bin. "Okay, Mr. Stone, you're headed for the holding tank. Let's go."

# Chapter 28

"Turn right outside the door, Mr. Stone."

The officer followed me down the hallway, which led to a door with bars on the glass in the upper half. The officer told me to go though, and it led to a large room with benches on two sides and a pair of steel gates. The opposite wall held a long counter with a half-door behind it. When we approached the counter, an officer took my bin and made me sign a paper. Another officer stepped around the counter with a set of keys.

"This way, Mr. Stone." My escort gently pulled my arm, and we headed toward the jail doors.

The officer with the keys used them on first one and then another lock in the door. The metallic clang resounded in the room and hit me like a slap as my heartbeat ratcheted up.

I looked at my escort. "Wait."

"No, Mr. Stone, don't start any trouble now." He put a second hand on my arm.

The officer at the door swung one door open with some effort.

"I'm not. But, don't I get a phone call?"

He stopped. "I was told you were ready for the tank. You haven't called anyone?"

"I've been sitting in that room for four or five hours by myself. You're the first person I've seen since they dumped me there."

"Okay, let's go sit you down for a minute while I

check this out." We went to the benches and he put a second set of cuffs on me, one end around the chain between my wrists and the other end to a steel loop embedded in the wall. The officer at the jail door locked it down and went back to his post at the counter. My guy disappeared the way we had come.

The clock on the wall over the bench told me he was gone for twenty minutes. He conferred with the two officers at the counter and came to unlock me.

"Looks like we owe you a phone call. Come with me."

We went back out the way we had come and made an immediate right turn into a small room. Along the wall four wooden chairs sat between privacy dividers that stuck out from the wall a couple feet. A steel bracket held an industrial-grade phone to the wall.

"You have ten minutes. When you pick up the phone, tell the operator the number you want."

He stepped out of the room and locked the door. Through the bars that covered the glass in the upper half of the door, I saw him take a post. I sat at a phone and gave the operator Chief Mackey's cell number.

"Chief, this is Mark. I need your help." My voice cracked.

"Are you okay?"

"I'm calling from the city jail. They're putting me in the holding tank."

"Whoa. What're you doing there?"

I told him about punching Beauchamp. I had to back track and told him about the truck. I described Beauchamp's threat about delaying Lee's investigation and that the Chief of Detectives had taken me to the jail himself. Mackey seemed surprised. I asked if he could contact an attorney for me. I had no idea whom to call. Lee and I had only dealt with a lawyer when we'd closed on our house years ago. He said he would try to help, but was sure there was nothing he could do tonight, and I might as well try to get some rest.

I hung up the phone and sat hunched over in the chair. A few minutes later, the lock snapped, and the officer stepped in. "Happy now?"

I stood and watched the floor as we made our way to the jail doors. I didn't look up when they opened. I stepped through, and both officers followed. The steel door banged shut. One officer led, and the other trailed behind me. I shuffled along for thirty seconds until the officer in front of me stopped.

I looked up at another door made of steel bars and sucked in a quick breath. We stood in a large room, maybe the size of a gym. The door was the entrance to a steel cage that sat in one half of the room. There was a space of ten feet between the walls of the cage to the walls of the room, which had barred windows at fifteen feet above the floor. The cage stood about twelve feet high, with bars for its ceiling. Fluorescent lights hung four feet above it. The other half of the room held individual cells that backed up to a solid wall separating them from the big cage in front of me.

The lead officer addressed the inmates in the holding tank. "Move to the center. You have a new cell mate coming in." He put his hand on his pistol in its holster and said, "Step over to this side of the door, Mr. Stone, and put your hands up on the bars."

As I did, I saw five guys in the cage move to sit on benches connected to a steel table in the middle of the space. They wore the same jumpsuit as mine. The trail officer unlocked the cage door, swinging it open halfway.

"Okay, Mr. Stone. Put your hands on the door."

The officer behind the door unlocked the cuffs and pulled them off. "Step in."

I turned and moved into the doorway and stopped. The door swung behind me, touching my back and butt and pushed me a half step into the cell. It snapped closed behind me. Two of the guys at the table slid off the bench and went to their bunks.

A heavy guy with a dark beard swept his arm in a wide arc toward the corner of the cell ahead of me. "You can use any of those." An upper and lower bunk hung on the solid wall to my left with another set further along the wall. A third set hung on the steel bars making up the far wall. All four walls held a pair of upper and lower bunks made of steel frames with a thin mattress and chains running diagonally from the outside corners back to the walls. A folded blanket and pillow sat on each one of the bunks the bearded guy had indicated. Through the bars on the outer wall, blackness filled the high windows, and I wondered what time it was.

I moved forward and glanced at the three at the table, passing the first set of bunks on my left. The inmates sat impassively. I stopped at the next set of bunks on my left. The lower bunk suspended three feet above the floor, and the upper one was at eye level. I put my hands on the edge of the upper frame and laid my head against them. I felt eyes on me, and I lifted my head and pulled myself up onto the upper bunk. I pushed the blanket aside and positioned the pillow at the end of the mattress toward the corner of the cage. I pulled off my shoes and laid my head on the pillow, staring at the bars six feet above my head.

I heard a voice at the table. "What I tell you? Pay up."

Above the bars, a lamp glared directly down on me. I put my arm across my eyes.

*\*\*\**

Harsh snoring pulled me awake with a start. I propped myself up on my elbows, disoriented, looking around to get my bearings. Three-quarters of the fluorescent lamps were off, including the one directly above me. The stark cell came into focus, and I moaned, dropping back onto the pillow. I relived the disappointment and anger of Beauchamp's lack of progress, the nervous strain of waiting in the interrogation room, and the fear of jail. The snoring continued at an even pace, an irritating and unnatural sound. I tried to ignore it, but couldn't.

After a few minutes, I barked, "Hey!"

It stopped immediately, and I heard a general rustling from around the room.

It took a long time for me to go back to sleep, especially after the snoring started up again.

### Saturday July 14

The windows in the outer walls shone with bright sunlight when I woke, and all the overhead fixtures glowed at full capacity. I squirmed to sit with my back against the solid wall. I noticed items sat on the horizontal bar near the bunks that held an inmate. There were books, toiletry items, and towels hanging from the diagonal chains at the end of the bunk. Everything in the jail cell was gray, from the epoxy coating on the floor to the enamel on the bars and table.

To my right, in the corner by the entry door, I noticed a solid steel room about four feet square. As I looked, its steel door opened, and one of the other inmates came out with a towel around his neck. Bolted to the wall next to it was a sink with a stainless steel mirror above it. Another inmate entered the little room as soon as the first one was clear. The entry door I had come through had a slot in it about waist-high, and a towel roll sat in the slot. I climbed down from my bunk, fighting a sore back. I walked toward the entry door and heard the bearded guy say, "That's yours."

I looked back at where he was sitting on his lower bunk, and he pointed his chin at the towel roll. I went over and picked it up. A thin towel held a toothbrush, toothpaste, comb, and a bar of soap.

I looked back at him. "No razor?"

He snorted. "Once a week. Under supervision."

I waited until the guy came out. I pulled my socks off and stepped into the little room. It held a showerhead and a stainless steel toilet.

When I came out, the rest of the inmates sat at the table eating. It looked like an oversized picnic table made of welded steel, except it had steel grating for the top surface and the benches. I set my things on my bunk and went to the table.

I ate cold oatmeal, cold toast, and cold coffee, black. I used a plastic spoon and drank from a paper cup. I'd had worse.

"Hey, man, what are you in for?"

I looked up at the bearded guy, sipping the bitter coffee. I set the cup down slowly. I looked at the cup for a few moments and looked back at him. "I slugged a cop."

A scrawny guy next to him said, "All right."

The bearded guy said, "I'm Terry. This is Jimmy. You?"

"Mark." I looked back at the coffee.

Someone cleared the table, but I didn't pay attention. Later, I heard an officer at the door. "Hey, bring that cup over here."

I looked up, swiveled to face the door, and saw all of the breakfast items on the tray in the slot. I eased up, favoring my back, and put the cup on the tray.

I stuck my hands in my pockets and walked toward my bunk, stretching my back. I turned and walked back toward the door. I couldn't climb back to my bunk and didn't want to sit. I paced.

A group of three sat at the table. Terry shuffled cards and looked at me. "Want to play?"

I shook my head.

The card game lasted a couple hours, and I sat on the lower bunk long before it ended. Lunch came and went. The cage got warm in the afternoon, and most of the inmates napped. Dinner was the worst meal of the day, and afterward the group played more cards but didn't ask me to join.

With my head on the thin pillow, the ceiling of bars filled my field of view, and the lights dimmed. I had kept from thinking about my foolishness but now I replayed my actions over and over. Hitting Beauchamp had been a mistake. I needed action, progress on Lee's murder. I had let her down again. I had let my anger take over, and I realized that I needed to keep my head in the future. I had to push my anger aside. I needed to look at every moment as factual - be observant, keep track, but no anger. I promised myself not to let it get a hold of me again. When I got out of here, I needed to apply my energies to the problem analytically and make good decisions. It was the only way I would catch Lee's killers and get any justice for her.

# Chapter 29

**Sunday July 15**

The next morning went the same as the previous morning, except this time, I put all my breakfast items on the tray at the door before the guard came to pick it up. I didn't play cards either. I spent the time reviewing the details I knew about Shacklee. Something tickled at the edge of my memory, but I could never catch it. Not a lot lined up with him being a thief and killer, but then, a lot did line up. I knew he was involved.

Just before lunch, two officers came to the door and one called my name. I went to the door.

"Get your things. You're getting out."

I went back to my bunk, grabbed my shoes, and went to the door. They went through the reverse of the process from when I'd come in. I felt the eyes of my cellmates on me, but I never looked back once they closed the door and we walked away.

I got my clothes back and changed, and an officer led me past the interrogation area to the anteroom where the Sergeant sat. Chief Mackey leaned against his desk.

"You don't look any worse for the wear." He chuckled and held out a hand. "You ready to go?"

I grabbed it and smiled. "Thanks, man, it's good to see you."

He turned as we walked out and waved. "I'll catch

you later, Sergeant."

We stepped out into the blazing sunlight and headed for the parking lot. "How'd you arrange that?" I asked.

"I have a good friend on the force. We served together on a tour of duty in Iraq. We discussed your problem, and he did a little digging. My friend, who will remain nameless, had a talk with the Chief of Detectives. Turns out, the Chief of Detectives didn't have you booked after he looked into your wife's case file. He was going to let you cool off for a couple days and charge you with a misdemeanor instead of felony assault. When my friend discussed it with him, he decided to drop it all together. No arrest record, no charges."

I smiled and shook my head. "Man, that's great. I can't ever thank you enough."

"You'd do the same for me. Don't worry about it."

We stood at his car. "Where did you park?"

I looked around, then did a complete revolution. My car was nowhere to be seen. "I left it right here."

We looked around for a minute and decided to go back into the station. Inside, I headed for the receptionist. She gave me a crooked eyebrow and said, "Yes?"

I explained that I had parked my car in their visitor lot yesterday and it wasn't there today. She opened a drawer, pulled a sheet of paper, and laid it on the counter in front of me. It was a photocopy of a map.

"You head over to the impound lot, here." She pointed with a pen. "If you left it overnight in our visitor lot, you'll find it there."

I looked at the map and into her face. She raised her gray eyebrows at me. Mackey chuckled. We left and went to his car. He started it up and kicked the air to maximum cool.

"You going to be okay once we get your car?"

I thought for a moment, realizing I wasn't any further ahead. "Chief, I'm positive that this guy Shacklee is involved somehow in Lee's murder. I just need one tiny little thing to lock it in. But, I don't know what to do."

"Look, I'm not close enough to the details to be any help. It seems like there's nothing to do about it, except let it ride out in the hands of the police."

Those were not the words I wanted to hear. My elation at getting out of jail vanished. He put the car in gear and asked which way to go. We crossed town and pulled into a lot behind a towing company. The Stratus sat front and center. Mackey waited while I went in.

He lowered the window when I came out and asked if I was all set.

"Sure, seventy-five bucks later."

"That'll teach you to go to jail." He smiled.

I jingled my keys. "I'm all set now. Thanks again. I don't know how to repay you, but thanks."

"Don't worry about it. I'll see you later."

# Chapter 30

I left the impound lot and headed home, even though I didn't want to be there alone. Inside, I walked into the living room, stopped, and looked around. It was a dead place. I felt like giving up. I had no options, no plan, no direction. I fantasized about going to Shacklee and putting my gun to his head, forcing him to spill his guts. I paced the living room, the scene throbbing in my mind. I tried to think of ways to get Tony to let me into the estate.

I grabbed my head in both hands and yelled, "Is this it? Threaten a man's life? And if he doesn't give me what I want, pull the trigger?"

I fell back on the couch, head back, hands still on my head. I squeezed my eyes shut and let the tears ooze from the back corners of my eyes. I wished for Lee. I slumped to the side and dropped my forearm across my eyes.

\*\*\*

I stepped into a room. It was very indistinct, dark enough to blur all sharp edges, but light enough to make out some details at close range. I couldn't tell anything about the floor except that it was solid. The walls were colorless. I made out the shape of an easy chair and stepped toward it. A sofa appeared in front of me. I looked for one end, but it faded into the colorless walls where a shelf held unknown objects. I moved toward the shelf and made out a football without seams. A trophy sat next to it, but I couldn't make out any detail. I saw the rearview mirror from a car on the shelf and an empty picture frame. I reached for the picture, but the shelf moved away. I looked left, and the shelf disappeared into the gray mist. When I looked right, a baseball rolled off the shelf and bounced away on the floor.

An explosion of thunder rattled the walls, and I jerked up from the couch, eyes wide open. Strobes of lightning shot through the full-length glass pane of the patio door. I squeezed my eyes against the blast of light. As the hot light image in my eyes began to fade, I saw the shelf and the baseball falling from it. I tried to keep the image of the shelf alive even as the thunder erupted in the background. The image bothered me, and I kept my eyes closed, trying to capture it, remember it. It felt familiar, but I didn't recognize it. With each flash of lightning, the after-image burned the vision away. I began to lose the odd feeling and the memory of items on the shelf. I felt the urge to try to record it and didn't stop to question why.

I slid to the end of the couch and twisted on the lamp. I went into the dining room and grabbed a pad of paper and pen, then returned to sit on the sofa. I closed my eyes to try to regain the image and made some notes. I felt driven to hang on to it. I sketched it, as a stick figure of my memory. The effort seemed to kill the vision. I set the pad down and leaned back.

I stared at the flat-panel TV mounted in the middle of our entertainment center. The TV was a black rectangle in the middle of a blond wood rectangle. Other blond rectangles complemented the center rectangle, and the whole unit became a large blond rectangle. The top of the entertainment center made a natural storage ledge. Lee and I had made it the only place where we allowed clutter, and we'd kept things there that we wanted to see. It was an odd collection of items, including framed photos.

A long, growling thunder built in intensity, and I turned to look out the patio door to see a snaking pattern of lightning. I snapped my head back and focused on a spot near the top left edge of the entertainment center. When I didn't see what I was looking for, I jumped up and walked over to the unit, but I still didn't see my target. I slid the coffee table over and jumped up on it to make a thorough search.

It was gone.

Years ago, our church had held a charity event. Lee and I loved baseball, and we had gone way overboard in bidding for an historic baseball that had been donated for the event. The baseball had been signed by one of our favorite players from the St. Louis Cardinals. It sat in a clear plastic box and came with an official certificate of authenticity.

I hadn't noticed it missing before, but now realized it had been taken along with the other valuable items during the break-in. I hadn't given the losses much attention. My real loss had been so great that nothing else mattered.

I went back to the couch and picked up the pad of paper. My autographed baseball seemed to be rolling off the shelf while I stood dumbly and watched it fall. The sketch showed a shelf a foot and a half below the ceiling of the room.

I dismissed the dream, forgot the sketch, but remembered seeing my autographed ball on Shacklee's trophy shelf.

I went into the master bedroom and into the walk-in closet. I found the metal box we kept there that held our important papers. I took it out and set it on our bed, opened it, and leafed through it. I found and pulled out the certificate of authenticity for our autographed baseball. The certificate contained a serial number that I knew was also embossed on the ball.

"Lee, I'm so glad we shared our love for baseball. This certificate will prove Shacklee is one of the killers."

# Chapter 31

"This is Anthony Marino." The voice on the cell phone sounded all-business.

"Tony, it's Mark Stone."

"Mark, it's over. The police were here Thursday, and the boss isn't happy. He doesn't want IGL involved in any more police business in any way."

"Tony, I have proof."

"Mark, the police interviewed Shacklee and then me. They have assured me that Shacklee is fully cleared." His tone remained firm.

"I'm telling you that I have proof, and I'm holding it in my hand."

The line was silent for a few seconds. "What kind of proof?"

"Shacklee has a trophy shelf in his living room. On that shelf, he has an autographed baseball for which I have the certificate of authenticity. He stole it when he broke in my house."

"How can you be sure the ball is yours?"

"I saw it."

"Mark, you're putting me in a tough spot. The boss wants this to go away. Now. And I'm supposed to believe you saw a ball you claim is yours."

"You want to live and work with a killer?"

"No, not if it's true. But, I have to balance that against relying on your memory and I question your emotional state." His voice lost its edge.

"It's a simple thing to prove. We go look at the ball on his shelf. He doesn't need to know we're there."

"Why didn't you tell me about it before? If you saw it, we could have avoided the visit by the cops."

I could tell that he wanted to find out but was compelled to protect his employer. "Look, I just realized it was missing. When I did, I dug out the certificate. There's even a photo of the ball on the certificate."

"I'll get back with you."

At mid-morning, Tony sent me a text message to meet him at the estate in the early afternoon.

When I arrived at the gate, Tony came out of the guard shack. "Mark, once you're inside the gate, follow me. We're going to park your car in the garage. I want to minimize the possibility of Shacklee spotting you or your car."

I agreed and followed Tony, who drove an ATV that was parked at the gate. We went around the back and into a ground-level garage under the massive pool deck. Tony hit the door closure button and turned to me.

"I don't want any of the other employees seeing you."

"That's fine with me." We went through the door into the mansion.

Tony looked back at me. "I don't think anyone else is mixed up in this, but I want to be extremely careful. Only Gloria and I know you're here. I've asked her to have Shacklee working on the far tip of the grounds today."

As we made our way into the business offices, Tony used his cell phone and I heard him directing a guard to his post at the main gate. He clipped the phone to his belt and we went out the door to the courtyard, where he stopped and scanned the grounds. From there, I could see through the open back gate out to the lake glittering through the trees. We made our way to Shacklee's bungalow. Once we were inside, Tony closed the door quickly behind us.

I went through the kitchen into the living room and walked to the spot where the clear plastic box that held my ball sat on the edge of the shelf. I put my hands on my hips and turned to Tony.

"Hold on." He turned and went back into the kitchen, returning with a hand towel. "Try picking it up on the edges."

I took the towel and gripped the box on opposing corners. I brought it down and held it so we both could look in the box. I could read an "A" and a "P" in the scrawl that was the signature, and rotated it to see the embossed certificate number. I set it on the back of the sofa, then pulled the certificate from my pocket and unfolded it. I read the number to Tony.

"You're right. This is it."

The kitchen door flew open. "What's going on here?" Shacklee yelled. He slammed the door and stomped into the living room.

I picked up the box with the towel and said, "This makes you the prime suspect in my wife's murder."

Shacklee swiped the box out of my hand and held it to his chest. "This is mine! Who said you could come in here without my permission?"

I clenched my fists to reply, but before I could say anything, Tony edged between us. "That's okay, you hang onto it." He glanced at me and eased the certificate from my hand. "When we take this certificate to the cops and prove that you stole it from his house, you'll be going down for murder."

"Oh, no, they're not going to pin any murder on me." He glanced at the ball, eyes wide. "This was given to me, and there's no way they can prove I killed anybody."

"Who gave it to you?" I glared at him.

Shacklee faced Tony, but his eyes flicked everywhere while he seemed to consider an answer.

Tony stepped back and slid the certificate in his pocket. He looked Shacklee in the face and pulled his cell phone from his belt.

Shacklee held up a hand and shook his head. "Now, look, a couple of buddies needed to haul some brush for a job they did, and I loaned them the truck. They told me they got the ball at the pawn shop and gave it to me for letting them use the truck."

He was lying. I asked, "Okay, so who are these buddies?"

Shacklee turned toward me his brows together and his lips pressed tightly. "Mister, you clear out of here. You're not the cops and I don't have to answer to you!"

# Chapter 32

I lunged toward Shacklee with a growl. Tony moved quicker. He grabbed my shirt in both hands near my neck and pushed me back. Shacklee stepped back, opening the gap between us. I jerked, trying to free myself from Tony's grip.

Tony pushed me against the back of the sofa. "I'm in charge here, Mark. Stop!"

"He knows who killed my wife!" I lurched forward, twisting toward Shacklee. Tony slipped to the side and pulled my left arm around behind me, grabbing my thumb and bending it back. Pain shot up my arm, and my knees buckled.

"Let's go. Outside." I heard the threat in his voice. Shacklee clutched the box and stepped back again. Tony pushed me forward and increased the force on my thumb. My legs wobble from the pain, and we staggered out of the living room.

I twisted my head to Shacklee and, grunting with the agony, yelled, "This isn't over!"

Tony made me open the kitchen door and pushed me out. He kept pressure on my arm through the carport, and we lunged into the courtyard. With a push he let me go, and I stumbled a couple steps while he said, "Take it easy. That was mostly for him. I have a plan."

I turned back, breathing hard, and took a step toward him. He grabbed my shoulder twisting me back toward the mansion without missing a step.

"Let's go. Just head over to my office. I don't want Shacklee to suspect anything."

His words finally got through the pounding anger, and I stalked across the courtyard. I rubbed my arm and thumb the whole time. In his office, he told me to sit and pulled the certificate from his pocket. He made a copy of it on a small machine on his credenza.

I let out a deep breath. "Okay, what's your big plan?"

"Mark, now I'm convinced Shacklee was involved. I still can't see him as a killer, but maybe some of what he said is true."

"He was lying. That ball came from my house."

"Yea, but maybe all he did was loan the truck to his buddies, and they were the ones who broke into your house."

"Then he knows who they are and what they did."

"Right. That's where I'm at on this. What I'm going to do is take this certificate and all that I know about your wife's murder to my boss. He's the owner of IGL."

I groaned. "What's he going to do, dock his pay for loaning out the truck?"

"Let me finish. The boss has known Shacklee for years. Shacklee's been with the organization for a long time, in various other positions well above his current position as a groundskeeper, which is his last chance to stay with IGL. When I lay it out for the boss, he won't sit still for any kind of nonsense from Shacklee. I guarantee the boss can put enough pressure on him to get him talking about who he loaned the company truck to."

"I don't know. I can't see the threat of losing his job as enough pressure to get him talking, if he doesn't want to talk."

"I didn't say he would use such a minimal threat."

I shook my head and looked away. I couldn't see what the boss could do that some of Tony's arm-twisting wouldn't do quicker.

"Mark, I'm telling you, the boss can't allow something like this to affect his business. I can't tell you why, but this is one thing that could have a huge impact on operations." Tony nodded. "And profits."

I looked up sharply at Tony. "What kind of business is IGL?"

He hesitated. "The company has representatives in most major cities in the U.S. as well as some major cities overseas."

"That's impressive, but you didn't say what IGL does."

Tony gave an imperceptible shake of his head while he seemed to consider. A few moments later he said, "IGL does specialized consulting. I can't say more than that, due to the confidentiality requirements of our clients."

I lifted my palms with a shrug. I had no idea what he meant.

"Sorry, Mark, but I can't say more."

"Okay, so your boss is going to beat it out of him, or cut his pay, or maybe Shacklee will come clean out of loyalty for the company. I just can't see it."

"Just let me handle it. I'll talk to him as soon as you leave, and we'll know something today or tomorrow."

I latched onto the confidence in his tone. "Okay. I guess I'll head out and wait to hear from you."

We backtracked to the garage in silence. A thought tried to struggle to the surface, and it finally clicked into focus as I stepped through the door and saw my car. I remembered talking with Dana and her mother Phyllis, who had seen an unfamiliar Dodge truck on her street when she had suffered her break-in. I stopped and turned to Tony. "If your boss can pressure Shacklee to find out who his buddies are, maybe he can also find out if he loaned it to them on other occasions."

"Okay, why?"

"I know someone else who suffered a break-in at her house before it happened to me. The woman told me she saw a white Dodge truck on her street on her way home when she discovered she had been robbed."

"Oh, man." He nodded. "Maybe Shacklee or his buddies used his truck for other robberies."

"That's what I'm thinking." I got in my car, and Tony hit the button, rolling up the garage door.

As I put it in gear, he said, "Don't stop at the gate on the way out. I'll have it open for you."

I waved and backed out.

# Chapter 33

I kept going at the gate and turned south at the county road. I didn't want to go home. I saw myself pacing between the kitchen, dining room, and living room. I didn't have my running bag with me, but I didn't feel like running, anyway. I felt like hitting somebody.

I didn't think I would hear from Tony anytime soon. Maybe his plan looked good to him, but not to me. The county road twisted and rolled, and I lifted my foot from the gas pedal to keep from slinging off the asphalt on a tight curve. As I got the car under control I realized that I didn't know where I was headed. I felt powerless. I had no next step, once again. But, Shacklee was the key. I needed a way to force him to tell me the truth, and all I could imagine was holding a gun on him, thinking he would fold and tell me what I needed to know. But then, I guessed he would say anything just to get away.

The road came to a T. The intersection held a new housing development on the right and a new strip mall on the left. Undeveloped Florida scrub flourished everywhere else. At the green light I turned east onto a new four-lane roadway with a drainage ditch separating the eastbound lanes from the westbound lanes. It had been years since I had driven out here on an old county road. A mile farther I was stunned to see a new Wal-Mart. I pulled into the parking lot and found an old oak tree on the edge of the lot that the builders had possessed the foresight to save. I parked in its shade.

I dialed Sue, wondering if she would talk to me after the way our last conversation had ended. She answered in a friendly voice and gave no indication that there was any lingering effect from my cruel words. I asked if she would be around if I was in the area and she told me she would be around all afternoon and evening and that I was welcome to come by. I told her I would see her a little later and thanked her.

*\*\**

I stood at Sue's front door, mentally rehearsing my apology, but the door swung open.

She smiled at me. "You know, the doorbell works better than telepathy."

It startled me, and I didn't reply as I tried to gather my thoughts.

"Oh, come on, it was just a little funny." She stepped aside. "Don't just stand out there in the heat. Come in."

Inside, I closed the door and turned to her. "Sue, before we go any further, I want to apologize for my harsh words and how I treated you last time we talked. I'm sorry. That's not who I am."

"I know. Now, forget it." Her sincerity came through in her tone and relaxed stance.

"Thanks. I'll try to keep from doing it again."

We went into the living room, and she asked if I wanted anything to drink. I declined until she said she was having ice tea. When she came back, I wondered if I had interrupted a day of chores. She wore jeans that fit well and a lightweight yellow blouse that looked more business than casual. Her short hair was pulled up, and she wore old tennis shoes without socks. She put a tall glass of tea in front of me and sat in an armchair opposite of me.

"I hope I didn't interrupt a busy day for you."

"No, no, I was just catching up on some things around here. But, it sounded like you wanted to talk?"

I realized I shouldn't burden her with my troubles, especially my recent stay in jail. She had a pleasant presence that made me relax. Her friendly attitude had pushed my frustration with Shacklee and Beauchamp behind a mental door. "I finally took your advice and took my photo of the killers' truck to the cops and told Beauchamp I had found the killer. Unfortunately, he had taken my list of four trucks and done his own investigation."

"Unfortunately?" Sue raised her eyebrows.

"Yeah, he had already interviewed the blue truck's owner, a guy named Gary Shacklee. Beauchamp informed me that Shacklee was cleared and in no way involved with the break-in at my house and the murder of my wife."

She covered her mouth with her hand. "No."

"I'm through with the cops, unless I have absolute evidence." I looked away, wondering if I should say any more. When I looked back, she seemed to know I had more. The expression on her face and the way she tilted her head seemed to pull it from me.

"I just may have the absolute evidence. But, I'd like to know what you think."

My cell phone buzzed, telling me I had a text message. I asked Sue to hold on a second and looked at the phone. Tony had sent it and it read: Sorry, you were right. Shacklee is sticking to his story. I replied to Tony with a note of thanks and a promise to talk later. When I finished, my pulse pounded, and my hands shook.

"Mark, are you okay?"

I stared ahead. "I'm fine."

"You wanted to know what I thought about your evidence?"

I took a few seconds to focus on my previous line of thought. Calmly, I told her about my dream of the autographed baseball and finding it at Shacklee's, his refusal to talk about it, and Tony's approach to have his boss put the pressure on Shacklee.

"That's incredible. You're very close now. I think the detective would jump on this."

"I don't think so."

"Your message?"

"Yeah, it seems Shacklee's not talking."

Sue sat on the edge of her chair. "Oh, Mark, please take it to the detective. You have all but solved the murder for him."

"No, I have to go after the killers myself."

Sue's shoulders collapsed. "Please….why not take it to them?"

"Beauchamp's already convinced Shacklee's innocent. He's not going to change his mind. He'll probably say that Shacklee's story is the way it happened. Look, Beauchamp's already shown that it's his way or no way."

"But, Mark, I'm worried about you. These guys are proven killers. What chance do you have against them?" Sue looked at the floor and shook her head slowly. "Mark, you're going to go too far with this. I'm afraid for you." She looked up at me. "If you aren't going to take this to the cops, I don't want to be part of it.

I snapped. "You're right. I don't have a chance against them." I stopped, pushing my rising anger into a hole. "But, I'm not giving up."

# Chapter 34

Driving home, I wondered if I had just lost a good friend. I'd gone to see Sue with an open mind, I thought, hoping for her unbiased opinion. I knew that she was worried for me, and I felt warmth for her because of it. But, when she'd kept advising I go to the police, I couldn't help but see Beauchamp's smug face and hear his disregard for me. She hadn't been the one to report to him each time and get shot down. I couldn't get her to see that. All I knew was she didn't look at me when she said goodbye.

My cell phone alarm sounded, and I flipped it over on the car seat. It was a reminder for a physical therapy session in a half-hour. I had forgotten all about it. It was a make-up session for one I had missed last Friday. I didn't want to go. I tried to come up with a good reason to cancel. But, Rachel worked hard, and I didn't want to leave her hanging after rescheduling once already. I changed course and headed for her office.

Halfway through the session, my shirt was soaked. I worked in quiet determination. She encouraged me and tried to make conversation, but I didn't play along. It didn't seem to effect her positive attitude.

Facing me, she held my arms over my head. She seemed to hold the position longer than I expected, and my shoulder muscles started to burn. I looked her in the eye.

She cocked her head with a smile. "So, you're going

to break your silence?"

I grunted, and she dropped my arms.

"You seem awfully quiet today, Mr. Mark. I hope it's not something I've done."

"Rachel, you don't want any part of my problems."

"I help people heal. It's my job. Sometimes, the healing is more than physical. Now, what's your problem?"

I looked for a place to sit and said, "You know I'm trying to do what I can to find my wife's killers?"

"Oh, yes."

"No thanks to the cops, but I've found a genuine suspect who was involved with the break-in and murder."

"That's incredible."

"The only problem is that he's been cleared by the cops. As far as they're concerned, he wasn't involved."

"Are you sure he was?"

"I have absolute evidence he was involved. He's in possession of one of the items stolen from my house that night. I know that doesn't mean he's one of the killers, but I'm sure he knows who they are."

She smiled. "If that's the case, why don't you track him? He'll lead you right to them."

"I don't think I can just go sit outside his house and follow him wherever he goes."

She stood and moved to her desk. "No, I mean track him using a GPS tracker." She started pecking at the keyboard.

I wiped my face on a towel. "What do you mean?"

"During my divorce, my attorney hired an investigator because I needed proof Martin was cheating on me. The investigator got a little device he called a GPS tracking key and hid it on my husband's car. He retrieved it a couple weeks later and downloaded all of the GPS coordinates Martin had visited. Sure enough, there were at least six visits to his mistress's home address."

"I've never heard of a tracking key."

"Neither did Martin, and now I have a decent settlement." She pecked away at the laptop and looked up. "What's your e-mail address? I'll send you a link to the website for the tracking key."

I told her she was a genius and thanked her.

When she finished, she said, "You ready to get back to work?"

"Sure am." I was sure she could tell a marked difference in my attitude for the rest of the session.

***

I was astounded by the information on the website about the GPS tracking key, made by a company called Platinum Cloud Systems. The key was a small electronic box with a USB connector and a waterproof housing that incorporated a powerful magnet. It was designed exactly for the purpose of tracking vehicles. Once it was enabled, it would record every GPS coordinate that the vehicle traveled. It included its own software and cost less than five hundred bucks.

I ordered one for express delivery.

It was still early, so I called Tony.

"Mark, I can't believe the boss couldn't crack Shacklee. I apologize and offer any assistance I can to help. This is beyond me."

"Tony, take it easy. I had a few hours of wallowing in my own self pity, but I've got something that'll nail him."

I explained the GPS tracking key, and he thought it was the perfect answer. We would let Shacklee lead us to the real killers.

I did three miles in the dark. I liked running late at night. Traffic was light and the air cooler. When I recorded it in Lee's notebook, I was pleasantly surprised to see that it was run number twenty-four.

## Tuesday, July 17

The tracking key arrived at the house the next day, and I called Tony to meet at a coffee shop. He was anxious to see all the details on the device. He took it when we split up and sent me a text message later in the day that said he had secretly planted it on Shacklee's truck. We would give it a couple weeks before getting it back and analyzing the data.

My run that evening felt good. I ran longer than I had planned, but it was easy. It left me with a feeling of accomplishment.

I thought about Sue and how we had left it. I couldn't seem to keep from hurting her. I called her in the evening. Hearing her voice, I wanted to apologize again, but there was no warmth in her responses. We agreed to have lunch in a few days and said our goodbyes.

## Thursday, July 19

I spotted Sue near a window overlooking the ninth green at the golf club restaurant. I said hello and sat across from her. She was friendly, but I could sense her reservation.

She smiled and patted my hand. "So, tell me how the investigation has been going."

I wanted to keep it low-key. "Nothing much has happened since the last time we spoke. Things are kind of slow."

She must have expected the opposite because she

hesitated, then relaxed. I admired her character, and had a question about it for her.

"Sue, I'd like to ask you a personal question, and I understand if you don't want to answer."

She drew back. "I'll try. What do you want to know?"

"I have always wondered how you are able to get by with out any resolution regarding your husband's murder. I'm not trying to pry into your life, but you seem to cope well. What's your secret, if you don't mind me asking?"

She looked out the window for several seconds, then turned back with a compressed smile. "It wasn't easy at first. But, as I got over the trauma, I was able to remember and relive some of the best times of our lives. I realized that Paul, my husband, had taught me how to cope years before. I often wonder about the coincidence of it."

She stopped and covered her mouth with her hand, looking out the window again. A few moments passed, and she regained her focus. "It's kind of a long story."

"I'm listening."

"We bought and lived in a house that had a line of bushes along one property line. The previous owners had never maintained the bushes and they had grown out of control for many years. The problem was that they were completely overtaken by vines. You know, the kind of vines that totally take over a tree or bush, wild and voracious ones. The bushes made a line a hundred feet long and twenty feet high. Paul fought those vines for years and never made any progress. He used to sit at the kitchen table at breakfast and gaze out on the poor bushes and shake his head. I saw him do it many times. He had no easy solution, and when we talked about it, he would tell me how much work it would be to cut and dig those bushes out by hand. He said you couldn't just dig out the vines - they were just too entwined with the roots of the bushes. He said it would take years of maintaining new ones to arrive at something he could be proud of. But, nothing ever got done on those overgrown bushes because they were so far down the priority list of things we needed to do to that house.

"The city bought the neighboring property and cleared it for a new park. One day, my husband was out looking at the progress on the new park, and he realized that park renovations seemed to have crossed the property line and come well into our yard. He also discovered the bushes seemed to grow at a diagonal across the property line with half of them on our side and half on the park side. We had a new survey done, and both conditions turned out to be true."

"He contacted the project manager for the new park, and they met out at the bushes. Together, they reviewed the survey, and the project manager admitted that they had made a big mistake. He immediately ordered workers to fix the problem and offered to make up for the mistake in any way that my husband would like. Paul told the manager that it wouldn't be necessary, but he did ask the manager what he wanted to do with the overgrown bushes on their side of the line. The manager asked what would we do, and my husband said he would dig them out.

"The project manager called a tractor on the radio and, when it arrived, gave the order to remove the bushes. Ten minutes later, they were dug up and in a pile waiting for a dumpster. It actually took four dumpsters to haul all of them away.

"The project manager told my husband that they had an excess of young trees and he could have any of them he wanted. In the end, Paul had them plant ten

Crepe Myrtles just inside our property line. Those trees bloomed magnificent magenta blossoms for all the years we stayed in that house.

"When we talked about it later he said he learned that all his worry and disappointment over the overgrown and vine-infested bushes had been for nothing. That he couldn't do it on his own didn't mean that it couldn't get done. That's what I think about his murder. If I worried about it, it would be for nothing, and, just because I can't do it myself, doesn't mean it can't be solved."

She smiled and looked me in the eye.

It was a good story, and she was right… but not for me. I couldn't live that way. I didn't want to ruin the moment or the fragile relationship we had. I said, "I can see that approach and understand it. It works for you, and I am glad." I shook my head gently. "But, I can't live like that. It was my fault Lee was killed. I couldn't protect her at the most dangerous moment of her life, and I just can't rest without justice for her murder."

"You need to ease up." Her smile disappeared.

\*\*\*

Driving home, I marveled at Sue's resilience and acceptance. Yet, there was no way I could stop now. I was too close to the killers.

For the next week, I took a break from the grind to find the killers. I had a plan. It was in motion, and all I had to do was wait. I relaxed and stopped thinking about the killers.

I ran every day. Some days were hard, but most felt good. I saw Rachel on Fridays and Wednesdays. Each time, she seemed to have a sense of glee about my improving condition and the effort I put into the session. She joked that she should turn me into a showcase for promoting her services. She was probably right: I hadn't had pain in the bullet wound for weeks.

## Tuesday July 31

Tony's text said that he had covertly recovered the tracking key and suggested meeting at the coffee shop the next day. It was a quick meeting, and Tony was excited to see the results of the GPS record and the possible lead to the killers.

I took the unit home and fired up its software. When I downloaded the data files, I found 171 raw entries over the two weeks it had been on the truck. I followed the recommended procedures supplied by the manufacturer and eliminated any entry that lasted less than three minutes, which essentially eliminated stops at traffic lights and other traffic-related stops. It left me with thirty-one entries to check.

I saved them as a single text file and fed it into a spreadsheet. I sorted the entries by GPS location, which gave me eighteen unique GPS coordinates. Of those, there were five locations that were duplicates or more. Three locations were repeated twice. One location had three entries. The final location was repeated four times. I started with the location that Shacklee had visited four times and entered its address into my online search program. It did a reverse lookup and came back with a bar in Orange County. I did the same lookup for the location that had been recorded three times.

It came back with the residence of a man named Liam Peterson, and my jaw dropped. I'd found one of the killers. I would never forget the name Liam. It was the name one of the killers had yelled at the other just before Lee was shot. I jumped up and gave out a shout, dancing around the dining room. I had found the killers.

# Chapter 35

It was time for some research on Liam Peterson. My subscription to the people search website had another ten months before it expired. It was amazing what you could find out about other people for $59.95 a year. When I had first subscribed I had done a test search of my own name, and it had told me things I had forgotten.

I entered Liam Peterson's name in the search box. Thirty seconds later, I began reading a six-page report on him. His home address was on the east side of Orlando. His home and cell phones were listed, but no work number. Liam was thirty-eight, divorced, with one kid. I was surprised to see his house mortgage had been paid off two years ago. Before Lee's death, we'd had another twenty-two years on our mortgage. The report listed eleven previous home addresses, most in central Florida, with the two oldest addresses out of state. His work history went back fourteen years, with nine jobs on the list. But, he hadn't had a wage-paying job in five years. His last reported job had been a two-year position as a landscape technician, which I translated as a "lawnmower." In the financial part of the report there were records of two evictions. When I got to the criminal record section, my stomach dropped. This guy was a criminal, and it hit me that he would probably take me out if I approached him the wrong way. But, his criminal record was clean for the past four years. Before that was a list of arrests for drug offenses, assault, robbery, and domestic violence. He had served jail time for a grand total of two years.

The report included a map to his house. I printed the report and the map.

I did another late-night run. I was never so glad to be done with a run. The logbook said it was number thirty-three since I'd begun trying to get back into shape. The run tonight confirmed I had a long way to go.

### Wednesday, August 1

At 8:00 AM, I took the Stratus for my first surveillance run. It took me forty minutes to get to the east side of Orlando, and I pulled into a subdivision that might have been ten years old. It still seemed new compared to other parts of the area and had well-kept homes with sidewalks and curbs. It probably had a good homeowner's association to enforce the rules. I turned east onto Newberry Avenue, the street that held Liam's house, to find it ran along the southern border of the development. A thicket of oaks and pines stood on a little rise in the land opposite the houses to the south. I drove down the street at a normal speed, glancing to spot the house numbers. When I spotted the right number I took a long look and kept going, keeping a watch for any sign of people who might be out for a walk.

I went around the block and around the next block the opposite way so I could cruise down Newberry from the opposite direction. I realized that there were no cars parked on the street, but most houses had one or two in the driveway. I didn't see anyone out, which encouraged me that I could drive by a few more times.

Liam's house was in very good condition, with a landscaped yard. There were no cars in the driveway.

As I studied his house I realized I knew which developer had built this subdivision by its style and the style of the houses around it. Liam's house was dark, and I guessed that either he was asleep or not home.

At the end of the street, I worked my way onto the street behind Liam's house. All the houses on Liam's street backed up the homes on this street. They all seemed to have good-sized yards. Most yards were fenced, and many of them had pools. I saw a dog-walker and a family in nice clothes loading into an SUV. Otherwise, this street was quiet. At the end, I turned left away from Liam's street. I wanted to give it a little more time before I drove down his street again.

I spent five minutes exploring the development. It had been built right and had been kept in good condition. No millionaires lived here, but it seemed to be a good place to live. I made my way back to Newberry Avenue. With no one in sight, I slowed to a crawl as I drove past his house. It had a two-car garage on the right side, a high-pitched roof, and a bay window on the left side. A three-foot-high chain-link fence started at the back of the house and ran to fences at both neighbors' houses. The house on the left had a six-foot high wooden panel fence, and the one on the right had another chain link fence. I didn't hear or see any dogs, but high-panel fences usually meant big dogs. Both of the neighbors' homes were quiet.

I made one more pass down the street and noted a few more details. I knew about neighborhood watch groups, and I was concerned that driving up and down the street could look suspicious, the last thing I wanted. I decided to come back later for another look. But, I didn't know what to do next. I didn't have a plan, but I knew what I needed. I had to have some undisputed proof of Liam's undisputed involvement with the break in and Lee's murder. I also knew that now was the time to be careful.

# Chapter 36

A deep blue filled the evening sky when I pulled onto Newberry Avenue in the BMW. There were no lights on in Liam's house, no hint that anyone lived there. I drove past and headed for a small park two streets away that I had seen on my explorations earlier in the day. The park had six slots carved into a small parking area, and I chose number three from all of the empty slots.

A half-block from the park, sweat poured from my face. It wasn't a hard walk, just a regular hot and humid Florida evening. With no street parking, I was glad to find a spot that would not be questioned. But, I wished it were closer. My goal was some form of evidence; I knew I had no real chance of finding anything tonight, but I needed to get familiar with Liam in some way. I didn't feel the pressure to make instant progress. I knew I had at least one of the killers in sight. I just needed to get closer. Sooner or later I would need to confront Liam; it seemed the only way to make progress on getting evidence. I just didn't know enough and didn't want that confrontation before I had some better background.

As I walked up Newberry Avenue to the east, I noticed a sign in the yard of the fourth house from the corner. It was for sale. Six houses separated it from Liam's house. I slowed my pace and scanned the house for sale. It was the reverse floor plan of Liam's model. I made out a dim light through the bay window from a room toward the back, but the light didn't have enough strength to brighten the vaulted ceilings. The house seemed empty.

Two houses further on, two dogs ran to the back yard fence. They began to bark when they heard my footsteps and saw me. I moved faster, trying to put the house between the dogs and me. I didn't want attention. The dogs knew I would be visible from the other side of the house and they were waiting for me, barking and running back and forth. I kept moving without looking like I was in a hurry. I passed in front of the next house and they lost sight of me and the barking wound down.

Liam's house hadn't changed. It seemed no one was home. It was totally dark and quiet. I stopped directly in front of it and looked up and down the street. No one was out in the yards or on the sidewalks. No one drove by. I stepped up to the front door, looking for the doorbell. I didn't plan to push it, but I wanted to look as normal as possible. From the front step, I looked in the front window and the two panes in the upper part of the door. It was too dark inside to see anything in detail. I looked around again, stepped off the porch, and walked across the front yard to the west. The neighbor's garage faced Liam's house, and I went around the corner to the yard between the garage and Liam's house.

I felt less obvious here, knowing that Liam's house was empty and the garage prevented the neighbor from seeing me. I took my time, stepping between bushes near the house and up to the first window. My eyes became accustomed to the darkness, and I could make out a very well done living room. The next window gave me a view of the kitchen. The cabinets and appliances looked new. Some dishes sat next to the sink, and trash filled a wastebasket next to a counter. I let out a sigh. It confirmed for me that Liam actually lived there. Up to now, I'd had a tiny suspicion that he might not be living in this house. I just hadn't been here when he was around.

The back window looked into a bedroom, but I only could catch a small sliver of it with the curtains down. It seemed like a guestroom, but I couldn't be sure in the dark. I hopped the three-foot chain-link fence at the back, where a screened enclosure stretched across the full width of the house. I tried the screen door, but it was locked. It would be nothing to pry it open with a car key, but I didn't want the noise or activity to draw any attention. I hopped the fence again and went up the other side of the house. I suspected that the master suite was at the back corner with the garage in front of it. Most of the windows had some type of curtains. With the dim light, I couldn't make out much. I tried opening every window I came to, but none of them budged.

I leaned against the house at the front corner of the garage and peeked around it. I didn't see anyone on the sidewalk or street. I moved around the front of the garage, bent down, and pulled up on the overhead door handle. The door made a clanking sound but didn't move.

"Hey, Liam, you lock yourself out?"

I looked over my shoulder and saw a man with a dog crossing the street two houses down. I jumped up and slipped back around the corner of the house, out of sight. My heart pounded. I froze, totally shocked. I heard the man yell, and I ran to the back of the house, hopping the fence in one motion. I ran across the back of the house and crouched at the corner of the screened enclosure. I could see the man standing on the sidewalk between Liam's and his neighbor's houses. He had a cell phone to his ear, but I couldn't make out much of what he said. But, I figured he was calling the cops.

The man dropped the phone in a pants pocket and moved in front of Liam's house. I crept to the fence in a crouch, listening for any sign of the man doubling back. A moment later, I vaulted the fence and slipped along the wall toward the front of the house. My shirt was drenched and stuck to my chest. I looked around the corner of the house to see the man walking briskly along the sidewalk, away from Liam's house. When he passed beyond the neighbor's house, I trotted across the yard to the corner of the opposite neighbor's house to the west. I looked around and took off at a trot toward the end of the block where I had come from earlier.

I jogged all the way to my car, unlocked it, and slipped in. I backed out and drove to the stop sign at the end of the street. A cop car with flashing lights sailed past in front of me. No question, he was headed to Liam's. I turned right and headed for the main road out of the subdivision at a normal speed. I kept to the speed limit all the way home.

# Chapter 37

**Thursday, August 2**

I drove the Stratus to Liam's in the middle of the afternoon. I parked in the driveway of the house for sale and made a very deliberate survey of it, the sidewalk, and the street. I didn't see anyone. The Florida afternoon heat discouraged people from being out. When I got out of the car, I did another scan of the area, then headed across the street. I climbed the gentle rise, dodged palmettos, and moved into the trees.

Pines dominated the little forest, but ancient oaks made up a large minority. Pine needles scattered with pinecones carpeted the ground, and an occasional spindly tree competed with the pines and oaks. Fifty feet back, the little forest abruptly ended at a barbed-wire fence that made up the perimeter of an open field. The field was mostly grassy, and I spotted cows at a great distance across it. The fence ran parallel with Newberry Avenue and I followed it until I guessed that I was opposite Liam's house.

I worked my way through the trees until I could see Liam's house easily. I stayed behind the cover of trees as much as possible. The trees blocked the sun, and I didn't feel even a hint of a breeze. I knew this kind of thing was suspicious and didn't want anyone calling the cops again. I just needed to see Liam. I knew where he lived, but I didn't really know anything about him. Getting a look at him would be a starting point for making a plan to confront him. But, I also had this nagging thought that I would recognize him. If I didn't recognize him because he was four hundred pounds or had a prosthetic leg or for any other reason didn't fit my memory of him from the break-in, then there was a chance that I was wrong and he wasn't one of the killers. I shook my head at that thought.

I searched for a spot that would keep me out of the sun while providing a good view of Liam's home. I needed something to conceal me from cars and people on the sidewalk. I worked my way east through the trees until I was across from his neighbor's house without finding anything useable. I backtracked and kept looking, trying to stay behind as much cover as possible. I would stop every few seconds to survey the street and houses. West of Liam's house I found a cluster of palmetto bushes that had crested the rise and grown well into the trees. A large branch nestled in a part of the cluster, and the overhead trees protected it from the sunlight.

I worked my way into the palmetto cluster and sat on the ground with my back against the big branch. I inched along it until I could see Liam's house through a gap in the palmettos. The top of the spiky plants came to a height just above the top of my head, and I didn't need to hunker down to be out of sight from anyone across the street. Gnats and mosquitoes found me instantly. The hot, humid air forced me to take a deep breath often just to make sure I got oxygen.

I sat for an hour with sweat running down my face and dripping from my nose and chin. I had left my cell phone locked in the car because I didn't want a call to come through and alert a passerby. There had been no activity at Liam's, but I didn't expect any yet. I planned to wait until midnight if I had to. He had to come home sometime.

An hour later, with no activity across the street, I wondered if I had drunk enough water to make it to midnight. The sweat kept flowing, and I felt thirsty. I guessed I had another two or so hours of daylight, which made me revise my plan. I decided to leave at dusk if I hadn't seen Liam by then. It was okay. I would come prepared with water next time.

An hour later, I heard an automatic garage door open, and I leaned up to see one of the garage doors on Liam's house moving up. A late-model luxury import car swung into the driveway. It hesitated while the door opened all the way, and then the car pulled in completely. Before the door started down, I saw a Corvette parked in the adjacent bay of the garage. The garage door closed, and I didn't get a view of Liam.

I leaned back, disappointed. I didn't care about the heat and discomfort. It bothered me that I hadn't considered not seeing Liam at all. Now, it all seemed quite reasonable that he would park in the garage and go directly into the house. I knew seeing him wouldn't provide me any real evidence, but I felt it was important.

I decided to stay in my spot until after dark. On my knees, I surveyed the area. I looked west, holding my hand at arm's length, with the bottom edge of it lined up with the bits of western horizon visible through the trees. The top of my hand lined up roughly with the sun's equator, which told me that the sun would be down in less than an hour. I settled back to think through my next steps.

Ten minutes later, I happened to be looking through the gap in the palmetto leaves at Liam's house when the front door opened. I straightened up and pushed the leaves back to get a full look. Liam came out the front door, and I immediately saw that he was one of the men who broke in and killed Lee. The body matched, and I was convinced.

# Chapter 38

Liam followed a curved walkway to the driveway, where he stopped and put a hand up to shield his eyes from the sun and looked directly at me. I eased the palmetto blade back, leaving a tiny slot for me to watch him. I knew I was out of sight, but I stretched my legs and lowered my body until I leaned on my right elbow.

Liam kept his hand up against the sun and walked to the end of his driveway, where I thought he would stop, but he kept coming, seemingly directly for me. A few steps into the street and he dropped his hand when he walked into the shadow from the trees. His stride seemed purposeful, and I had no idea what he was up to. I decided to lie still, expecting him to stop. There was no way he knew I was there.

By the time he was three-quarters across the street, I knew he was coming up to where I lay hidden. My heartbeat jumped. I couldn't get caught here. I crawled on my stomach along the big dead branch to the far end of the little opening. I knew I had to stay low and couldn't stand up. The palmettos made a solid wall, but I found a gap between two plants. I crawled on my stomach and wormed my way along the ground between the base of two of them. I tried to plot my escape route once I made it out of the palmetto thicket. I pulled through the two plants and got to my hands and knees, still moving forward.

I'd started to rise to a crouch when I saw two feet

step in front of me. I looked up and saw an evil grin and the flash of a baseball bat swing toward my head from my left. I jerked back, but heard the sickening crunch of the bat against my head.

# Chapter 39

A slit of light grew from a blur to a sharp outline as I blinked. The crack of light wasn't much brighter than its surroundings. My left temple throbbed, sending pulses of sharp pain into my face and down my neck. The opposite side of my head rested on a hard floor as I lay on my right arm. I raised my left hand, and pain shot from my wrist. I recalled the instant when I'd seen the swinging ball bat and jerked my left hand up to shield me from the blow. I touched my temple and found the painful lump just above it. The bat had gotten my wrist and head. I pushed up on my elbow and stopped, dizzy. It passed, and I focused on the lighted slot. After a few seconds I guessed it was the gap at the bottom of a door and, I looked around and saw the shapes of a bathroom.

I got to my knees and pulled myself up using the vanity. I tried to step toward the door, but it turned into a lunge. I leaned on the doorjamb and put my hand on the doorknob. It didn't move when I tried to twist it, but a sharp pain exploded in my wrist. I let out a whimper and squeezed my eyes shut. After a moment, I focused on a sound and made out the voices of two men. The killers. They sounded as though they were a couple of rooms away. I held my left wrist, leaning on the doorframe just above the light switch. I flipped it on and squinted. The light intensified the pain in my head and I touched it gently and saw blood on my fingers.

I moved slowly to the vanity and turned on the cold water to drizzle. I wanted to be as quiet as possible. There was no point in letting the killers know I was up and around. I rinsed my fingers and gently wiped my head. In the mirror above the sink, I examined the bump. It was just above my temple, and the skin was split open. I looked at my left hand and found my wrist swollen. I knew that I'd have been dead if I hadn't gotten my hand up in time. I dabbed cool water on my head for a few minutes. I leaned down, cupped my right hand under the faucet, and took a long drink. When I turned off the water, I heard one of the voices yelling in anger.

This had to be Liam's house. I couldn't be sure, but it didn't make sense to drag me somewhere else. I was sure they intended to kill me. The guy with the bat probably thought he had killed me. Probably disappointed he hadn't. My knees buckled from the fear that this would be my last moments, and I dropped to a knee, leaning against the vanity. I imagined them flinging the door open any moment and shooting me dead. I moaned with the pain and hopelessness. It brought back the horrible sight of Lee lying back in our bed with blood across her chest and hair in her eyes. Tears burned my eyes then dripped from the corners. The memory overcame my self-pity and restored my resolve to make the killers pay.

I pulled myself up, wiping my face on my sleeves. I turned to survey the room. The toilet was on my left in the corner of the room. The wall next to it had a small window and I stepped over to it. It was made from glass block. I peered through a part of the glass block that was somewhat clear and made out a screened enclosure, another clue that this was Liam's home.

Opposite the window was the locked door. To my

left was a tub with a sliding shower door. Inside, a dried bar of soap sat in the corner. Beyond the tub was a linen closet. I moved to it and opened its door. I searched each of the six shelves and found absolutely nothing. I moved to the medicine cabinet above the sink. Someone had also cleaned it out completely. Inside the lower cabinet doors on the vanity, I found a dried cleaning rag draped over the drain gooseneck and some bits of toilet paper. The vanity had drawers on either side of the sink, and I inspected them. In the back of one, I found a pencil three-quarters of its original length. I stuck it behind my right ear, and somehow it lifted my spirits. I closed the drawer and turned around, leaning against the vanity. I touched the throbbing bump on my head, thinking again that I was caught, just waiting for the killers to come and finish it.

I turned around again and opened the cabinet door on the vanity. I could rip the door off its hinges easily. It had a total of eight tiny brass screws holding it to the pressed-wood vanity frame. I considered it as a weapon, picturing how I could use it to slam into the head of the first guy through the bathroom door. It was the second man through the door that blew my plan. I had no doubt that two of them against me would end with me losing. I closed the cabinet.

They were ruthless. I knew they had beaten me. I was trapped. There was no way out. My stomach knotted and I felt helpless. I pictured my dying body in a pool of blood on the bathroom floor. Lee would never see justice and my efforts would be a waste. I slid down the wall to sit with my head in my hands.

I heard Lee whisper to me. "That's not what you promised."

I looked up.

I didn't see her, but she came to me again. "And

what about not letting your emotions get in the way? Quit feeling sorry for yourself. Now, get up, and solve this."

I stood and looked around the bathroom again, searching behind the toilet, stepping into the tub, investigating the linen closet again, and studying the plumbing under the sink. Nothing. I went to the door and listened, but I didn't hear any voices. I leaned on the wall between the door and the vanity, desperate for an idea.

The wall gave slightly from my weight against it. That was the answer. The bowing wall triggered a thought that the builder had probably followed his normal construction practices and used thin drywall sheet on a two-by-four frame with twenty-four inches from one two-by-four to the next. It was a cheaper way to build than the normal half-inch drywall on sixteen-inch centers. Cheaper meant weaker. I turned around and pressed on the drywall with my hands, allowing my weight to bear on it. It gave perceptibly. I bounced my fingers on and off the wall, watching the painted sheet flex. I moved horizontally, pressing the wall until it didn't flex, and I knew I had found where the wooden stud supported the drywall sheet from behind. I moved back the opposite way until I found the next place where the wall became stiff and verified that the wall framing was built at twenty-four inch centers.

I could punch a hole in drywall this thin. Once I had a hole, I could open it up by breaking off sections of sheeting until I had a hole big enough to get through. Then I could do the same to the drywall sheet nailed on the opposite side. But, pounding it with my fist would be loud. The first time I hit the wall, the killers would come running. The other risk was the possibility that one or both of the killers had gone into the room on the other side of the wall. I knew the drywall sheeting was the weak point, but getting through it had to be quiet.

I looked around the bathroom again, evaluating each wall for my starting point. The wall with the tub wouldn't work, since there was no free wall space. The wall with the window was a concrete block wall, typical to all exterior walls on Florida homes. The wall with the door didn't have enough room on either side of the door to make a big enough hole. It probably led to a hallway and was the closest to the sound of the voices. I chose the wall between the vanity and the door and crouched down. I went through the same testing and found a stud about six inches from the vanity. I pulled the pencil from my ear and made a vertical line on the wall from the floor to a height of about two and a half feet. I tested until I found the next stud about two feet to the left and drew another vertical line. I then drew a horizontal line connecting the top of the two vertical lines. I had the outline of my escape door.

I kneeled on the floor and used the pencil to poke through the drywall just inside the top of the vertical line on the right. I pushed and rotated it, but it wouldn't punch through. I put my weight behind it and tried again, grunting. The tip broke off, and the wooden pencil soon became blunt. It wasn't going through. I leaned back on my feet and looked around the bathroom. I needed something metal to use as a cutting blade. I stood and opened the vanity door. I could rip it off and try to use a corner of the door to scribe a line in the drywall, but it might make too much noise. I looked at the brass hinges and thought that I could tear them off and try to cut the drywall with one of them. They might not be easy to rip off the door once it was free of the vanity and they were also small. It might be hard to grip them tightly enough to get them to cut the drywall. I closed the cabinet door and decided they would be my last resort.

I examined the shower doors carefully. The towel rack could do the job, if I could just unscrew it from the door. It didn't make the list, since I couldn't figure out how to take it apart. I briefly considered breaking the medicine cabinet mirror to create a glass knife, but I couldn't figure out how to do it without making noise.

I looked at the toilet and took a quick step toward it. I lifted off the tank lid and set it on the floor, leaning against the wall. I reached in and touched the flapper valve arm. It was brass. I was ecstatic. Many new homes used cheaper fixtures, and toilets often came with plastic parts. I held onto the flusher handle and unscrewed the brass nut that held the handle to the flapper valve arm. I set the handle down and unclipped the little chain from the end of the arm. I held it up and looked at it carefully, finding that the end that held the chain was flat. It was the right tool for the job at hand.

I knelt at the outline of my escape door and began to work the flat end into the drywall sheeting. It punched through in no time. I moved it down a fraction of an inch and punched through again. I moved it down again and again. In a few minutes, I was sweating and breathing hard, but I had a six-inch cut completely through the sheeting. As I worked down the wall, I had to go back occasionally to fix a cut that I'd thought had gone through.

When I got to the horizontal line at the floor, I quickly realized that I couldn't keep kneeling and cut at such a low level. I got down on my right side and braced my left foot against the tub. The work was very difficult and much slower going than the vertical line, but I soon had it cut. A ring of sweat soaked my shirt, but I kept punching holes. As I started on the opposite vertical line, I took off my shirt to wrap it tightly around the skinny brass arm, and it made the work easier. My right hand was sore, and my left was weak from the ball bat.

The angle was better at the top horizontal line, and I cut across the top quickly. The piece of drywall did not fall out easily. I used the brass arm to pry at the top and found a number of places where I needed to go back and cut through small sections that still connected it to the main sheet. It finally popped free, and I grabbed it along the top edge. I worked it completely out of the hole and set it behind me.

I looked into the hole and saw the two wooden studs and the backside of the drywall sheeting of the wall of the next room. It wasn't painted, and I could see the bare paper that made up its skin. I found a piece of heavy house wiring stretching from a hole in one stud to a hole in the next one. It hung about two inches below my opening, and I knew I could get past it once I had an opening on the far side drywall sheeting.

I wanted to make sure the room on the other side of the remaining drywall was empty. I crouched down and began quietly to work the brass arm into the sheet until it punched through. I made a few more cuts to create a hole a half-inch wide. I got up and flipped off the bathroom light. When I came back, I got as low as possible, pulled the small plug from the hole, and looked through it. It was dark. Either no one was in there or someone was there with the lights off, maybe sleeping.

I started at the lower left of my planned hole and began to cut vertically up the wall. I stopped about six inches up and cut six inches along the bottom. I cut between the two and worked the piece of drywall out. I turned out the light again, pulled the piece out, and peered into the room. When my eyes adapted to the dark, I could tell that the bed was empty and there was no movement in the room. I flipped the light back on and got to work quietly and quickly. The padding from my shirt really helped, and I think I cut the second hole in less time than the first one.

I worked the cut piece out of the hole and carefully brought it into the bathroom, setting it next to the first one. I went back to the hole and found a dresser covering the right half of the hole in the bedroom. I slipped my shirt back on and got to my knees. I pushed against the dresser but it didn't move. The dresser legs seemed to be hung up in the carpet. I put both hands on it and pushed but had no leverage because I was kneeling. I tried to use one hand to brace against the vanity, but the pain in my left hand cut that short. I got down and looked into the room at the opening left by the dresser and tried to gauge if I could squeeze by it. An image of me caught in the hole convinced me that I had to move the dresser.

I lay on my back and stuck both feet through the hole until they found the dresser. I inched closer to the hole, drawing my knees up. I reached over my head and braced against the wall with the tub and linen closet. I slowly increased the pressure from my legs until I felt the dresser budge. I needed to move it slowly and quietly. I pushed again, and it moved. I inched it away from the wall a little at a time, until it looked clear for me to get through the hole.

I reversed my position, stuck my hands through the hole, and worked my head through. Then I inched my whole body through the hole. I crawled clear of the hole and rolled on my side on the bedroom floor, panting into the carpet.

# Chapter 40

Sweat rolled across my face, and I wiped at it, smearing grit from the drywall on my cheeks and forehead. I rolled on my back and brought the front of my tee shirt up to wipe my face. I lay still, trying to get my breathing under control. I heard the voices through the open door mixed with the sounds of a TV. I wondered why they had locked me up and not taken care of business. I thought about it a few moments.

*They must be waiting for something. Or someone.*

The bedroom door led to a dim hallway. The bedroom contained a bed, a nightstand on both sides, and a lamp on each. The only other item in the room was the dresser. The carpet was thick. The wall behind the bed contained a curtained window, and another one sat in the wall next to it. The wall next to the door held a closet. This had to be the guestroom on the west side of Liam's house.

Breathing calmly, I rolled over and got to my hands and knees. I stood and moved to the window at the head of the bed. The carpet soaked up any noise from my movements and I was grateful. I pulled the curtain aside and looked out the window at the neighboring property, recognizing the garage. It verified what I had been thinking, and I knew exactly where I was. I assessed the lock on the window and the screen outside it. I could open the window and punch out the screen easily. It would provide a quick and easy getaway. I slid the other side of the curtain aside and stopped.

A security sensor hung on the window frame. I knew the way they worked. When the window was closed, a magnet energized a switch in the main sensor. Opening the window allowed the switch to close, and it would immediately set off the alarm if it were set. If it weren't set, then the control pad would emit a warning that the occupants could hear, and they'd come running. I eased over to the window on the other wall and found it held a similar sensor. The window opened to the screen enclosure at the back of the house. A small, kidney-shaped pool took up half of the enclosure.

I looked closely at the sensor in the dark and tried to imagine a way to get the sensor and its magnet off the window frame in a way that wouldn't allow them to separate far enough to set off the alarm. The sensors on my house were screwed in place, and the screws were under the covers of the devices. With tools, there might be a chance to get both parts free, but I couldn't take the chance of ripping them off with my bare hands.

I looked around the room. I was running out of time and needed to get away. I felt a twinge of panic and moved quickly to the door, stopping behind the frame. I took a quick look into the hallway, hearing the voices and TV. The floor was covered with ceramic tile, like the bathroom. The hallway was about eight feet long, fed to the bathroom door, and opened to a darkened room. I slipped around the doorframe and eased past the door to the bathroom. I moved slowly, placing each foot carefully and quietly. I crossed to the right wall and crept to the arched opening.

The room in front of me seemed to be a recreation

room, dark and quiet. A pool table sat in the center of the space, with a couch and chairs on two sides. Vertical blinds stretched along the back wall from a door on the far left. The door must have led to the screened enclosure and pool. I peeked around the corner of the opening and saw a short hallway to the right leading to a kitchen, also dark. Indirect light filtered into the opposite side of the kitchen through a wide opening. The voices and sound from the TV also came through the opening, which was along the far end of the wall to the left. I couldn't see through it, but I guessed it was a dining room that led to a living room at the front of the house. I made out most of the conversation with two men talking.

"Take it easy. You know Gary can't just leave."

"Why not. It's a free country."

"We've been over this, George. Since that guy has been snooping around, they are watching him closely."

"He ain't gonna to do any more snooping. He's out cold, and he may never wake up, if I have anything to do about it."

I recognized the voice. It sounded just as deadly as the last time I'd heard it. There was no question: George was the one who'd killed Lee.

"You should have seen him fold. That felt so good. I've always swung a mean bat," George chuckled.

"Well, you may have killed him with that swing. It sounded like you were smashing a watermelon."

"I hope I killed him."

I wanted to go in there and break his neck. The killers sat no more than fifty feet from me, and it made me realize that what I needed was hard evidence. I was sure that they had guns, and mine was locked in the car a half-block away. I knew I couldn't go in there and have a chance against them.

I heard someone moving in the other room. "Well, Liam, you know I'll kill him anyway."

If one of them came back to check on me, I'd be in trouble. I took a quick look around the corner and didn't see any shadow in the light filtering into the kitchen. I stepped across the short hallway to the kitchen so that I stood against the opposite wall. I thought that if someone came back, I would be behind him when they came through the kitchen.

I glanced at the back door. Maybe now was the time to get out. Come back another time, now that I knew the killers were guys named George and Liam. I checked around the corner and watched the light for a few seconds. I didn't see any movement, and the conversation had died. I edged away from the wall and slipped past the pool table, swiveling my head back toward the kitchen as I moved. I kept out of the direct line of sight from the kitchen and approached the back door.

It had a double lock. A deadbolt with a rotary lever sat above a brass doorknob with a center twist lock. A security sensor was mounted on the upper corner of the doorframe. I knew the killers would be alerted as soon as I opened the door. I wondered I could get out the door of the screened enclosure before they came running from the living room. It would be a race.

I twisted the deadbolt lever slowly, but it let out a click as it opened completely. I glanced back and stepped back. My heart pounded as I waited at least a minute. I moved closer, slowly tightened my grip on the doorknob, and gently twisted the lock in its center. It rotated silently. It was now or never. I turned the doorknob gradually.

The doorbell rang. I let go of the knob and jumped back. I heard George's voice. "It's about time."

Someone moved in the other room, and I knew he

was heading for the door. It came to me that when he opened the front door, it was my chance to open the back door. It might provide me enough diversion to get out the door on the screened enclosure.

I moved back to the door and put my hand on the knob. As the front door opened, I heard George growl, "Gary, what took you so long?" I pulled the door, making sure it didn't slam against the wall, and darted out. I didn't hear anything from inside as I ran around the right side of the pool. I made it to the screen door and slammed against the handle. Pain lanced from my wrist up my arm, as the handle didn't move. I heard a yell from inside the house. I rattled the handle with my right hand and felt panic rise. I looked at the handle and spotted the tiny nub that engaged the lock on it. I used my left hand to try to release it, but my hand was numb. I heard a yell from just inside the back door. I slid left and jammed my right index finger nail against the locking nub and heard it click. I slammed the opener, and the door flew open. I sprang out the door and ran to the left.

# Chapter 41

I ran along the back of the screened enclosure through thick St. Augustine grass. At the corner I turned toward the chain-link fence, thinking I would hurdle it and head toward my car down the street. I saw motion through the screen and glanced to see two men pour out the back door of the house. In the next step I jerked my head to the right, seeing the six-foot wooden fence and turning toward it. If the third guy came out the front door, I'd be trapped between the two houses. I sprang onto the wooden fence and grabbed the top of it in both hands. I kicked and pulled until my head cleared the upper edge. I hooked my left arm over it and pushed with all my strength until I got my chest and left knee on top, and then I rolled over and fell. I slammed against the ground and rolled, pushing myself up. I ran.

The two after me yelled, and I heard one of them slam against the wooden fence, but I didn't look back. I tried to find a spot on the opposite side of the yard to try to get over the fence again. A few trees followed the fence line and I sprinted toward an opening between two of them. I jumped up on the fence, grabbing the top edge. My left wrist wouldn't work, and I pulled with my right, trying to go over this time on the opposite side. As I balanced on my chest, I took a quick look across the yard to see one of the two killers doing the same. I pushed over but held on to let myself down instead of falling. As I did, I saw the killer on the other fence back down into Liam's yard instead of following me across the neighbor's yard. I liked it.

I turned and ran. Halfway across the yard, I saw that the far fence was a four-foot metal fence with pickets made of square tube. A dog blasted from a doggie door and started barking as it chased me. I sprinted toward the fence, but the dog was fast. A light came on in the house, and the dog's bark turned ferocious. Bushes lined the fence, and I jumped at the top rail through them and used my momentum to leapfrog over it. I crashed down in a thicket of bushes along the fence and stared back across it into the teeth of the angry dog. It barked as though it wanted to eat me alive, and I knew I had to get away from the clamor it raised.

I backed out of the bushes on my hands and knees, then stood and turned. A pool surrounded by a flagstone deck filled the space behind the house. I darted to the right to go around the back of it and a light came on in the house while the dog kept up its howling. I cut across the deck behind the pool and headed for the back left corner of the lot. Past the line of bushes that ran along the property line, I saw that the next house didn't have a fence and backed up to a house whose lot also didn't have a fence. I made it to the back corner of the lot, pushed through the bushes at the fence, and vaulted it. I crouched and snuggled up to a tree, sweat running down my face. I wiped it on the sleeve at my shoulder.

I surveyed the way back toward Liam's house and could see through the two yards to the high wooden fence in the yard next to his. The dog continued to bark, but not with its previous intensity. No one came out of either of the houses where the lights had come on. I scanned the area toward the street. Nothing moved. I figured they wouldn't give up. They knew that I knew who they were, and I had some pretty convincing wounds to blame on them. I needed to get to my car and get out of here without them knowing. My car sat in the driveway two houses away.

I looked over to the next yard and saw that it had a four-foot metal fence like the previous one with the dog. I didn't want to jump that fence. I would be exposed, and I didn't want to take the chance of another dog broadcasting my whereabouts. The yard also had a pool with a lot of open space. I could see through the yard to the back of the house where my car sat, but I couldn't see the car. A line of trees and bushes ran along the property line between the house where I crouched and the yard that backed up to it on the next street. I turned and surveyed the yard behind me. It didn't have a fence or a pool, but it had heavy landscaping, trees, bushes, and decorative plants throughout it. It was very well done. Pathways of thick grass wound through the yard. The house next to it was fenced with a big pool and no trees except for Crepe Myrtles that marked the property line with the far neighbor. I saw a way to get to my car.

I crawled on my hands and knees through the hedge and into the yard with the great landscaping and wiped my face again. I crouched as I trotted down a sweep of grass between the trees, heading toward the front corner of the yard. I inhaled the scent of jasmine and spotted a thick growth of it engulfing a latticework archway. I stayed low and kept moving toward the front. I stopped at the base of a huge oak and squatted, leaning against it. I surveyed the yards I had come through and continued my visual sweep to the house where I had parked. I spotted the right rear fender just past the edge of the house for sale. I didn't hear the dog bark anymore, and the only sound was a light rustling of the oak leaves in the cooling breeze.

I tried to keep to the shadows as I made my way to the front. I moved toward the fence on the line and followed it until it ended. I stopped, squatted again, and studied the street and front yards of the houses. All was quiet. I headed left and kept near the front of the house. I made it around the front of the house and moved to where the fence started under the row of Crepe Myrtle trees. I stopped and looked around once again. I didn't know where George, Liam, and Gary were, or what they were doing, and it made me very wary. I didn't think they would just let me go, but there was no sign of them.

I listened intently for a few more seconds and turned to make my way down the treeline. All of the branches were well over my head and I moved from one trunk to the next quickly. The tree trunks didn't provide much cover. At the end of the lot, I stopped again and faced the back of the house where I had parked. The yard was empty and very simple. Three palms grew in a random pattern, and a deck of brick pavers stretched across the back.

I decided to head for the right rear corner of the house. With no fence, the house would shield me from view from up the street toward Liam's house. I stayed where I was under the last tree for another thirty seconds, listening and watching. I expected to see at least one of the killers stalking the neighborhood, especially out front along Liam's street. Nothing moved or made a sound. I moved along the fence to my left taking advantage of the shrubs inside it for cover. I crept slowly and strained to listen, but I only heard the swishing of the heavy grass as I moved along. When I came even with the back of the house, I crossed from the fence to the back corner. The deck had a shingled roof patio cover. Adirondack chairs made a half circle in the middle of it, and I crossed between them and the house to the other corner.

I wiped the sweat from my face and eased my head around the corner of the house, searching for any movement or sign of my pursuers. I had to rise to see past the bushes and foliage that ran along the side of the house. I didn't see any sign of the killers or hear anything beyond the humid breeze in the bushes. I kept lower than the height of the bushes and worked my way toward the front of the house. I had to be very careful now. If they had made the connection that it was my car in front of this house, they would be waiting for me. I got down on my hands and knees, snuggled closer to the bushes, and crept the last ten feet to the front of the house. I eased down on my stomach and peered under the last of the bushes to study my car in the driveway. There was nothing suspicious. I looked under the car to check for feet on the opposite side, but there was nothing there. I swept my eyes to the end of the driveway, across the street, and up into the dark line of trees there. I studied every foot of ground I could see down the street before the house to my right blocked my vision. I repeated the survey the opposite way. I turned and looked behind me. I saw nothing beyond the dark, humid night. I could not believe I had lost them so easily.

I stayed on my stomach, nearly motionless, tucked up against the base of the bushes for five minutes. I kept sweeping my field of vision, moving my head in slow increments. Finally, I stood slowly in the shadow of the wall and looked over the top of the bushes. I saw Gary Shacklee's truck, five houses away in Liam's driveway. Nothing moved at Liam's house. I started to crouch down to move to my car, and I saw Liam's car back out of his garage. I dropped to the ground and rolled up against the bushes again. I could see a section of the street by looking under my car, and I watched Liam's car come down the street toward where I was parked. It rolled past my car and kept going, apparently not seeing me.

I knew I had to get out of the subdivision. Sooner or later, they would find me, especially when it started to get light. I stood and scanned the area again, crouched, and ran to my car. I kept low and gently slid the key in the door lock, turned it, and slid it back out. I smoothly pulled on the handle, and the door clicked open, snapping on the dome light. In the next moment, I heard Gary's truck start, and I jerked my head up to look through the passenger window. The truck headlights blinked on, and I jumped into the Stratus. I started the car and shoved it in reverse. The front wheels chirped and the car shot backwards. I slammed the shifter into drive and jammed the gas pedal to the floor. The car jumped ahead and I raced away from the house. I hit the brakes hard at the corner and spun the wheel. In my rearview mirror, the truck headlights bounced down the street from Liam's house. I kept the pedal down as I slung around the corner and built speed as I flew down the block. I knew the other car would be on me soon. They were surely on the phone with each other.

At the end of three blocks, I stood on the brakes from at least sixty miles per hour and tried to make the left turn onto the main street that led out of the subdivision. The car slid sideways, all four tires screeching. I made the turn without hitting the curb and jammed the gas pedal to the floor again. I could see the main entrance ahead and built speed. In the side mirror, I saw the truck bounce around the turn behind me, but I had to look back quickly. I swung to the left to make the right turn at high speed and flashed out into the empty intersection.

# Chapter 42

I kept the accelerator to the floor and glanced at the digital clock on the dash. At 1:48 AM, the four-lane boulevard was nearly empty. I roared past the only car on my side of the road and cut in front of it. I approached a major intersection, and the light changed to yellow while I was still a half block from it. One car waited on the right cross street and I flew through the intersection, hoping Shacklee would have to stop. A block farther I hit a red light with cross-traffic filtering through the intersection. I made a quick right turn, falling in behind a small car. I pulled around it and glanced in the mirror. I didn't see the truck but knew it wouldn't be long. I cut left at the next intersection, drove a block, and went left again. I hit the boulevard that I had been on and went right.

I knew this kind of maneuvering would eventually get me caught, so I decided to head for the highway, a toll road that cut from the east side of Orlando to the extreme west side. I didn't think the truck could keep up with the car. I found the on-ramp heading east and whipped the car onto it, building speed. I flew up onto the highway and checked the mirror. Shacklee's blue Dodge came around the turn and started up the ramp.

The car built speed, and I found myself doing eighty-five. The four westbound lanes held enough traffic that I had to weave from lane to lane to maintain my speed. I concentrated on maneuvers for a few minutes and then got the chance to check the mirror. I couldn't make out the truck but knew it was back there. It felt good to know I had a cushion of cars separating me from the truck. I focused on inching up my speed to build the cushion. I knew that the toll road would intersect the Florida Turnpike in a couple miles, and I decided to take it to the north, generally in the direction of home. If I could keep the speed and put more cars between us, I might lose the truck.

I slowed to take the sweeping turn north and fought the forces that wanted to sling me off the road. I braked but flew past another car in the right lane. I took a look back along the curve and didn't see the truck. I glanced forward at the ramp to the Turnpike and checked the side mirror for traffic, which was clear, and floored it. I took another quick look back along the long, curving entrance ramp, then jerked the wheel to slip past a vehicle in the right lane.

The Stratus bore down the highway at least twenty miles per hour faster than the light traffic, but I continued to weave from lane to lane to keep up the speed. A mile ahead, the 429 highway crossed the Turnpike. It was a superhighway like the Turnpike that fed the northwest corner of the Orlando area. I wavered between taking it or staying on the Turnpike. If I took it, I would have a clear shot home. If I stayed on the Turnpike, I wouldn't lead the killers to my house. I didn't know how closely they followed me. At the last second, I swerved across two lanes of traffic and headed north on 429.

The exit ramp made a large, sweeping turn perhaps a mile and a half long, making it easier to take it at high speed. The highway was deserted as I merged onto it, and I looked back along the exit ramp. I shuddered when I spotted Liam's silver import glide onto the ramp from the Turnpike. I kept the accelerator to the floor, but panic overshadowed my thoughts. Clearly, Liam would catch up. I needed a different destination than my own house. Once I stopped the car, I would be dead.

Where was a cop when you needed one? Fifteen minutes of high-speed maneuvers should be a neon invitation for cops to descend on me. I thought, if they couldn't find me, I would go to them. I knew exactly where the station was; I just needed to stay ahead of the killers to get there.

I realized I might not need to get there. I could call 911 and get them out here. I glanced in the mirror to see the car making steady progress on catching up to me. It was probably Liam, but I couldn't make it out in the dark. I reached for my cell phone in the door pocket, and the car swerved. I grabbed the wheel with both hands and steadied the car. I pressed the gas pedal and tried for the phone again. At my speed, the car demanded full attention, and I risked it to transfer the phone to my right hand. I tried to dial one-handed between glances from the road to the phone. I finally got the three numbers punched in and went to push the call button. The phone slipped and flipped to the passenger floor. I steadied the car and checked the mirror.

Liam seemed about ten car lengths behind me and closing. I looked up at the roadway and spotted a sign showing an exit a mile ahead. I recalled the road that ran under the highway and thought about how to lose Liam at the exit. I judged Liam's speed and estimated the distance to the exit. It seemed too fast for my plan, and I eased off the gas. Liam flew up behind me and pulled into the left lane. I hit the accelerator again. The exit ramp came into sight. It led down off the elevated highway in a straight line. I glanced in the mirror, couldn't find Liam, and then jerked my head to the left, seeing him creep up alongside of me. The Stratus didn't have anything more.

The two cars raced side by side down the empty highway. The exit ramp appeared beside me. I hunched forward with both hands gripping the wheel. I looked over at Liam's car and saw two men in the front seat, but I turned back before I could tell who they were. I glanced at the exit ramp and back at the road. At the moment the ramp ran out, I slammed on the brakes and cut to the right. The car shot over the shoulder and went airborne for a few seconds before it landed on the grassy slope next to the exit ramp. I hit the pavement and flew across the ramp, heading for the slope on the opposite side. I kept my foot on the brake and edged the steering wheel to the left. The car skidded sideways, and I let off the brake. The tires caught the pavement, and I raced down the ramp. I slowed and looked to the right, checking for traffic. The raised highway blocked the view to the left. It had worked; Liam had shot past the exit.

I stood on the brake pedal, and the car slowed enough for me to make a left turn at the bottom of the ramp. Both directions were clear, and I rolled through the stop sign. I went under the highway, whipped the car onto the southbound entrance ramp and jammed the pedal to the floor.

The car flew up the ramp, and I blasted onto the highway. There was no sign of Liam in the rearview mirror. I looked forward to see Shacklee's blue truck bounding over the grassy center median, aimed directly at me a quarter of a mile ahead. There was no doubt that Shacklee and Liam were in constant phone contact. I took my foot off the pedal. The truck came onto the two lanes in front of me. It swerved and stopped, blocking both lanes. I jammed on the brakes but felt like the car wouldn't stop in time. As I got near, I jerked the wheel to the left, and the car started to slide sideways. Blue smoke billowed around me, and the Stratus slowed. It screeched to a stop with a slap of the two vehicles together side to side.

When the car rocked back, I hit the gas pedal and plowed into the center median. The car bounced up onto the northbound pavement, and I cut to the left, wheels spinning. I didn't look back for a moment as I built up speed. I took a glance in the mirror to see the truck making a three-point turn on the southbound lane.

As I approached the exit ramp I had just used, I considered taking it to try to lose Liam and Shacklee. I knew that if I took the ramp, it would blow my plan to head to the police station. I had no time to fully consider it, and I flashed past the exit ramp and over the bridge. The on-ramp flew by, and I lost sight of the truck. I thought I just might have a chance.

A half-mile past the ramp, I checked the mirror and saw a set of headlights climbing the ramp like a rocket. They looked like Liam's.

# Chapter 43

In a couple minutes, I confirmed it was Liam. He continued to close on me, and it was only a matter of minutes before he would overtake me. The police station was still at least ten miles away.

Liam came up alongside of me, and I hit the brakes. I knew I couldn't stop, but I was trying to keep him off balance. He hit his brakes, and I slammed on the gas pedal. He came alongside again and crowded me. I jerked the car to the right, ran with half the wheels on the shoulder, and slowed.

I saw another exit sign, a road that I barely recognized. Liam slowed in response to me, and I speeded up again. As the exit approached, I pulled onto it while Liam kept his position next to me. At the bottom of the ramp was a stop sign for the crossroad. A two-lane service road ran parallel to the highway at the bottom of the slope and intersected the crossroad fifty feet from the ramp. We drove far too fast for the exit. Halfway down the ramp, I hit the brakes hard. Before Liam could react, I cut to the right and barreled down the grassy slope toward the service road. The car skidded and fishtailed in the grass, and I was afraid it might flip over.

At the bottom, I cut to the right and hit the road with my front wheels spinning. I couldn't spot Liam's car behind me. I raced down the service road, trying to remember where the road led. I knew it was the wrong direction for the police station, but if I could get turned around, or even find a place to hide, I might lose the killers.

I remembered a road named Country Road 456 intersected the service road a mile ahead. It was a left turn only, since it didn't cross under the elevated highway. I kept the speed and searched for the intersection. Other than my headlights, the road was unlit.

I spotted the intersection at the same moment I spotted a pair of headlights coming from the opposite direction. I took my foot off the gas and touched the brakes. The other set of lights came on fast. I planned to take the turn at as high a speed as possible. The oncoming lights turned into Shacklee's truck, and he cut toward me as I neared the intersection. I jerked the wheel to the right and jammed on the gas. The Stratus bounced off the right-hand side of the road as Shacklee flew past, barely missing the back of my car. I kept spinning the wheel and turned down County Road 456.

As I sped down it, I remembered being on this road once before. I shook my head, recalling that it led out to the country. I couldn't remember any way that the road led toward the city. They would be on me in no time. I decided that if I had to, I would stand my ground and fight it out.

# Chapter 44

I flew by a shabby quick shop near the intersection and an occasional house. The worn pavement markings were almost invisible without any streetlights. My headlights found a sign for a golf course, which brought a memory of a county park a few miles farther away. A small set of headlights popped into my rearview mirror, and I knew Liam was on to me.

I needed a place to lose the killers, and I tried to spot something in the dark at high speed. I thought about pulling in at one of the few houses and running for the front door, but I had no hope that someone would open the door for me. I considered finding a heavily wooded spot and trying to lose them. I couldn't see that working out, either.

The county park ahead had to be of some help. Beyond the park was totally unknown territory for me. I recalled the park had a large parking lot with a concrete walkway flanked by bushes running from one end to the other. It also had an asphalt bike path that had been converted from an old railroad right of way. The path was a popular route for joggers because it ran twenty miles out into the country and had markers every half-mile. Lee and I had visited the park once for a free outdoor concert. Visualizing the parking area, I thought about a way to lose Liam.

I found the entrance and slowed while gauging how fast Liam would get there. For my plan to work, I couldn't pull in too soon, and I kept braking. I kept rolling and let Liam get as close as I dared. I floored it and jerked to the right, heading for one end of the parking lot. Liam pulled in as I made it to the end of the lot. He committed to following me, and I swung wide around the end where the protected walkway became a narrow crosswalk. I jammed the gas to the floor and raced for the other end of the lot. I approached the narrow section by swinging wide and holding my speed. When I looked back, I finally caught a break. The maneuver bought me a cushion. It caught Liam unaware and forced him to a slower speed.

I jammed on the brakes at the entrance and spun the wheel, bounding back onto County Road 456, this time heading back the way I had come. The car skidded sideways and I jerked the wheel, correcting and accelerating. A set of headlights came on a quarter mile down the road and I knew it had to be the blue Dodge truck. I kept the pedal down and aimed for the lights. It accelerated toward me with the same intent. We closed the distance in a matter of seconds.

I cut the wheel to the left, trying to fake him, and pulled quickly back to the right. His reaction was slow, and I thought I had a chance. I pulled close to the road's edge and ran with one set of wheels in the grass. The truck swung back toward me at the last instant. I jerked the wheel right, and the truck just clipped the back end of the Stratus.

The car whipped into a skidding circle, and I had no control except to jam on the brakes. For an instant it seemed the car would make a full revolution and end up heading down the road west, but the front caught on the down slope of a deep drainage ditch. It jerked to the right and slammed nose-down into a foot of water in the bottom of the three-foot deep ditch. The impact set off the air bags. It felt like a heavyweight punch to my face. I lost my grip on the wheel and slammed back into the seat.

The bag deflated quickly, and I shook off the shock. I grabbed the wheel, throwing the car into reverse. The left front wheel spun madly, but the car didn't budge. I jammed it into drive, flooring it with no luck. I put it in reverse again, and the tire spun again, but the car didn't move. I glanced in the mirror and saw the truck still wobbling down the road away from me. I didn't see Liam's car.

I flung the door open and flipped around, climbing onto the driver's seat. I searched the floors for my phone, but I only found the Walther under the brake pedal. I grabbed it and backed out of the car. I killed the engine and lights, sliding my keys into my pocket, and slammed the door. I lifted my head and did a quick survey of the area.

# Chapter 45

The blue truck pulled into the park and stopped halfway in the entrance as Liam pulled up to it. I crouched next to the stuck Stratus and tried to clear my head. Across the road, a barbed wire fence ran along an open field. Behind me, the park offered little shelter from sparse pines and picnic tables. The parking area lay just inside the road, three hundred feet back from the way I had come. The bike path was on the other side of the parking area, where it ran past a public restroom made of concrete block. I slid down into the watery ditch and climbed the opposite bank.

I stayed low, watching the two vehicles a quarter-mile away, and made for the nearest pine tree in the park. Liam pulled onto the county road and approached the Stratus slowly. The truck swung left into the lot and headed toward the end near my car. I slipped from behind a twelve-inch trunk and darted to another. I kept moving further away from the wreck, toward the interior of the park.

Liam stopped in the road next to the Stratus. Two men jumped out and circled the car. One yelled that I wasn't there and waved to the truck. They jumped back into Liam's car and headed down the county road for a few hundred feet, then made a quick three-point turn. The car came roaring back toward the park. I kept low and moved further away from the road. The truck backed up, using its headlights as searchlights sweeping the area I was trying to cross.

I made it to the swath of land that had been cleared for the railroad and now held the bike path. From the treeline where I crouched across the bike path to the opposite treeline was about fifty feet of open ground. I dodged to another tree and tried to get a clear view of the woods on the other side of the path. It seemed to be heavier growth and maybe a better place to try to lose the killers. I heard both vehicles circling the parking area and glanced back. If I could time it right, I might be able to dash across the bike path to the woods. The parking area was a hundred yards away. I jumped from behind the pine tree and ran up a little slope toward the bike path. When I got to the path, a headlight beam swept across me, and I nearly froze. I darted down the opposite side, and another beam caught me. I looked at the trees, searching for a way to hide.

I heard the truck engine rev up and climb over the curb. Caught between the bike path and the thin woodland, I looked back and saw the truck bump onto the bike path. I turned and ran. The grass gave me no traction and I jumped up onto the asphalt path, sprinting away from the truck. Its lights danced around me as it growled after me. I knew I couldn't outrun it, but I pounded away, searching for any chance of safety.

The path curved gently to the right and seemed to head into thicker woods. I ran at top speed and knew I wouldn't last long. If I hadn't started to get in shape weeks ago, I wouldn't even have made it this far. I realized that they had guns and as soon as I ran out of strength, they would shoot. I ran faster than I had ever run and felt that I couldn't get enough air. I pumped and pounded down the path as it curved back to the left.

My foot hit something raised in the asphalt, and I

flew forward with outstretched arms. I hit the path and skidded, then rolled to a stop. I was breathing so hard that I couldn't focus my vision. I pushed up and looked back at the truck. It bounced down the path toward me relentlessly, with one set of wheels in the grass and the other set wandering down the asphalt strip. Its engine howled. I jumped up, quivering with exhaustion, and headed away from the truck.

Around the curve, I saw the asphalt path change into a wooden bridge that disappeared into the night.

# Chapter 46

The bridge gave me hope, and I raced toward it. It turned out to be more of a boardwalk than a bridge, but what I liked about it was that it looked too narrow for the truck. The killers in the truck must have thought the same thing, because I heard it speed up. I felt the lights grow brighter around me and knew it was closing fast. A hundred yards from the boardwalk I glanced over my shoulder. It was five feet behind me, and I knew I was dead.

I jumped off the asphalt to my left as the front fender skimmed across my back, shoving me hard. I flew through the air down the slope and tumbled in the slick grass. I came to a stop next to the trunk of a pine tree. I wasn't hurt, but I couldn't breathe from running. I thought I would pass out. The truck stopped, but its lights faced the path. I crawled around the base of the tree to hide. I needed a few moments to get control of my breathing.

The truck doors opened while it continued to idle, and I heard voices. I edged away from the tree, sliding in the pine needles to one farther away. The two men moved to the front of the truck. I was sure they would have heard my heavy breathing if the truck hadn't been idling. I stayed in the shadows and moved away to another tree, where I knelt in mud. A swamp edged up to the biking trail and cut off my retreat away from the path. The men must have come up with a plan, because one stayed on the path while the other came down toward where I had fallen.

The few minutes I'd rested had worked wonders on my breathing. It was down from the panic level to something I could control. I watched the men and estimated their movements. I thought I had a small window to dash from the trees to the boardwalk. I also considered standing my ground and opening fire. But, that would give my position away, and I would either get shot or shoot them. Even if I shot these two, I knew Liam was back up the path, and I couldn't guess the odds of getting away clean. A third thought interrupted my assessment. Even if I survived, I needed real evidence to prove two of these guys were Lee's killers. I looked at the entrance to the boardwalk and jumped from the tree, dashing along the tree line.

When I emerged from the shadows into the truck lights, one of the men saw me and yelled. I scrambled the final twenty yards to the entrance and pulled myself around the handrail. My feet thudded against the boards, some of which were loose. It was a fully wooden construction, with railings standing three feet high. Cyprus trees grew alongside it in shallow water covered with lily pads and other dark forms. I heard the feet of the men come hammering onto the boardwalk.

I needed to lose them somehow. In the darkness ahead, I glimpsed a sharp right turn in the boardwalk, and it gave me a thought. I ran toward it and patted my pocket. As I closed in on the turn, I saw a concrete block pylon standing six feet above the water behind the turn and guessed that it used to support the train tracks. I spun around the corner, grabbing the right side handrail, and stopped. The banging footfalls of the killers sounded loud and uneven. I hoped they were getting winded.

I pulled the pistol from my pocket and chambered

a round. Leaning on the handrail, I aimed back toward the sound of the killers and pulled the trigger. The gunshot cracked through the air. I pulled it again, and when the sound died away, I heard the men scrambling for cover. I backed away from the handrail, gun level in both hands, and fired another shot. I turned and sprinted.

I had no idea how long the boardwalk went on or if there was any cover on the other side. I'd gained a small breathing space between the killers and me but didn't know if it had done any good. I knew I couldn't run at this speed all night but realized that the killers might be worse off than I was. I slowed to listen and heard their feet slapping the wooden planks unevenly behind me.

A glint to my right caught my attention, and I looked as I ran. Moonlight rippled on a wide lake a hundred yards from the boardwalk where the swamp gave way to deep water. I made a quick decision and slipped the pistol back in my pocket. I slowed, grabbed the handrail facing the distant lake, and heaved myself over the top. The water below me was black and quiet, choked with plants. I got both feet on the edge of the deck outside the rail and jumped in. The splash was minimal, but I sunk in mud to my hips with the water lapping my chest.

I couldn't move. I jerked my legs, but the mud held tight. I twisted and pulled against the grasp of the mud, but it held its grip. I panicked and began to thrash, moaning and growling. I twisted around and grabbed the middle rail of the handrail, pulling toward it. It wrenched my back, but I felt a leg move. I stretched my right arm to the top rail and tried to pull but didn't have enough strength. I grabbed my right forearm with my left and pulled again. My right leg inched up from the grasp of the mud, and I kept bending my knee and pointing my toe. The sound of feet hammering the boardwalk filled my ears. My right knee broke free from the mud, and I swung my left hand to the top rail and pulled with all I had. The left leg sucked free of the muck, and I pulled up to rest both knees on the decking of the boardwalk. I saw the two men staggering toward me. I pulled up, and set both feet on the decking, and pushed off backward, arching a few feet over the water. I splashed down in the shallow water between two cyprus trees and went under, feeling the mud against my back. I seemed to glide over the mud in about a foot of water. I flipped over and started to claw my way forward, ripping plants and digging into the mud with each stroke. When I got even with the Cyprus tree, I pushed off it with a leg while continuing to claw through the swamp.

My thrashing and splashing echoed through the swamp, but I heard one of the killers behind me yelling that I had jumped into the swamp.

George shouted, "Someone needs to go in after him."

"I can't even see him."

Gunshots rang out, and I pulled harder, sliding behind the wide base of a Cyprus. The mud I clawed up stunk. I threw it behind me with every stroke. When I could, I used a tree to help me slide forward. I jammed my fingers into the roots of some water plant but kept moving away from the boardwalk. The gunshots died off. None of them had come close.

The mud seemed to be tapering off as I had more water under me. It still made swimming hard, but I made better progress. I heard their voices, and I was sure they could hear me splashing, but all I cared about was getting free.

The number of Cyprus trees thinned as the water

got deeper, and I swam more naturally. I spotted a large Cyprus tree with a huge root system and swam toward it. I went around the side away from the boardwalk and pulled myself onto the roots for a rest. I looked back the way I had come, trying to see the boardwalk. Trees and plants blocked most of it, but I made out the horizontal line of the handrail in a few spots. I didn't see the killers.

# Chapter 47

I hugged the base of the tree, resting my head on a knobby root. With the raucous background noise of chirping tree frogs and buzzing insects, I could barely make out the killers' voices. My heavy breathing dominated all of the sounds in my ears. I needed this rest. I found roots underwater with my feet and put some weight on them. After a few minutes, I turned around and leaned against the tree, crouching in the water with my weight on the roots. The water felt like a warm bath.

A layer of clouds filtered the sharpness of the partial moon, which hung off to my right. I traced the outline of the lake to my right and saw more of the same swamp and Cyprus trees through which I had fought. To my left, the swamp continued a quarter of the way around the lake, where it gave way to a solid shoreline. I guessed it was a half-mile directly across the lake, where the hazy sky reflected unseen lights that seemed well beyond the woods lining the shore. The lake was surrounded by genuine wilderness. That meant alligators.

I scanned the lake carefully from left to right, searching for a ripple in the glassy surface. I looked around the Cyprus tree and as much as I could see behind it. I would never see a lone gator if he attacked. If more than one came after me, I might see one of them. The lake was home to wild gators, I was sure of that. I just had no idea if they were out hunting food. With all the commotion I'd made in the swamp, I was afraid that it might have been a wake-up call for hungry alligators. I needed to get away. I needed a plan, and I couldn't go back the way I had come.

I looked hard at the part of the lake to the far left, where the swamp seemed to end and solid land took over. I guessed I could swim the distance if I took it easy, especially if I didn't have to claw my way through muddy swamp water. Dry land was safer, and I decided to go.

The odor from the mud nauseated me, and I slid down in the water to my neck. My tee shirt billowed out, and I caught my elbow in it. I pushed back up, and it stuck to me. It was smeared with swamp mud, and I decided to get rid of it. I slipped it over my head and wrapped it around a part of the cyprus tree roots that stuck up out of the water. I slipped back down into the water and pushed off the roots toward the open lake.

I swam with gentle strokes, scraping the mud a few times before hitting deep water. I flipped on my back and eased farther out, looking back at my tree. I hoped never to see it again. I spotted the moon and kept it directly behind me, swimming parallel to the swamp trees. I used an easy sidestroke to keep the trees in view. I made a concerted effort to keep my mouth closed, except when I took a breath. The mud smelled bad, and the water couldn't be good for me.

I stopped for a few moments, listening for the voices of the killers, but all I heard were the sounds of the wild. Looking around, I guessed that I was halfway to my goal. I started up again and switched to the floating backstroke to save energy. After a few minutes, I would flip back over and swim stronger. When I was on my back, the cloudy sky filled my vision. I imagined a gator swimming up and latching on to me. I kept repeating to myself that alligators are not considered to be man-eaters. Swimming forward, I could see ahead and to the sides, and it provided a small assurance that I might see an attacker.

I swam on my right side, checking around me and gauging the distance to the tree line. My arms and shoulders began to burn from the effort, and I flipped and swam on my left side. I checked the moon and the shoreline ahead of me. When I got about fifty feet from the shore, I stopped and tread water. My foot scraped the mud, but I didn't want to try to stand. I did a quiet crawl and came within twenty feet of the shore when I scraped a hand into the mud. I stretched out and tried to paddle in closer.

Water plants crowded the edge of the water. Some were three or four feet tall, and others had broad, flat petals. The vegetation created a thick barrier, but I could see onto the land. The vegetation flourished on the gentle rise from the water and eventually fed into woodlands. I was glad to see real earth and not the mushy swamp. I paddled in until my hands and knees dug into mud. It oozed and didn't provide any support. I crawled and floated until I reached the first line of plants. I grabbed onto the strongest ones and pulled myself into them. I clutched another one and pulled again until I felt my knees supported. I crawled on hands and knees through the plants until I began to feel real dirt under me. The vegetation on shore crowded and tangled every inch of land. I tried to stand and push through the foliage. It ripped at my skin as I worked through it up the embankment toward the tree line.

Plants and vines filled every square foot of land among the trees. I pushed through deeper into the trees, finding the foliage and vines thinned out the farther I struggled away from the lake. When I could walk easier against the foliage, I turned to look at the lake, thirty or forty feet away. I leaned against a pine tree and caught my breath. The rest felt good for about thirty seconds. Then mosquitoes found me in droves. I wiped and brushed my skin constantly, feeling their needles all over. I needed to move.

I worked back toward the lake and spotted the moon again. I walked through the trees with the lake on my right, trying to keep in contact with it. I wanted to get to an area opposite from my Cyprus tree in the swamp. I guessed that it would be the best place to start away from the lake, heading for the lights of the city. As I walked, I thought about the car wreck. I didn't feel any lasting injury from it. Fatigue bothered me the most. My wrist hurt, but not as badly as earlier. As long as I didn't touch my temple, it didn't hurt, either. My hands and knees burned from the fall on the asphalt bike path. I really wanted a shower. I would gladly clean my injuries with soap and water and suffer through the sting it would cause. The lake water and mud were certain to cause infection. I stank. No wonder the mosquitoes had found me so quickly; it was like advertising.

# Chapter 48

As I worked my way around a quarter of the lake, I wondered what I should do. If I went home, the killers could be there, waiting. If I went back to the Stratus, they could be waiting there. They could be at both places. I realized they probably had my phone. Even without it, they knew who I was.

I slammed my head on a low branch and took two steps backward. I needed to get out of the woods and to a place where I could orient myself before considering my next moves. I worked my way closer to the lake and checked on the moon. I looked along the lake as far as I could see to try to find the illumination in the hazy sky that pointed to the city. I barely caught a glimpse of it and decided to head farther around the lake.

I worked my way through the woods inland enough to contend with as few bushes and vines as possible. I caught glimpses of the lake and the hazy moon shimmering off of it. Animals skittered in the underbrush as I walked, because I made much more noise than the critters in the woods. It was dark, humid, and full of bugs. I regretted leaving my shirt. My shoes squished with each step. I tripped every third step, it seemed, and I used the trunks of trees as support and balance.

I headed toward the lake and came across a mushy, low spot choked with water plants. It was the edge of a small, swampy area. I backed away and followed the edge toward the lake. I pushed aside broad, spiky leaves, and a gator growled as it flipped, twisting away into the muck. I sprang backward with a yell, tripped, and fell into a tangle of vines and plants on my butt. I kicked, pushed up with my hands, and spun away. My heart raced, and I dodged behind a tree. Breathing hard, I leaned against the tree watching for any activity.

Nothing moved for a few minutes while my panic drained away. I backed away from the tree and headed deeper into the woods. I gave the swampy area a wide berth and looked for a clear way to get back to the lake where I could check my location. I found a spot where the water's edge seemed clear and carefully worked toward it.

I checked the moon and surveyed the lake. I could make out the swampy area across the lake and where it seemed to end off to my right. It seemed like the right place, so I turned, heading directly away from the lake. If my rough guesses were right, I was heading east. I hoped I moved in a straight line, but with navigating around trees, brush and fallen branches, I had no idea. It seemed to grow darker away from the lake, but the thinner underbrush allowed me to move quicker.

After a while, I sensed a break in the dark ahead. Through the forest of tree trunks, I could see swatches of space without trees. I worked my way toward it and found that the woods came to an end. I walked up to a clearing and saw a county road. The woodlands picked up on the opposite side of the road. I walked out of the trees on a gentle slope that led to a drainage ditch. I hopped it and climbed a couple feet to the shoulder of the road.

I guessed heading right would be north and turned that way. I walked for maybe a half-hour without a car passing me from either direction. I walked past a couple of block homes set off the road by a hundred yards. After a while, I saw a light ahead and came to an intersection with another two-lane road. I recognized the name of the road and headed toward the city.

In a few minutes, I came to a 24-hour gas station with a convenience shop. I recalled that I had been in this station before and went inside.

The attendant behind a counter with a thick glass divider looked up. "Whoa, man, you okay?"

I realized I looked a mess and had no shirt. "It's okay. I'm okay, but I really could use your phone." I approached the counter.

"I didn't see no car pull up. You got car trouble?"

"Yeah, had an accident down the road. Where's your phone?"

He hesitated. "You lose your shirt in an accident?"

"I ended up in a muddy ditch, and it ripped when I climbed out, so I pulled it off. How about the phone?"

"I can't let you behind the counter."

I pulled my car keys from my pocket and held them up. "Let me use your cell phone, and you can hold my car keys." I jiggled them. "I really need to make a call. Help me out, will you?"

He shook his head but pulled his phone from the counter and held it up. "Just slide your keys under the slot."

I gave him my keys, and he slid the phone out. "Thanks, I'll only be a minute."

I walked away from the counter, trying to remember Sue's number. I punched it in, and it rang. After four rings, it went to voicemail. I hung up and hit redial.

She picked up on the third ring. "Hello?"

"Sue, it's Mark."

"Are you okay?"

"I need your help. Can you pick me up on the south side?"

"What happened? Are you hurt?"

"I've tracked down the killers, but now they're after me. I've had an accident, and the Stratus is out of commission."

The line cracked for a few seconds. "Mark, please, call the police. I'm sorry, but it's too dangerous for me. I can't get mixed up in this anymore."

The line went dead. I looked at the phone and put it to my ear again. She was gone.

# Chapter 49

The phone display showed 4:41 AM. I thought about calling Chief Mackey. Sue was right. I should call the cops, not involve Mackey. It might be dangerous for him, maybe involve him in something that could be a lasting entanglement. But, I really could use a ride.

"Hey, man, you done with my phone?"

I looked over at him and made the decision to keep Mackey out of it. I stepped over to the counter and put the phone in the tray. "Thanks."

"You call the cops?" He dropped my keys in the slot, and I picked them up.

"No, I got someone coming."

"You want me to call them for you?"

"No, I got it under control. Thanks. Where's the men's room?"

He pointed, and I went down the aisle and into the men's room. I splashed cool water on my face. Nothing had ever felt so good. I wadded up a handful of paper towels and soaked them under the faucet, wiping them on my neck, chest, and arms. They came away streaked with mud. I got more towels and did it again and again, until my skin was clear of mud and slime from the swamp. I tried it on my shorts, but that didn't work. I washed my hands with soap a couple times, then used soapy towels to wash the scrapes on my knees and the split skin at my temple. Before drying off, I splashed my face again. I cupped my hand under the faucet and drank deeply.

I went out past the counter and thanked the guy. Outside, I got my bearings and headed down the street. I figured it to be a thirty-minute walk to my house. The first street wasn't too familiar, but I knew where I was and soon turned onto a residential street that I knew. I was amazed at the things I could see walking that I didn't see driving.

I thought about the killers waiting for me at my house. At least two of them had some familiarity with it, and that bothered me. I looked at it logically from both sides. Whether they were there or not, I would have to verify it before getting too close. I made a plan to do surveillance on my house from all points of the compass. If they weren't there, I would go in and call the cops first thing. If I could prove they were in my house, or waiting outside in a car, I would sneak down the street to a neighbor's house and use their phone to call the cops. As I thought it through, I hoped that they were there. I'd love to see the cops come tearing up the street and nail them. It would be over.

I turned onto a residential street a few blocks from my house. The moon winked through a slit in the clouds. I expected the killers to be waiting and it was exhilarating to think that they could be inside my house, at the scene of Lee's murder. To have the cops catch them there would be the beginning of the proof that they were the killers. If Gary were with them, he would be implicated, too. He was part of the crime, regardless of what Beauchamp thought.

I stopped in mid-stride and slapped my head. I should have called Tony from the gas station. He would have helped me. Even more so, he would have clearly put the facts together and come to the same conclusion. He would be my second call once I got home.

# Chapter 50

Two blocks from my house, I moved from the sidewalk to the shadow of a large tree. I scanned the street for anything abnormal, especially the sight of Liam's car or Gary's truck. If they were at my house or near it, waiting for me, I needed to approach undetected. Each step, I concentrated on stealth, stayed off the sidewalk, and moved through my neighbors' yards from the shadow of one tree to the next. Each time, I stopped and looked around carefully. The neighborhood was quiet except for the cry of tree frogs and chirping crickets.

I approached the general spot where Liam had parked Gary's truck on the night they'd killed Lee. I crouched behind a car parked at the street and watched my house for ten minutes. The whole time, nothing moved inside or outside. I studied the street as far as I could see and couldn't make out either vehicle. I concentrated on the windows to the living room. Even though the lights were off, I expected a vague shadow to move behind the curtains if the killers were inside. A small ripple in the curtains would also be a sign someone was inside. I watched for another few minutes, checking the dining room, living room, and bedroom curtains for any hint of motion. I kept low and backed away from the car the way I had come.

At the end of the block, I went down the street to the one that ran a block behind my house. I came up along the street in front of my house from the opposite direction, stopping a block away in the shadow of a massive oak. It had a good line of sight to the kitchen and back bedrooms to my house. I surveyed the street first, looking for the killers' vehicles. Afterward, I turned my attention to my yard and then the house. Nothing moved. Nothing was out of the ordinary. I stayed low, studying the house for several minutes.

Seeing nothing, I backed away carefully the way I had come. I wanted one more look. I made my way around the block behind my house and stopped in a neighbor's yard. I crept along the neighbor's house to a spot in his backyard, where I hid behind another tree and watched my house. The back showed no movement or sign of anyone inside. I was disappointed. I'd wanted them to be there, so I could call in the cops. I needed to be sure. I crouched by the tree for probably another ten minutes and saw no indication of anyone in my house.

It bothered me that they hadn't come here. I knew they couldn't let me go. I knew too much about them. There was no doubt that I was a dead man the next time we met. I tried to imagine what they had in mind and where they could have gone. I concluded that they might be coming for me later.

I cut across the neighbor's backyard to where it intersected a side street. I walked down it to my street and turned toward my house. It was clear to me that they weren't in my house, so I made no effort to hide my approach. I cut across my side yard to the front door, where I kept the screen door latched from the inside.

I stuck a key between the lightweight screen door and the frame and pried the door free from the latch. I held it open with my left leg, slid the key in the front door lock, and opened the door. I stepped in and closed the door behind me. I heard the security system control panel begin to beep in the kitchen, waiting for me to disable it. As I turned, a flashlight snapped on and caught me in its glare. A gun thundered, and my left knee exploded. I fell back against the font door and slid down, slamming my head on the tile. When I opened my eyes, the flashlight washed over me. A dark-eyed man with a week-old stubble covering his face stood over me.

"You're not getting away this time," George said.

# Chapter 51

"You're a dead man." George straddled me, both hands wrapped around the grip of his 9mm, smirking as he pointed it at my forehead.

I squeezed tears from my eyes, breathing hard at the sheer agony in my knee. I lay on my side, holding it, and felt warm blood oozing under my left hand.

George looked away quickly. "Liam, close the door, kill the flashlight, and get the overhead light." When it came on, George knelt on one knee to the side of me. He put the muzzle of the pistol on my forehead, and I inhaled the scent of gunpowder. He kept the gun on my head and patted me down with the other. He found my Walther pistol and wrenched it from my pocket. He lifted it into the light and laughed.

"You were going to try to stop us with this?"

Liam stepped into my field of vision. "What is it, George?"

"Looks like a 32. Maybe I'll keep it as a souvenir." He shoved it in his belt, finished patting me, and said, "I need the code for your security system."

I closed my eyes, taking a long breath. The system continued to beep, but soon it would erupt in alarm mode if it wasn't disabled.

He put his free hand on my neck and squeezed. "You can die right here. It's no difference to me." He pressed the pistol against my forehead and twisted. "We just need to shut it off so we can use the doors without setting it off and calling the cops."

I gritted my teeth and stared into George's eyes, unable to breathe.

"Okay, we'll leave you here dead, lying in your own blood and head out the way we came in. No one will ever know who killed you." He barked a laugh. "Or your wife."

She flashed before me, a bloody, lifeless mess.

She gave me a message. As long as I was alive, there was still a chance, a chance for justice. My lungs heaved, and I tried to mouth the code.

George released his grip on my throat. I sucked in air and coughed.

"So, you see it my way?"

I gave a nod with a couple final coughs. My eyes watered. "Eight, five, seven, three, one."

Liam went to the keypad in the kitchen next to the garage door and punched in the code. It became silent. George stood, and I rolled onto my back, inhaling deeply. My knee throbbed with severe pain.

George shoved his pistol in his belt next to the Walther. "Liam, I'm going for the car. Cover him." He stepped around me and put a hand on the front doorknob. "If he makes a sound, kill him." He drew the door open a foot and looked left and right. He left, pulling the door closed quietly.

Liam held a pistol easily in one hand, pointing at the floor. He stood six feet from me. I looked him in the face.

He shook the pistol at me once. "You've been a big problem."

I turned away and closed my eyes. The pain in my knee had all my attention. Nothing else seemed to matter, but I couldn't do anything about it except know it was there. I panted from the pain and focused on controlling my breathing. A couple minutes passed before I could slow it down.

I turned back to Liam, wondering how they had beaten the home security system. "How did you get in without setting off the alarm?"

Liam chuckled and shook his head. He pointed the pistol at the set of French doors leading from the dining room to the patio. There was a hole cut in the middle top pane and one in the pane at the door handle. The security sensor normally at the top of the door was missing. He pointed at the floor next to the door and I spotted the security sensor taped to its magnet. Liam pulled a chair at the dining room table and sat.

"You shouldn't put so much faith in technology." He held up the pistol. "This is where I put my faith." He laid the pistol on the table and leaned back.

I rolled my head away and looked at the ceiling. I noticed the hard pressure on the back of my head. It was the first feeling that competed with the agony in my knee. I pushed up on my elbow and looked at my blood-smeared knee. The bottom of my shorts was soaked with blood. The entry wound covered the inside front of my leg behind the kneecap. It gaped at me, and I reached for it with my right hand, gently covering it. It screamed with pain, and blood seeped from it. It hurt so badly, I couldn't tell if there was an exit wound. I ran my hand along the outside and up my leg and couldn't feel an exit wound where the bullet would have come through. I fell back panting, and fought to control my breaths.

\*\*\*

I jerked from a sharp pain in my ribs and realized I must have passed out. George stood over me, chuckling. He turned and walked away, saying, "I'm going to take the light out of the garage door opener before I pull the car in. Back in a minute."

Liam grunted from his chair.

A few minutes later, I heard the garage door open and a car come in. The garage door cycled closed, and George reappeared. He came up to me with a large plastic ziptie in one hand. "Cops aren't the only ones who can benefit from these. Liam, come here, and keep your gun on him while I get him turned over."

George kicked me again. When I convulsed from the pain, he gripped my shoulder, pulling me over roughly onto my stomach. The movement jammed my knee under me and sent a shock of pain up my leg. He put his foot into my back and pulled one arm, then the other, behind me. He wrapped the ziptie around my wrists, inserted the end through the lock, and pulled it tight. Fighting the waves of pain, I knew the plastic tie had far more strength than I could ever muster.

"Grab that arm," George said. Each of them looped his arms through mine and lifted. They dragged me across the dining room to the kitchen and through the door to the garage. Liam's silver luxury car sat pointing toward the garage door with the trunk lid open. They pulled me to it.

"Hold on, George. I don't want a bloodstain in the trunk."

They dropped me. Liam went back in the house, and George leaned against the car. Liam came back with a bath towel and the same duct tape they had used on the security sensor. He doubled the towel and wrapped it around my destroyed knee, covering it with a few turns of duct tape. They bent to me and lifted, pushing me head first into the trunk. When they bent my legs to fit in, I screamed at the pain.

"Shut up." George slammed the trunk lid.

I lay in the dark, crying with the pain.

# Chapter 52

I lay on my side, curled up with my throbbing knee on top. My feet pushed against the side wall of the trunk, my head against the opposite side. The car jerked from side to side, slamming me back and forth. I careened forward, jamming against a spare tire whenever the car braked.

The towel was the best thing that had happened to me that night. It padded my gunshot knee from the pitching car and helped stop the flow of blood.

The way the killers treated me was barbaric. I knew I was a dead man, and it didn't matter to them. As soon as they had the right circumstances, I would be dead. I knew it was my own fault. I was not prepared for them, and now I knew I would never be. I couldn't stoop to their immorality and disregard.

Later, the lurching car movements calmed, and it seemed that it traveled on a stretch of highway, with a rhythmic, gentle bouncing. A lengthy stretch of time went by without any turns or brakes, but I had no measure of time. The pain in my knee pounded with each heartbeat, and it occupied my thoughts. I had no idea if I passed out again or not, but the car jerked and lurched again, throwing my body around.

The car bumped and swayed, hitting potholes that slammed the suspension to its limits. I hit the trunk lid and slammed down. The tires ground along a roadway, which sounded as if it was made of gravel. I prayed the ride would end.

# Chapter 53

**Friday, August 3**

The car slowed, made a right turn, and stopped. I pulled in a few deep breaths, relaxing in the calm. I heard the car doors and the trunk lid release. George and Liam stuck their heads over the trunk, and beyond them I saw treetops in a dawn sky. They reached in and grabbed my arms, trying to pull me out. I was a dead weight in a very difficult position, and they struggled and cursed. In their frustration, they jerked me over the edge of the trunk and dropped me on the ground.

I landed on my face with a grunt, in weeds growing between two dirt tracks that made up a driveway.

George gave a laugh. "Let him lie there. Let's open the garage doors."

I rolled onto my side and looked around. There were no streetlights at the road and no other houses around. I looked toward the house and saw the killers opening two wooden, hinged garage doors. The lot around the house was thick with weeds and sat in a small opening among tall pine trees. The concrete block house hadn't seen paint for decades.

They came back, dragged me into the garage, and dropped me between a pallet of five-gallon buckets and a stack of used tires just inside the doorway. The place was overloaded with junk. They each pulled a door closed, and George threw a latch. They grabbed me again and pulled me along a path between greasy engine parts, boxes, tires, and garbage, my heels tracing lines in the dirt. A four-foot long fluorescent fixture hung by uneven chains from wooden trusses in the middle of the space. Two of four bulbs burned.

George huffed. "Leave him out here."

"Yeah, he ain't going anywhere. And I'm tired of dragging him around."

"Check the zip tie, will you?"

They jerked me forward, and Liam yanked on the zip tie. He grabbed the end and pulled it a few clicks tighter. "He ain't getting outta that."

They let me fall on the edge of a small step in the concrete floor, knocking the air out of me. My head bounced against an old tire. They went though a door and closed it behind them. I rolled to ease the pressure on my body and inhaled deeply.

# Chapter 54

The step was about six feet wide and stood about three inches above the main level of the floor. A rusty clothes washer and dryer sat on the step to my right, and a deep sink stood behind me. I straddled the edge of the step with my legs on the main floor and my arms pinned under me. The angle put pressure on my bad knee, and I needed to move. I used my right leg to squirm, inching my way to a position where my hip rested on the same level as my chest.

This had to be George's place, and I knew I would never get out of this garage. I had no idea of the killers' plan, but this was the perfect place to get rid of me. I had to do something.

I twisted my head and looked around the garage. A pile of junk blocked my view of the garage doors, and I swiveled to look toward the door they had used. An old refrigerator stood against the wall near the door, and next to it was a pile of wooden crates. I turned back and looked along the length of the step toward the opposite wall. A freestanding storage shelf covered the wall. Rusty paint cans, pesticides, and other containers lined shelves thick with dust. I scanned each shelf for anything that would help me get free, but I couldn't make out the contents on the upper selves. I dropped my eyes to the floor. There was a three-inch gap between the bottom shelf and the floor. In the darkness the gap, I made out the handle of a screwdriver buried in cobwebs. The discovery jolted me with optimism. I knew my time was short; the next time I saw the killers, they would probably kill me. But, the tool was there for me. I needed to recover it, somehow, and use it to save myself.

# Chapter 55

Lying across the edge of the small step twisted my body and cut like a knife up my back and across my arms. It forced me to draw in each breath. The vision of a knife along my back clicked into focus. I squirmed on the edge of the concrete step until the corner pressed against the plastic tie wrap. Arching my back, I dragged the plastic tie against the edge a few inches up toward my shoulders. I pushed it back toward my hips. I did it again, concentrating on the sound of the plastic grinding against the sharp corner of concrete. My aim wasn't great, and the rough floor scraped my arms. I moved my arms up and down a few more times, pressing hard against the edge. After a dozen moves, I dropped back down, breathing hard.

I had no idea of my progress, but I guessed the plastic would cut quicker if I scraped it faster. I took a couple deep breaths and arched my back again. This time I moved my arms quicker, counting up to twenty moves before I had to rest. The inside of my right arm was raw from rubbing on the concrete, and the tie cut into my wrists. I arched again and pressed against the edge, rubbing with all my strength. I could hear the plastic grinding with each stroke. It seemed there was a chip in the edge of the step. On each pass, I heard a tiny snap and felt the plastic strip jerk as it worked against the step. I lost count of the strokes but kept at it. I rested again, my heart pounding and sweat running into my eyes.

I bent my good leg under and gained more room to rub the plastic tie against the edge. I moved fast. The pain in my wrists and chafed arm turned to numbness, and all I could think of was to rub the tie faster and faster. I felt heat from the plastic strip where it bit into my wrists and I knew it meant progress. The heat told me I couldn't rest. The hotter it got, the quicker it would break.

I panted with each stroke, and my shoulders burned with fatigue. I concentrated on the sweet sound of the plastic strip scraping across the concrete edge. It made a final snap and my right arm shot free, rolling me off the step. I buried my nose in the greasy floor, pinning my left arm under me, breathing hard.

I sat up and rested on the edge. Half of the plastic tie dangled from my left wrist, the other half lay on the floor next to me. I grabbed them both and flung them into the trash across the garage. I checked the bloody mess of my right arm and massaged the depressions where the strip had cut into my wrists. Sweat dripped off my face.

I turned toward the storage shelf. Using my hands and good leg, I pulled myself to it and reached under for the screwdriver. I slid my hand flat under the lower shelf and tried to flip it out. It moved but didn't come out, and I jammed my hand under farther, flipping at it again. It rolled out. I pulled my hand free and grabbed it.

I gripped the four-inch handle in my fist. Six or seven inches of rusty steel blade swayed before my eyes. The tip was flat with a quarter-inch broken off. I smiled at it and visualized a plan to get free of the killers. I quickly discarded it for a better plan to get free and to establish unquestionable evidence that they had killed Lee.

I eased back toward the position where the killers

had left me bound on the garage floor. When I reached what I thought was the spot, I spent a few moments examining the edge of the concrete and found a sharp chip in the step with a smear of blood around it. I ran my thumb across the chip with affection.

I heard voices and quickly lay back with my tortured arms under me and closed my eyes.

# Chapter 56

I heard the door scrape open, and it muffled George's voice. I let my head roll to the left and moaned. Footsteps approached, and I felt a sharp kick to my ribs. I jerked and cried out.

"Time for your morning stroll."

I looked up at George, blinking my watering eyes and trying to take a breath. He pointed his 9mm pistol at my face. My Walther was still crammed under his belt. I inhaled a short and quick breath. Rolling my head away from him in pain, I glanced at Liam, who stood just outside the door from the house. His pistol remained under his belt.

I calculated my chances of survival if I got up. I would be going to my own death. If I stayed on the floor of the garage, I would probably still get killed. It would make it harder on them, and they would probably have a lot of work to do to sanitize the scene, but it would buy me some time. More importantly, if I tried to get up, they would discover the screwdriver. I knew I couldn't use it on both of them before getting shot again. It was time to roll the dice.

I rolled my head back to face George. "I can't get up. Just shoot me here."

George's eyebrows shot up as he stepped back. He pulled up the gun barrel. He looked at me, and a smile grew on his face. The gun came back to its dead-on position.

"No, it's too messy in here for that. Besides, you have to go to the gators. They won't come in here for you."

I looked him in the eye, ignoring the gun. My breathing slowed to normal. I kept an impassive face and stared. Ten seconds, fifteen, thirty seconds passed and his face reddened. He began to breathe harder, and the gun shook.

He kicked me again and yelled, "Get up!"

I twisted, absorbing the pain. I let out involuntary sobs, grunting through clenched teeth. I knew the kick had been coming. I took a few moments to let the waves of pain subside.

I took a deep breath. With a wavering voice, I blubbered, "Look, why don't you use my gun and get it over with?"

I watched through my grimace as George grinned and put his hand on the Walther. He barked out a single laugh. "This thing is for sissies. It's only a 32. No, you're going to get it with this." He waved the semi-automatic at me. "It's sure to get the job done, just like it did on your sweet little wife."

I groaned and turned away. I mentally checked it off. Step one of my plan had worked. If I could survive, I had him.

# Chapter 57

I turned back to George. He probably couldn't tell that I had a hint of a smile forming on my lips. On to step two.

My voice cracked. "I'll tell you why you can't do it here. You can't look me in the eye and pull the trigger." He looked at me sharply. I could see his anger rise again, and I continued. "You want me out in the swamp, where you can shoot me in the back."

He jerked the gun at me. "You shut up."

"No, you're just a wimp and a coward. Nothing without a gun."

He swore at me and bent forward, and I flashed with panic.

Liam yelled. "Just grab him by his hair, and let's drag him out."

It seemed to click with George, and he straddled me, his pistol hand swinging wide. He bent and grabbed a handful of my hair, his face a mask of hatred.

I winked.

He hesitated.

I twisted off the little concrete step, freeing my right arm, swung it out from under me, and plunged the blade at an upward angle into his chest, just under the point where the ribs meet. The handle thudded to a stop as it hit the bone.

His eyes shot wide, and he dropped the pistol. It clattered away as he moved to grab at the screwdriver.

I slid my right forearm up under his chest, hanging tightly onto the handle. He released his grip on my hair and grew slack. I pulled my left arm free and pushed against his growing weight. I heard Liam yell. George grunted and drooled on me. He slid forward, and I braced my left arm against the concrete to hold his weight and began grabbing with my left hand for the Walther in his belt.

"George! George, what are you doing?" Liam's voice held panic.

George stopped moving, and I couldn't hold the slack body as it eased down on top of me. My right hand around the screwdriver made a pedestal, keeping his body from blocking my effort to grab my pistol. His head came down next to mine, cheek to cheek, and I pulled the gun from his belt. The pressure of the screwdriver handle on my chest threatened to squeeze the air out of me.

"George, you okay?" Liam, yanking his pistol free, stepped forward.

I slipped the pistol from between us and snapped it up at Liam, firing a shot. He kicked back, spinning to the right, and fell backward over a cardboard box.

# Chapter 58

I took my finger off the trigger, brought the gun in my fist to George's right shoulder, and shoved him with both hands. He was loose and heavy. I struggled to pivot him onto his back next to me and release the handle of the screwdriver.

I could hear Liam floundering, thrashing his legs off the crushed box and I looked over to see him twist to a kneeling position. I sat up and swung the pistol toward him. I realized I had no time to transfer it to my right hand and decided to hold it steady on him. He angled up and spotted me.

I looked him in the eye. "Hold it!"

His gun continued to swing toward me, and I yelled, "The next bullet is going right between your eyes."

He stopped, and I put the pressure on. "You're going to be the next dead man in this garage. Look at your dead buddy, here." I saw his eyes dart to George. Mine stayed steady. I was ready to pull the trigger. I felt like killing him and fought the urge to squeeze the trigger again and again. I teetered on the edge of blowing him away. Adrenaline, pain, and anger boiled in me. I had no rational thoughts except to squeeze the trigger at a hint of movement.

Liam held a hand on his right hip, covering a bloody spot. He grimaced but stayed quiet.

His silence gave me hope, hope that I wouldn't end up any better than him, a killer.

"Listen, Liam, he's the real killer. You want to risk your life for him?"

Liam's face fell. The gun faltered.

"Put the gun down, and I won't kill you." My voice growled with conviction, but my stomach churned.

He pointed the muzzle toward the rafters and lowered it to the floor.

"Slide it over. Slowly."

He pushed it a few feet across the floor and collapsed to the side, pushing up against the wall to a sitting position. He moaned. "Man, I'm going to bleed to death."

His whining galvanized a streak of anger that recharged my strength. I held the Walther on him, not giving him the slightest chance. I slid over to his gun and wiped it off the concrete step to a spot a few feet into the mess of the garage.

Liam sat behind the crushed, box making pitiful noises. I pushed back until I found support from a crate piled against the side wall. I saw the crushed box as an ally. It had tied him up long enough for me to get my gun on him first.

We were close to the final step of my plan. "Hey, you have your cell phone?"

Liam stopped whining and looked at me. "In my pocket."

"Get it out."

He whimpered. "Man, I'm hurt bad."

"Get it out. You're not getting any better like that." I lifted the pistol. When he saw it, he moved to work the phone from his pants pocket. He held it up.

"Don't give it to me. Put it on speaker, and call 911. Set it on the box, and I'll do the talking."

When the operator came on, I said, "There's been a shooting, and we have three injuries. We need three ambulances."

"I understand, sir. Is this Liam Peterson?"

I nodded at him, and he said, "Yes."

"What is your location?"

I nodded again, and Liam replied, "We're at 153 Brown Creek Road."

"I see that's in southeast Orange County. Is that right?"

"Yes."

"Okay, we have three ambulances on the way. Can you describe the injuries? I may be able to help with first aid."

"Operator, this is Mark Stone speaking. I am holding Peterson at gunpoint for my own safety."

"One moment, Mr. Stone."

A few moments later, the operator came back on. "We have dispatched SWAT to the scene. Are you able to maintain control of the situation?"

"Yes, operator, but I need Detective Beauchamp of the Apopka Springs Police Department to come to the scene and take charge. This situation is directly connected to a current murder case he is working. I don't want SWAT to interfere, because there is sensitive evidence here at the scene."

"Okay, Mr. Stone, I understand your request and will try to coordinate it immediately with Detective Beauchamp. But, I can't guarantee we can meet it."

"Operator, you have to make it plainly clear to SWAT not to fire on me because I am holding a gun."

"Mr. Stone, we have procedures for these kinds of situations. Please, remain calm."

I didn't reply but kept my focus on Liam. I didn't want to risk a glance at George. He hadn't made a sound since I'd pushed him off of me onto his back. I would deal with it if he made a move toward me.

"Mr. Stone, are you still there?"

"Yes as is Liam Peterson."

"Would you like to describe the injuries?"

"We're not in a position to do anything about them, so let's just wait for the EMTs."

# Chapter 59

"Peterson, hang up and dial another number."

He moaned as he leaned for the phone. I gave him Tony's number and said, "Put it on speaker, and set it on the box again."

"Tony Marino."

"Tony, this is Mark. Listen, I'm holding one of the killers at gunpoint, waiting for the cops to arrive, but you need to know that Shacklee was fully involved with the robberies and worked with the killers last night, trying to kill me. You need to be careful. He is very dangerous."

"Okay, but are you sure?"

"If he's there, the truck will have body damage on the driver's side rear where he played chicken with me last night. The damage will have some paint the same color as my Stratus."

"Hang on. I'm headed out of my office to the side door to see if the truck is parked is at his bungalow."

The phone speaker tapped out his quick footsteps. "Yeah, the truck's here. I've got to go to check it out. Hey, wait, are you okay?"

"Somewhat. Tony, you need to take care. Once the cops have these two in custody, they're going to be coming after Shacklee."

"I'll get a fix on him and lock the place down. Not until I verify the truck damage."

"Talk to you soon."

"Thanks for the heads-up, Mark." The line went

dead, and I nodded at Liam to hang up.

He squeezed it and let it lay on the box. "Hey, man, we didn't mean to kill your wife. It was an accident."

I looked him in the eye. "It was murder."

"No, no, George, he…"

"You broke in to steal and you ended up stealing and killing. You're filth."

"No, George and I didn't normally work together, and it just got out of hand."

"Really? You sure wanted to kill me ten minutes ago. If you had this gun, I'd be dead right now. So, don't tell me you're not a murderer."

"No, I swear, that was all George's doing. Gary and I had to go along with him. He said we had to take care of you, or we'd spend the rest of our life in prison."

"Shut up. The truth will come out, and that's all that matters."

The garage was warm, and I guessed the sun had cleared the trees to start broiling the place for another day. I rested my forearm on my bent right knee, keeping the pistol on target. The phone chirped, and we both looked at it.

Liam leaned toward it and said, "Yeah, I know, speaker."

He took his hand away from it, and I said, "Mark Stone."

"Stone, this is Detective Beauchamp. I got your message, and I'm on the way with a small army. We're about twenty minutes out. Can you hold on?"

I kept my eyes on Liam. "Yeah, I've got one of the killers at gunpoint. And, unless he gets stupid, he won't get shot."

"Mr. Stone, is there another one there?"

"He's wounded, probably pretty bad. He's not moving."

Beauchamp cleared his throat. "What about you?"

I grunted. "What do you mean?"

"Are you okay?"

"I've been shot again and have an assortment of scrapes and bruises, but I think I'll survive until you get here."

"And, ah, your hostage? Is he okay?"

"He's got a .32-caliber slug in his hip, but otherwise, he's fine. Look, detective, there's a third party involved in this mess, and he worked with these two here to try to take me out last night."

"Right. We got a report already that your car was wrapped around a tree."

"I think you need to send a couple units to pick up this third party. Once he finds out his buddies are in custody, he's going to disappear."

Ten seconds of background noise came over the speaker.

"Mr. Stone, I can't do that on your say so. It will have to wait until I get there and fully assess the situation."

I caught Liam with a smile creeping onto his face, and I let another ten seconds of silence transmit Beauchamp's way. "Fine."

I pictured the ambulances, SWAT, and cops arriving at the address like a scene from "Police Academy." "Detective, you need to know that none of us are mobile and can't come out to meet you. We're all in the garage on the south side of the house, and the garage doors are closed."

"Okay, no problem."

"I'm telling you this because I'm keeping this gun pointed at one of the killers until you get here. But, I don't want the SWAT boys or some gung-ho cops blasting in here and taking a shot at me just because I have a gun in my hand."

"Mr. Stone, please." His petulance came across the speakerphone. "Give us a little credit for knowing what we're doing."

I wouldn't reply to that one.

"Mr. Stone, I'll coordinate with the team and also with you once I arrive. I'll call you back."

In the quiet moments that followed, I heard the wood slat roof creaking from the growing heat but didn't look up. My focus stayed on Liam. When he made a face as if to say something, I said, "Shut up."

My left knee throbbed. I wondered if I would walk again. I ran my left hand slowly over my right collarbone and realized it had been a while since I had felt pain there. It gave me hope for my knee. My thoughts flowed to the night a bullet had ripped through there, and Lee floated into my memory. It wasn't the picture that usually came to mind lately, the one of her slumped over and covered in blood on our bed. Instead, she smiled at me and flipped dark hair from her cheek.

Liam moved, and the crushed box scraped a fraction of an inch. I changed the angle of the pistol from his chest to his face. He got the message and stopped. I glanced over at George. He wasn't moving. His face was pressed against the concrete floor in a distortion of life. I turned back toward Liam with the image of George, ski mask obscuring his face and pointing his gun between my eyes as I lay defenseless on the bed next to my frightened wife. I adjusted my grip on the pistol and gave Liam a slow smile.

The modulating sound of cicadas filtered in from outside, and it surprised me that I noticed. In the next second, I realized the cicadas were sirens.

Liam's phone rang, and Beauchamp came on. "Mr. Stone, we're outside of the house at 153 Brown Creek Road."

"Detective, we're all the way in the garage up near the house. I think we should stay on the phone until your team can get in here."

"Right. They're coming in now."

The garage brightened as one of the doors swung open, but I kept my focus on Liam. I could hear the intermittent sounds of SWAT cops moving and saw shadows on wall behind Liam. In my peripheral vision I caught a glimpse of one taking a knee, rifle pointed at us. In the next second, another appeared six feet in front of me. He held an M16 and was dressed in full body armor.

He said, "Mr. Stone, we have the room secure. Put your weapon on the floor. Both of you raise your hands."

The cop gave orders, and his partner retrieved my pistol and dropped it into a plastic bag.

I nodded at Liam. "His gun is behind you about four feet."

The other SWAT cop retrieved it and bagged it.

"Any other weapons?"

I lowered my hands and pointed at George. "His gun is on the floor somewhere on the other side of where he's lying."

A third SWAT cop stepped past me and went over to George. He looked around, picked up George's 9mm pistol, and bagged it.

The lead SWAT cop keyed a shoulder mic and said, "All clear."

We heard Beauchamp over the cop's speaker. "I'm coming in."

The cop near George squatted next to him and laid a gloved finger on George's neck. He looked at the screwdriver in his chest and over at me. He pulled his finger away. "Sergeant, this man's dead."

Beauchamp stopped next to me, looking at George.

Liam spoke up. "Hey, I'm dying over here. I need a doctor."

Beauchamp nodded at the sergeant who keyed his mic. "Send in a paramedic team."

# Chapter 60

Beauchamp looked down at me, and I followed his eyes flick from my face to the blood-soaked towel around my left knee. He shook his head. "Mr. Stone, you've really made a mess out of this case."

"I don't think so." I shifted against the crate, pulling myself more upright. "I have indisputable evidence that the dead guy over there killed my wife, and this other guy was his accomplice."

Paramedics rolled a stretcher up to where Beauchamp stood, forcing him to step around me to stand next to the Sergeant. They looked at the three different potential patients.

I looked at Beauchamp. "They should probably take care of Peterson and get him out of here. I'm not saying any more with him around." I jerked my head at Liam.

Beauchamp pointed at Liam. "Take care of him, but get another team in here to look at that one." He pointed at George.

The detective looked at me. "I'll be happy to hear your story, Mr. Stone. But, until this is sorted out, I'm afraid you will have to be considered a suspect in all this, ah, mayhem here."

I shook my head slowly. "Fine. Can I get a bottle of water?"

In a few minutes, the EMTs had checked out Liam and rolled him out on a stretcher. Another stretcher held George's body and they rolled it out. The SWAT team had retreated, and a third rolling stretcher was parked a few feet from me. The EMTs started to fuss over me.

I held up my hand. "Hold on a minute, guys." They stopped. Beauchamp stood in the same spot with his arms folded across the bulge of his belly.

"Detective, I want you to hear this before we leave the scene."

"I'm listening."

Time for the final step in my plan. "Now, your Crime Scene Investigators are going to be looking at three pistols. Of course, one of them is mine, and you'll find a bullet from it in Peterson's hip. I put it there instead of letting him put one in me. He may try to lie and dispute it was self-defense, but if your CSI guys check out the trunk of his car, I'm sure you'll find evidence that I was in the trunk. They shot me, dumped me in the trunk, and brought me out here to kill me. Of course, one of the other pistols belongs to Peterson. You can verify that easily. I'm sure you'll also find George's fingerprints on my gun. He took it from me when they kidnapped me. I took it back from him moments before they were going to execute me."

I took a slow pull from the water bottle and closed my eyes for a few moments. "The evidence proving George killed Lee is the third gun. It's his, and you'll find his fingerprints on it. When you match the bullet from my knee to it and then match the bullet from my wife to it, you'll find he's the killer. He shot her, and he shot me."

"Very good, Mr. Stone."

I squinted up at Beauchamp. "If things had gone just a bit different here today, I'd be dead, and he would have gotten away with murder. Twice."

The End

Defenseless is also available on kindle:

www.amazon.com/dp/B00N7UE7KY

To discover more great books like
Defenseless by Matt Lenz visit:

**thebookfolks.com**

Made in the USA
Middletown, DE
22 July 2015